TALES
of the
TATTOOED

TALES
of the
TATTOOED

An Anthology of Ink

edited by

JOHN MILLER

This collection first published in 2019 by
The British Library
96 Euston Road
London NW1 2DB

Introduction and notes © 2019 John Miller

Cataloguing in Publication Data
A catalogue record for this publication is available from the British Library

ISBN 978 0 7123 5330 4
Limited edition ISBN 978 0 7123 5345 8
e-ISBN 978 0 7123 6720 2

The frontispiece illustration shows stages of a tattoo
design by Sutherland Macdonald, from 'A Tattoo Artist' by
Gambier Bolton in *Pearson's Magazine* August 1902.

Cover design by Mauricio Villamayor with illustration by Luca Ortis

Text design and typesetting by Tetragon, London
Printed in England by CPI Group (UK) Ltd, Croydon, CR0 4YY

CONTENTS

By the time the first tattooed Barbie was released in 2011, any sense that getting a tattoo was a radical anti-social gesture was already long gone. Even so, the idea that something as apparently edgy as a tattoo could adorn a figure as conventional as Barbie represents a watershed moment in the history of tattooing. Once the mark of the renegade, tattoos have entered mainstream consumer culture as never before. On the one hand, this is good news for the burgeoning tattoo industry and testament to the extraordinary creative evolution of tattooing over the last twenty years. On the other hand, the status of tattoos as something like fashion items has provoked plenty of nostalgia for a time when tattooing had the unequivocal power of rarity: a time when a tattoo, especially a large, prominent tattoo, could cause a sudden intake of breath, or make people unsure whether to stare or look away, or might even generate direct hostility. In 2001, one of the first people I showed my first tattoo (a Dylan Thomas poem on my ribs) told me with total confidence that it was totally disgusting. Now very few tattoos have the force to be disgusting.

There is an old joke that the only difference between tattooed people and non-tattooed people is that tattooed people don't care if you're not tattooed. There are doubtless still people who disapprove of tattoos, but (at the risk of generalization) in metropolitan Western society at least, the joke no longer holds; no one cares if you've got tattoos. Even formerly extreme tattoos on the neck and hands ("job-stoppers" as they are sometimes known) have lost a good deal of their transgressive energy. Now that Barbie is tattooed, what is there to be offended about? Tattooing is available to everyone. Consequently, at the risk of being too hard on her, Barbie has killed tattooing as a form of outsider art, marking the end of its meaningfulness as a sign of difference and individuality, bringing about the final decay of its subversive beauty.

Despite tattooing's ubiquity in a celebrity driven popular culture, however, it is an exaggeration to say that tattoos have entirely lost their mystique and disappeared into bland, corporate uniformity. There may be some designs tattooed so frequently as to appear mass-produced, but part of tattooing's enduring appeal resides in the negotiation between artist and client to produce an entirely singular artwork that cannot be sold on (though there is reportedly a market in Japan for dead tattooed skin) and might well never be repeated (though given tattooing's visibility on social media, tattoo plagiarism is always possible). As a great many commentators and artists have pointed out, if tattoos are commodities, they are a very different kind of commodity. It may be an obvious point, but getting tattooed is much more painful than shopping, and, unlike most things we buy in our disposable age, tattoos are very difficult to get rid of. Ironically, it is precisely this difference—the sense that a tattoo might be something deep and real in a culture overwhelmed by media illusions—that makes tattooing so thoroughly commodifiable. Everyone wants to be unique, just like everyone else. So the twenty-first-century tattoo is something of a paradox. Tattooing has become mainstream *because* it is alternative.

There is a danger, of course, in pronouncing in the abstract about the reasons people might get tattooed, or what their tattoos might mean to them, or how their life experiences relate to fashion and consumerism, what secret traumas or pleasures their tattoos bear witness to, or what grand promises they reveal. It is too easy and reductive to think of the tattoo renaissance (as it is sometimes called) as simply the emergence of attention-seeking hipsterism. Personally, in the course of acquiring a full bodysuit tattoo over the last eighteen years (mainly the work of the brilliant Luca Ortis who designed the cover to this book), I have never really had any clear idea why I wanted to get tattooed except that I find tattoos profoundly beautiful, alluring, joyful, strange and interesting. In getting tattooed, we participate (often unwittingly) in fascinating, complex, controversial, suppressed and entwined histories. The meanings of tattoos may be deeply personal, but they are also more than personal: signs in an ancient and continually expanding network of signs.

Tattooing has been around for over five thousand years and has developed across the extent of the globe from the Arctic to the Tierra del Fuego. Behind the tattoo renaissance are longstanding and culturally significant practices involving magic, medicine, community, ritual and spirituality. Tattoo history is also, since at least the eighteenth century, a colonial history in which tattoo practices have been subjected to repression, as well as becoming caught up in less violent global processes of cultural exchange. Today, many indigenous tattoo traditions, especially in the Pacific, have become resurgent after being demonized and outlawed by imperial regimes, though there are now also anxieties about the appropriation of socially specific designs in our globalized mass culture. From a Western standpoint in which tattooing has long been associated with social margins, it is tempting to conclude that history is not written by the tattooed (though how can we be sure?) But at the same time, tattoos *are* history: in a specific sense in Maori culture, tattoos denote social and genealogical affiliations; more generally, tattooing unfolds through an amalgamation of tradition, adaptation, invention and reinvention.

Tales of the Tattooed brings together stories that shine a light on aspects of this history. Many of the tales collected here are little-known; some are probably entirely unread since their initial publication in periodicals and magazines. They emerge from an intriguing window in tattooing's history. The earliest story collected here is from 1882; the latest is 1952. Like our own time, these were heady days for tattooing. In the 1870s, tattooing began to take shape in Europe and America as a profession, practised by committed artists. By the 1880s an earlier version of the current tattoo renaissance had taken hold (though on a far more limited scale than today's tattoo fixation). Most commonly, this "tattoo craze" was associated with wealthy socialites in Europe and America (the press drew particular attention to a number of tattooed royals and aristocrats), but its reach was in reality much wider, aided by significant developments in the craft of tattooing. The first electric tattoo machine was patented in the U.S. by Samuel O'Reilly of New York in 1891 and a British patent was taken out by Sutherland MacDonald in 1894. MacDonald was one of the earliest British professional tattoo artists (possibly the earliest) whose shop above a Turkish bathhouse in Jermyn Street in London's West End played an important role in the history of tattooing in the U.K. Surviving photographs reveal the remarkable precision, detail and depth of MacDonald's work; contemporary accounts of his studio note the lush interior and readily available "cooling drinks" and cigarettes to soothe the tattooee. Fiction was quick to catch on to the tattoo craze with the first full-length novel featuring a professional tattoo artist published in 1886. *The Mark of Cain* by the anthropologist Andrew Lang includes the admittedly rather dubious figure of Dicky Shields who makes a living in London tattooing sailors.

As the maritime focus of Lang's novel reveals, while new tattoo demographics were formed in the late nineteenth century, tattooing's key myths remained persistent. Kings and princes may well have established tattooing as a practice with a foothold among the social elite, but at the same time there remained a strong connection between tattooing and a small number of distinctive social groups. Alongside the naval connection, tattooing has long had an intimate connection to criminality. To this day, tattooing has been unable to shake a link to crime expressed recurrently in popular culture, especially in TV crime dramas. Of the more than seventy short stories I have uncovered about tattooing from the late nineteenth century to the Second World War (and there are certainly more to find), the most common literary genre for the tattoo tale is crime or detective fiction. Half of the tales collected here involve some kind of crime. As much as anything, tattoos are extremely useful plot devices: culprits may be identified by their distinctive ink, or some hidden message (not infrequently the location of some misbegotten swag) might be secretly tattooed on the skin (and not always on human skin). Such narrative strategies emphasize tattoos as codes to be deciphered, but also consolidate the idea of tattoos as improper and disturbing. To be normal is to live with an unmarked skin; to mark the skin is to announce yourself as a deviant, quite possibly with criminal tendencies. As much as the tattoo developed a certain anxious credibility at the end of the Victorian era, it was still seen as a mark of psychological and social otherness. Heavily tattooed people were most commonly in evidence in freak shows and circuses (like the curious figure of Monsieur de Montillac in T. W. Speight's "The Green Phial") and if they were the source of curiosity (and even desire) they were also seen as resolutely "other".

Consequently, in most of the stories collected here, tattooing is still thoroughly weird. Even a small tattoo had the power to shock, as in Alfred Payson Terhune's story "Branded" in which a discreet heart on a lady's wrist infuriates her po-faced husband. Indeed, there

is a particular frisson in the involvement of women with tattooing
in the period. One of the most prominent aspects of the Victorian
tattoo craze (and the same point has often been made about our
more recent tattoo renaissance) was that more women were getting
tattooed, a prospect which occasioned horror among a patriarchal
moral majority who saw tattooing as a blemish on deeply entrenched
ideas of femininity. There are also, however, tales here with a less
conservative take on tattoos and gender politics. Arthur P. Hankins'
detective story "The Tattooed Eye" goes so far as to feature a female
professional tattoo artist (quite possibly the first work of fiction to
do so), in the form of the sassy and resourceful Nan Sundy.

With one exception, the stories republished here are from Britain
and America, although there is a global dimension too. At the risk
of over-simplification, tattooing is sometimes thought of as being
divided into three major world traditions: Euro-American tattooing,
Japanese *irezumi* and the Pacific tradition (and of course it is from
Polynesia that we get the word "tattoo"). Each of these is represented
here: most, as the stories' national origins would suggest, are focused
on Euro-American tattooing, but the Japanese tattoo is represented
by Jun'ichiro Tanizaki's "The Tattooer" and in Terhune's "Branded"
(as well as more peripherally in some others). Polynesian tattoos are
a more marginal presence and are confined to the appropriation of
Maori designs by de Montillac in Speight's story, an act that tellingly
reveals a historical insensitivity to the specific significance and roles
of tattoos in Pacific cultures.

It is important to note that the literary representation of tattooing in the nineteenth and early twentieth centuries, and particularly
of Pacific island tattooing, involves some brutal racism. Take R. M.
Ballantyne's children's classic *The Coral Island*, for instance, published in 1857. Encountering an extensively tattooed Polynesian man,

Ballantyne's hysterical narrator Ralph denounces him as "the most terrible monster I ever beheld" (p. 174). Tattoos are seen here and in many other texts as the sign of a savagery that is routinely opposed to Euro-American civilization so that the representation of tattoos forms part of the construction of imperial hierarchies. Such violent racial stereotypes do not form part of this collection. Nonetheless, there are colonial attitudes traceable in *Tales of the Tattooed*; it would be impossible and somewhat naïve to produce an anthology about tattooing between the 1880s and 1950s without providing testimony to the ways in which the popularity of tattooing emerges out of and through colonial interactions, in part through the close connection of tattoos and the sea. The association of tattoos with sailors is at the centre of two stories collected here, W. W. Jacobs' "A Marked Man" and Arthur Tuckerman's "The Starfish Tattoo" and in the background of several others.

Tattooing's connection with empire is complex, however. There is much more to the colonial history of tattooing than the demonization of indigenous tattoo traditions. In contrast to Ballantyne's blunt racism, the heavily tattooed Fijian harpooner Queequeg in Herman Melville's *Moby Dick* from 1851 is a rich and sensitively drawn character. As much as concerns about the increasing popularity of tattooing in the period operate through ideas about racial difference (and especially through ideas of the primitive or the savage), they also show the instability of nationalist ideas about the body. The unmarked, "normal" and implicitly white Victorian (and later) body is not a "natural" entity, but rather is an idea that needs to be constantly reinforced and insisted upon by the exclusion of "other" bodies. This makes tattooing a significant topic for a postcolonial critique of the violent and broken logic of empire. This also reminds us of the crucial role narrative plays in tattoo history: explaining, blaming, fantasizing, obsessing. Tattoos and stories go together, whether we think of the story behind a single tattoo or of the larger story of tattooing's development, a story of which these tales are a mostly forgotten part.

JOHN MILLER

FURTHER READING

R. M. Ballantyne, *The Coral Island* (London: Nelson, 1898 [first published 1857])

Lee Barron, *Tattoo Culture: Theory and Contemporary Contexts* (London: Rowman and Littlefield, 2017)

Jane Caplan (ed.), *Written on the Body: The Tattoo in European and American History* (Princeton, NJ: Princeton University Press, 2000).

Wilfred Dyson Hambly, *The History of Tattooing* (Mineola, NY: Dover, 2009 [first published 1925])

Herman Melville, *Moby Dick* (Oxford: World's Classics, 1988 [first published 1851])

Margot Mifflin, *Bodies of Subversion: A Secret History of Women and Tattoo* (New York: Juno Books, 1997)

TWO DELICATE CASES (1882)

James Payn

James Payn (1830–1898) was a prolific essayist and novelist who was widely admired by many of the most distinguished writers of his age, notably Charles Dickens, Arthur Conan Doyle and Henry James. Despite the great popularity of Payn's work during his lifetime, his writing quickly fell into obscurity after his death. According to his obituary in *The Spectator*, Payn was "was not a man of genius, not a great novelist, not even a considerable litterateur", but a man who "interested and amused an entire generation". Today he is best remembered as editor of two of the most important periodicals of the era, *Chambers's Journal* and the *Cornhill Magazine* and for a single entry in the *Oxford Dictionary of Quotations*. It is to Payn that we are indebted for the profound realization that toast always falls buttered side down.

"Two Delicate Cases" centres around the character of Dr. Nicholas Dormer, author of the definitive monograph on the "comparatively unknown but picturesque art of Tattooing". While Payn's tale ostensibly approaches the topic of the tattoo from within a sober medical context, there is plenty of sensational material here to titillate Victorian readers, particularly in the colourful form of Matthew Stevedore, who is tattooed from head to foot as a form of punishment he is subjected to in "Chinese Tartary". Payn's creation of Stevedore is directly based on the intriguing life of Georgius Constantine, an Albanian who (like Stevedore) is "discovered" in

Vienna exhibiting his extensive tattoos. Constantine's claim to have been forcibly tattooed after being held captive during a gold-prospecting mission in Burma was the subject of some scepticism, though penal tattooing was a well-documented historical practice. Payn's recreation of Constantine epitomizes tattooing's function in the late nineteenth century as an alluring but troubling (and now very problematic) sign of the violent and the exotic.

I F YOU HAVE NEVER READ MY WORK—DR. DORMER'S MASTER-
piece, as I am told it is termed by the profession—upon the Skin,
in connection with the interesting subject of tattooing, you had
better get it, because the book is becoming exceedingly rare. I may
say without vanity that it is by far the best monograph on the subject
that exists; for it is the only one. Others—hundreds of others—have
written, of course, upon skin diseases. Indeed, the question I found
myself putting to myself on commencing practice in London as an
expert in that branch of the healing art, was, "What have they *not*
written about?" There are nowadays but two methods of getting
one's name known and establishing a medical reputation in London:
one is by taking a house in Mayfair with an immense doorplate, and
setting up a brougham and pair in which you sit well forward and are
driven rapidly as if you had not a moment to lose; the other is by the
publication of some exhaustive treatise, with coloured plates. Most
of these last, though often striking (indeed, once seen, you will never
forget them), are to the unprofessional eye by no means attractive,
and it was not my object to recommend myself to the profession
only. Instead, therefore, of any glowing account of the nature of
Carbuncles, or genial essay on Port-wine Marks, I devoted myself to
the comparatively unknown but picturesque subject of Tattooing.

It was not, it must be owned, one of very general application, but
it had some general interest, and if only that could be aroused and
concentrated upon Nicholas Dormer, his future would be assured.

I had the honour of being the first man to introduce to the public
(through the columns of the *Medical Mercury*) the case of Matthew

Stevadore, the most highly coloured and artistically executed individual known to science. He had been made prisoner in Chinese Tartary and sentenced to be put to death, but his punishment had been commuted (or extended) to tattooing. Five others suffered with him, but he was the only survivor of the operation, which combined the horrors of sitting for one's portrait and vivisection. The victim was held fast by four strong men, while a fifth, the artist, worked away upon him with a split reed, like a steel pen, for hours. At the end of three months he was considered finished, and would doubtless have been "hung upon the line" if the Chinese Tartars had had a Royal Academy in which to exhibit him.

The pigments used are doubtful; it is certain they were not powdered charcoal, gunpowder, or cinnabar, the colours used by our native artists (chiefly marine) for the same purpose, inasmuch as "none of the particles remained entangled in the meshes of the true skin (corium)", or "became encapsuled" (see article in *Medical Mercury*) "in the nearest lymphatic glands". One must conclude that the work was performed by the simple agency of the juice of plants. Yet the effect produced was perfect. "So it ought to be," poor Matthew used to say with a groan of reminiscence, when complimented upon his personal appearance. Indeed, I have no doubt that the operation hurt him very much. If he had known that he was going to be a contribution to science, or even to have formed the subject of an article in the *Mercury*, he might (perhaps) have borne up better. But as it was, those consolatory reflections were denied him. He had only the satisfaction of feeling that (if he survived) he would be the best illustrated man in Chinese Tartary.

He looked, when in nature's garb, as though the whole of his body was tightly enveloped in a robe of the richest webbing. From the crown of his head to the tips of his toes he was covered with dark blue figures of plants and animals, in the interspaces of which were written characters (testimonials, for all I know) in blue and red. The hands were tattooed on both surfaces, but only with inscriptions; probably a condensed biography of the artist himself, with a catalogue of his other works. The blue figures stopped short at the insteps, but the tattooing was continued on the feet in scarlet to the roots of the nails. Through the very hair of the scalp and beard could be seen "designs" in blue. On the whole body there were no fewer than 388 figures: apes, cats, tigers, eagles, storks, swans, elephants, crocodiles, snakes, fish, lions, snails, and men and women; of inanimate objects such as fruits, flowers, leaves, and bows and arrows, there was also a lavish supply; and upon his forehead on each side were two panthers "regardant"—that is, looking down with admiration (as well they might) upon this interesting and unrivalled collection.

Such were the attractions of my honest friend Matthew Stevadore, who made a good deal of money by the exhibition of them in Vienna, where I went on purpose to see him. It may certainly be said of him, if of anybody, that "we shall never look upon his like again". It has been remarked that "beauty is only skin-deep," but in his case it was at all events more lasting than usual. If it was not "a joy for ever", he retained it as long as he lived.

Of course I incorporated my notes in the *Mercury* upon this case—after what had been written *upon* him, Matthew didn't care twopence what was written *about* him—in my work upon Tattooing, which also contained a full-length portrait of him in colours. It had an immense success, but, strange to say, did not increase—that is, commence—my professional practice. I published another book of a more scientific kind with the same result; that is to say, it had none. It was tolerably successful as medical works go—it cost the

author not more than fifty pounds or so; but, as was remarked by
the senior surgeon of our hospital, who has the misfortune to be a
wag, "it didn't beat the tattoo"; while the general public of course
never so much as heard of it.

One day, however, grim Fortune relaxed into a smile which I
took for good nature, though, as it turned out, it was only cynicism.
A carriage and pair drove up to my door, out of which stepped an
eminent personage. There is a temptation to leave that description of my visitor as it stands; but I scorn to deceive the public,
and therefore hasten to add that it was *not* a member of the Royal
Family. He was not at that time even a peer of the realm; but nevertheless he was a man of great importance. I knew him by sight as
one of the life-governors of our hospital; and I knew him by report
as being one of the greatest financiers in the city. A tall soldier-like
fellow, very upright, though he bore on his own shoulders many a
gigantic speculation, and with an air of command that was quite
Napoleonic, as befitted the master of millions. Being so very rich,
there were naturally many stories afloat concerning him, and all to
his disadvantage. The same thing happens in the case of all our great
men, from statesmen to poets. His mother was in the workhouse;
his brother in penal servitude; he had murdered his first wife, and
was starving his second. He himself—as a slight drawback to the
enjoyment of his ill-gotten gains—had a disease previously unknown
to the human species.

If so, I only hoped he had come to consult me about it. A surgeon's duty is to heal, not to give ear to idle rumours. Still, I could
not help regarding him as he took his seat in my study with a certain
curiosity. His name was Mostyn, or rather his card asserted as much;
his features were Caucasian, and suggested Moses. His speech was
very calm and deliberate, either the result of indifference to any

change of fortune that might possibly befall him, or a precaution-ary measure to restrain a natural tendency to talk through his nose.

"My visit here, Dr. Dormer, is a strictly confidential one. I trust to your honour as a member of a chivalrous profession—and I will also make it worth your while—not to reveal the nature of this application to any human being, during my lifetime."

I gave my promise, and kept it. Mr. Mostyn—Dives Mostyn, as the world once called him—has long since been gathered to his fathers, whoever they were. He died in Paddington Workhouse.

"In my early days," he went on, "I bore a very different character from that which I have since acquired." Here he stopped: he was obviously in a difficulty. I hastened to help him out of it.

"You mean, perhaps," said I, smiling (as though it were of no consequence), "that you bore an indifferent character?"

"Just so," he answered; "thank you. Not that I ever did anything positively discreditable."

I waved my hand to intimate that even if it had been so (which was incredible), it would make no matter to me. This kind of "treat-ment" in such cases (to speak professionally), I have always found to afford immense relief.

"In youth, however," proceeded my visitor, "I was what is called a ne'er-do-well. I could not settle to anything. Finance—of which, if I may say so, I have shown myself to be a master—was a calling not at that time open to me. I never had more than a few shillings to call my own, and any attempt to persuade other people to let me have the management of *their* shillings would have been hopeless. The man was ready," said Mr. Mostyn, drawing himself up, "but the hour had not yet struck. I quarrelled with my family and enlisted."

Here he stopped again, and I nodded; not exactly approval, I hope, but acquiescence. The thing had happened so long ago that it was ridiculous to censure it; and besides, it was not my business.

"The life of a soldier, Dr. Dormer, is attractive to adventurous spirits, and though I never was an adventurer—far from it—I had my dreams of military glory. They lasted about three weeks, when I deserted."

"That was serious," I observed.

"It was very serious, sir, in its consequences. I was detected, brought back again, and—it was in the old times, you see"—he hesitated, and once more I had the satisfaction of helping him out of his embarrassment—

"I think I guess what happened," I said. "It may be indicated by a single letter, may it not?"

"You are right. The letter *D*. It is branded between my shoulders. You are the great authority upon 'brands' of this description. I am come here to have it removed."

"Well, really, Mr. Mostyn," said I, "I'll do my best. But I never did have anything of this precise character to deal with—just let me look at it."

He took off his coat and things and bared his shoulders.

"What's it like?" he inquired. "I have cricked my neck a dozen times in trying to look at it. At the time it—it happened—though it was by no means a red-letter day for me in the usual sense—I had an impression—a very strong impression—that it was red."

"It is white now," I answered, "or nearly so; only when you strike it—see—"

"I can't see," returned the patient testily.

"Quite true: I beg your pardon. You must take my word for it that when you strike it, it becomes red again."

"It's quite visible, I conclude, whatever colour it is? eh, doctor?"

"Well, yes, I am bound to say it is."

"You could read it ten feet off, I dare say? Come, be frank with me."

"I am not near-sighted, my dear sir," I replied, "and therefore could read it at twenty. It's a very large letter."

"I don't doubt it," he answered grimly. "It seemed to me at one time that I was all D. I must look like one of those sandwich-men who go about with capitals between their shoulders."

"Well, Mr. Mostyn, of course I should never have ventured to make use of such a parallel, but since you mention it, it *does* remind one of some sort of advertising medium. There are many things so advertised," I added consolingly, "of a most respectable character."

"No doubt," he answered drily. "My D must look like something theological and denunciatory."

"Or a certain famous sherry," said I, falling into his humour.

"Ah, but that's *not* brandied," he answered bitterly.

I confess I compassionated my visitor sincerely. To a man in his position, it must have been very disagreeable to have this telltale memento of the past about him. And, after all, I knew for certain nothing worse about him than that he had had a distaste for the army which, indeed, I shared with him. He had evidently a great deal of humour, which, in a private soldier, must be a very dangerous possession. "There is no discharge in that war," as the preacher says, unless you can purchase it; so that really he had had no alternative but to desert.

I think my visitor read something of my thoughts, for he observed: "You see, this may be a very unfortunate thing for me, Dr. Dormer. People may say things behind my back and welcome, but if they *saw* things?"

"Well, you don't bathe in public, I conclude," said I consolingly.

"No, but there are always risks. I might be run over by a cab and taken to a hospital. The idea of the possibility of disclosure makes me miserable. The higher I get in the financial world, the more dangerous my position appears to me. I have been twice 'decorated' by foreign Governments; just imagine if it should come to be known that I had been decorated by my own, though (as we say in the House of Commons) 'in another place'."

I had forgotten that Mr. Mostyn was in the House. Indeed, that circumstance was merely a sort of pendant or corollary to his eminent position. He was essentially a man of mark, though until that morning, of course, I had never known how very literally he was so.

"The question is, doctor," he continued gravely, "can you take it out?"

The phrase he used was a ridiculous one; a mark of that sort was not like the initials on a stolen pocket-handkerchief, to be picked out and smoothed away, and I frankly told him so.

"The trace of the branding-iron is then indelible, I conclude?"

He was very cool, but I noticed his voice trembled in alluding to the instrument of his disgrace.

"I am afraid so. Science—or at least *my* science—knows no means of eradicating it. There is, indeed, one method by means of which your secret may be preserved."

"Name it, and then name whatever fee you please," he exclaimed excitedly.

"Well, you could be branded again in the same place with something different—some mark of good conduct, for example."

He shook his head and put on his hat and other garments.

"Thank you for your obliging offer," he said, "but I have had enough of that."

It was obvious that he had quite made up his mind upon the point, so I did not press it, and we parted excellent friends.

The great financier's visit, even had I done him any good, could, from the nature of the case, have been of no advantage to me in the way of advertisement; and as matters stood, except for his fee, I was not a halfpenny the better of it.

For six months afterwards I had no patient of any importance, and almost began to think that my studies in tattooing were to have no practical result whatever. And yet the old house-surgeon at St. Kitts Hospital, who was reckoned a sagacious man, had given me this advice: "My dear Dormer, be a specialist; do not attenuate your intelligence by vague and general studies; apply yourself to one thing only—'the little toe and its ailments', for example—and stick to it."

One day a young lady called to consult me. She came in a hack cab, but I saw in a moment that she was used to a carriage and pair.

"I cannot give you my name," she said, "and I hope you will do me the favour not to seek for it."

I bowed and assured her that I had no vulgar curiosity of that kind, though, on the other hand, it might be necessary, for professional reasons, to be made acquainted with her circumstances.

"My case," she said, smiling, "is scarcely one to require such a revelation. However, my position in life is good. I am engaged to be married to a gentleman of title. It is on account of that circumstance that I am paying you this visit."

She looked so beautiful and blushed so charmingly, that if I had not been a professional man I should have envied that gentleman very much. Indeed, I could not help building a little romance about her in my own mind: perhaps she didn't like the man, who, being of title, was permitted by her family to persecute her with his attentions; and it might be that she was come to me to be tattooed in some temporary manner in order to choke him off. Her next words, however, showed that this supposition was quite unfounded.

"I love the gentleman, you must understand, doctor, very truly, and all my hopes are centred in him; but,"—here she began to stammer in the most graceful manner, like some lovely foreigner speaking broken English—"but, a long time ago" (my visitor was not more than eighteen at most), "many years, in fact, I formed a girlish affection for my cousin Tom."

"That very often happens," I said encouragingly, for she had come to a dead stop. "First love is like the measles (except that you catch it again), and leaves no trace behind it."

"I beg your pardon," she replied; "in my case, it left a very considerable one."

"Perhaps you had an exceptionally tender heart," I said, turning my hands over in professional sympathy; "such scars, however, are not ineradicable."

"Quite true," she said; "and even if they are, they are not seen, which is, after all, the main point."

Then I knew of course that she was a young lady of fashion, and that sentiment would be thrown away upon her.

"The fact is," she continued with some abruptness, "I may confess at once that I made a great fool of myself with Cousin Tom, and in a moment of mutual devotion we tattooed our names upon one another's arms. In his case it mattered nothing, but as for me, I was very soon convinced of the folly of such a proceeding."

"You quarrelled with your cousin, perhaps?" I suggested slily.

"Of course I quarrelled with him; but whether that happened or not, the inconvenience of such a state of things would have been just the same. The idea of putting on ball costume was out of the question with a big 'Tom' on my arm, such as schoolboys cut on the back of a tree. I had to affect a delicacy of constitution which compelled me always to wear high dresses. Think of that, sir."

"A most deplorable state of things," I murmured.

"Well, I got used to *that*, and might in time have come to regard the matter with calmness; but, notwithstanding this comparative absence of personal attractions, I have had the good fortune to secure the affections of a very estimable young nobleman, and hence the affair becomes much more serious. Some day or another, he is almost certain to find out that hateful 'Tom' upon my arm."

"There is no doubt a possibility of it," I assented gravely.

"Well, that would be a dreadful blow to him, I'm sure; he is very sensitive and slightly jealous; and I have come to you to have that dreadful word erased."

With that she turned up her sleeve, and on her white shoulder it was true enough the word "Tom" was very legibly engraved, though fortunately not quite so much at large as she had led me to expect.

"It does not look to me to have been done in gunpowder as usual," observed I after a careful scrutiny.

"It wasn't," she answered peevishly; "it was done in slate-pencil, which we scraped together (idiots that we were) on the same plate."

"It's very well done," I answered; "that is, from a tattooing point of view. May I ask if the Christian name of your cousin Tom has any resemblance to that of your intended husband?"

"No, not the least. Why do you ask?"

"Well, if it had been anything similar—such as John, you see—we might have converted Tom into John, and nobody would have been any the wiser; indeed, the young man would have taken it as a very pretty and original compliment."

"That would have been a capital plan," assented the young lady admiringly; "unfortunately, however, his name is Alexis."

As substitution was impossible, I was compelled to try erasure, and even that was a very difficult job. I had no idea that powdered slate-pencil could be so permanent. In the end, by persevering with infusions of milk, I contrived to tone down the objectionable "Tom" to a vague inscription such as to a man of research would have suggested Nineveh or the Moabite stone; in the case of Lord Alexis, however, I suggested that it might be attributed to the result of an unusually successful vaccination, and I have good reason to believe that that was the view he took of it.

As for the young lady, she showed her gratitude in a very practical way, and I owe a considerable portion of my present extensive practice to her good offices. In my whole experience, however, I have never had a more delicate case than hers.

THE GREEN PHIAL (1884)

T. W. Speight

Thomas Wilkinson Speight (1830–1915) is a little-known author of gothic, crime, weird, and science fiction who balanced his writing with a career on the railways.

"The Green Phial" is a flamboyant and improbable mystery story containing elements of Victorian spiritualism, along with reference to some of tattooing's most prominent associations. The ostentatious tattooed figure the story revolves around is one Monsieur de Montillac, the son of a French magician who, falling on hard times, accepts the position of "New Zealand chief" with an English circus. The facial tattoos he receives to establish himself in this role exemplify the way in which indigenous tattoo cultures have been appropriated throughout colonial history. *Ta moko*, the Maori practice of tattooing, signifies specific cultural and genealogical relationships which make the use of traditional designs by non-Maoris extremely controversial. In part, then, Speight's tale demonstrates the ways in which the significance of tattooing in the late nineteenth century was filtered through colonial politics. To the naïve narrator, de Montillac's tattoo appears as a generic sign of savagery, a prejudice which renders the tattoo a site of conservative anxiety. The tattoo also, however, provides a source of fascination and desire (with some unequivocal homoeroticism into the bargain).

I T WAS AT THE HOUSE OF THE REV. PERCIVAL MILBURNE, WHERE
I had gone to read, that I made the acquaintance of Victor
Langholme, who was my senior by about three years. His parents
were dead, and although he was rich he had no home. Mr. Milburne
having been one of his father's oldest friends, Victor had taken up his
quarters at the rectory for a time, pending the settlement of certain
claims connected with his inheritance. Despite the difference in our
ages and the dissimilarity of our dispositions, Langholme and I,
being thrown much together, soon struck up one of those youthful
friendships which are so pleasant while they last, but are scarcely
calculated to stand the wear and tear of life in after-years.

I had been brought up in a country house where hunting, shooting, boating, and cricketing were looked upon as the legitimate
amusements of English gentlemen, and were pursued with a degree
of energy conducive alike to health of body and mind. But here was
a young man, rich and of good family, who cared for none of these
things; a young man addicted through choice to vegetable diet, who
made one suit of clothes last him a year, who kept himself aloof
from polite society, who had never been on horseback in his life,
and who held the cultivation of his intellect and the acquisition of
knowledge as the only ends worth living for. The contrast puzzled
me at first, and ended by attracting me, the result being the friendship of which mention has been already made.

In person Langholme was tall, thin, and fragile-looking, with a
slight stoop of the shoulders probably induced by poring so many

hours over his books. He was an intellectual egotist, living the intro-spective, self-contained life of an Eastern mystic, and regarding with indifference or ill-concealed contempt all those minor accidents and circumstances of everyday life by which the majority of people are so powerfully swayed. He was of Scotch extraction, and he possessed to some extent the gift of second sight. Young though he was, he was already an adept in the use of opium, and he would sometimes relate to me with as much earnestness as though they were based on fact some of the singular visions induced by the imbibition of that dangerous drug. He devoured books, rather than read them, of any and every kind, and was the only reading man I ever knew who had no favourite authors.

When my twelve months came to an end I bade adieu to my good friends at the rectory and set out for Cambridge. Langholme announced his intention of shortly proceeding to Paris, there to study anatomy and walk the hospitals in furtherance of a certain crotchet which of late had found lodgment in his brain, but would probably die there of inanition before many months were over.

So each of us set out on his own road in life, and after some half-dozen epistles had passed between us we lost sight of each other for several years. Letter-writing was always my detestation, and Langholme was too deeply immersed in his own mental experiences to care greatly about keeping up a correspondence with one who, as he probably thought, had passed out of the circle of his observation for ever.

II

Several years passed away, and the image of Victor Langholme had all but faded from my memory, when one autumn evening, while rambling through the streets of Heidelberg, I suddenly encountered him as he was emerging from a second-hand book store. We recognized each other in a moment, and after a hearty greeting I walked back with him to his hotel, where we dined together and had a pleasant gossip about old times.

Langholme looked even taller and leaner than of yore, and was as eccentric in manners and dress as I always remembered him to have been. He had come abroad for the benefit of his health, which had been injured by over-study, and he was now wandering from one town to another in a desultory aimless sort of way, not caring greatly where he found himself so long as his craving for variety and continual change of scene was gratified. We were both of us so well pleased with the renewal of our broken friendship that we agreed to join company and wander about together till my holidays should be at an end.

A few days later found us at Kaiserbad, at which place we decided to make some little stay, neither of us having visited it before.

Kaiserbad was, at the period of which I write, and probably is now, one of the most enjoyable of places to those who visit it for the first time. The town in itself is charming, and is surrounded by some of the loveliest scenery in Germany, in addition to which there were at that time certain phases of society to be seen there the like of which could be encountered at few places elsewhere.

Neither Victor nor I gambled. It is true that we now and then ventured a little loose change on the red or black, but when the croupier's rake had swept it away we shrugged our shoulders and contented ourselves with being lookers-on for the rest of the evening.

We were strolling through the Kursaal as usual one evening watching the company, when Langholme stopped suddenly in front of one of the tables and plucked me by the sleeve.

"Observe that man," he said, indicating one of the players on the opposite side. "Notice him particularly; I shall have something to tell you concerning him when we get back to the hotel. Strange that I should encounter him here!"

We drew nearer the table, and placed ourselves directly opposite the spot where the stranger indicated by Langholme was seated.

The face of the man in question was certainly an uncommon one—one which, once seen, would not readily he forgotten. His features were bold, well formed, and regular; his eyes were large, black, and piercing; black also were his thick moustache and imperial and his close-cropped hair. The singularity of his appearance lay in the fact that both sides of his face were artistically tattooed, after the fashion of various savage tribes, with an elaborate pattern picked out in dark blue. He was lame, one of his legs having recently been broken by the kick of a horse, as we learned later on, and he was now seated in an invalid chair, behind which stood a servant in livery ready to wheel him away whenever he should grow tired of the game. He was dressed in the extreme Parisian fashion of the period, and wore a cluster of brilliants on one finger which had cut through his tightly fitting primrose-coloured glove. He was nervously anxious about the play, although he strove hard to assume a mask of impassibility, and his keen black eyes lighted up with gleams of avaricious joy, or shot forth lurid, angry flashes from under his thick brows, in accordance with the varying chances of the game, while a slight trembling of the hands whenever a fresh rouleau was handed to him by his servant indicated still further how futile was his assumption of indifference.

But he only gambled indirectly and by deputy.

Immediately in front of him, but so as to allow him a clear view of the table, sat a lady, young, fascinating, and richly dressed, who did all the work of winning and losing. She was very handsome after a certain sinister style of beauty—a style which has for some men such an attraction that they yield themselves body and soul to its influence, while others there are whom it repels, who, warned by some instinct of harm, shrink from it as from something baleful and malign. Small regular features; a complexion which by that light looked as pure and delicate as the tints of the wild rose; large grey eyes shaded by dark eyelashes; a magnificent profusion of yellow silky hair—not auburn or golden, but genuine pale yellow—plaited and coiled round her head after some strange snaky fashion which looked thoroughly original; a figure lithe and slender, but not too tall. There she sat, drawing to herself the eyes of every one in the room.

"Unhappy the mortal round whom yonder siren weaves her spells," muttered Langholme in my ear. "Not until she has compassed his utter ruin will she rend the magic web that binds him to her. Had she lived three centuries ago she would have stood a chance of being burnt as a witch. For you may rely upon it, if we could only drag out of the past and see enacted over again a few of those trials for witchcraft which, especially when the victim was young and beautiful, seem to us so strange and barbarous, we should find that the popular conscience which gave utterance to the verdict was in many cases justified to some extent by seeing, or believing that it saw, in its victim such half-hidden but veritable signs of the fiend's own marking that its rough, sharp justice and summary method of purgation are hardly to be wondered at."

"The stranger calls himself Monsieur de Montillac," I heard some one behind me remark, with a sneering emphasis on the *de*. "He is reported to be immensely rich, and the lady is his wife, or passes for such."

"Adventurers both," muttered Langholme contemptuously.

Madame was certainly an accomplished player as far as preserving her coolness went. Not the quiver of a nerve, not the trembling of an eyelid, betrayed her whether she won or lost, and yet there was an avidity about her style of play which seemed to indicate that she was a thorough gambler.

We wandered about the rooms and the alleys outside for an hour or more, and then we retraced our way to the table, where we found De Montillac and his wife still busy. They had won largely, and there was quite a crowd round the table watching their run of luck. De Montillac could not hide his exultation; but Madame sat as cold and impassive as some marble goddess behind her rapidly increasing pile of gold. And still the croupier's everlasting croak went on.

No sooner, however, did the finger of the clock point to ten than De Montillac touched Madame lightly on the shoulder and whispered a word in her ear. She rose at once, and while her husband swept the heap of winnings into a velvet *sachet*, she pulled off the gloves in which she had been playing, dropped them under the table, and proceeded to draw on another pair. A minute later they were ready to go. The servant behind turned the chair and proceeded to wheel it slowly down the saloon, followed by Madame with downcast eyes, still patiently drawing on her gloves.

"I told you that I had seen De Montillac before," said Langholme as soon as we were alone in his room at the hotel; "but I did not tell you when and where. I saw him six months ago in a dream."

"And you pretend to recognize him again! You must be dreaming still, *mon ami*."

"So be it," answered Langholme quietly. "But pretermit your further observations till you have read something I am about to show you."

Without a word more he unlocked his writing-desk and drew from it a thin morocco-bound book—his diary, in fact—in which he quickly found the passage he wanted. He then laid the book open before me and bade me read. The passage pointed out by him bore the date of March thirteenth of the current year, and ran as follows:—

"Last night I had a singular and very vivid dream, the particulars of which seem to me worthy of finding a record here.

"All at once, as it seemed to me, and with that strange absence of any known foregone cause capable of leading up to such a result so common in dreams, I found myself among the ruins of some moyen-âge castle or baronial residence, the features of which were utterly strange to me. I was digging a hole with spade and pick in one corner of the courtyard. The scene was dimly lighted by an old-fashioned horn lantern, whose function would shortly cease, for a dull, grey, ghostly light was beginning to broaden in the east and night was nearly over. It had been revealed to me by some occult means that below the spot where I was digging lay buried an ancient treasure of immense value, the finding of which would make me rich beyond the dreams of avarice. But underlying the feeling of exultation induced by the hope of finding the treasure was a secret dread of discovery—for, in such a case, discovery meant death. Still, I kept on digging while the dawn slowly broadened, bringing into sharp relief against the clear sky every fantastic feature of the grass-grown ruins. At length my pick struck against something hard. I carefully removed the surrounding earth and laid bare a small iron box. There was no need to open it; it was what I had been told to search for. I knew that its contents consisted of diamonds and rubies of incalculable value unsunned since the reign of Charlemagne. I wrapped the box in my cravat and hid it away within the folds of my vest, buttoning my coat over it for further protection.

"Leaving my implements behind me I emerged from the twilight corner where I had been digging, crossed the courtyard and the castle fosse, and came out on a steep grassy mound which sloped down to some level meadows, beyond which lay a little town, whether French or German I could not tell. I paused for a moment to consider the path I ought to follow. That pause was fatal to me. Suddenly as if it had dropped from the clouds a thick cloth was flung over my head and shoulders. The next moment I was seized tightly round the body, my feet slipped from under me on the damp grass, and with a loud cry I fell heavily to the ground.

"Scarcely had I touched the earth when the cloth that enveloped my head was withdrawn and some one was seated astride my chest—a man whom I had never seen before, who glared down at me with black eyes that were at once mocking and malignant. Judging from his dress, he was a gentleman; his hands, too, were white and delicate and laden with rings; but his face was a remarkable one, not from any peculiarity of features, but from the fact of both his cheeks being tattooed, stamped with a network or reticulation of thin blue lines arranged in some fantastic pattern, after the fashion of a New Zealander or Malayan chief. I struggled desperately but unavailingly to throw him off. He waited without speaking till I sank back breathless and exhausted, then, drawing a small green phial from his pocket, he held it up to the light for a moment. The golden stopper flew open and the mocking light in his eyes deepened as he proceeded to press the phial to my nostrils. A delicious odour seemed to fill my brain and to steal away my senses not unpleasantly. I felt myself sinking softly into a sleep against which I had neither the power nor the wish to struggle. Softly and slowly I seemed to be sinking down through delicious dreamy spaces into a sleep within a sleep—when I was recalled suddenly and rudely from the land of shadows by an importunate knocking at my bedroom door, and on the instant all my cobweb fancies vanished into thinnest air.

"My dream was gone, but the impression left behind it was a particularly vivid one, owing, doubtless, to the fact of my having been so suddenly awakened while its pictures were still painted freshly on my brain.

"*Mem.*—One would like to know whether the curious-looking stranger with the green phial has a real existence, or whether he was merely a figment of my own distempered fancy. Further, if there be such a person, whether he in his turn dreamt that he played the part which I in my dream saw him enact."

"Then you wish me to believe," said I with a smile, as I gave the diary back to Langholme, "that the man you saw in your dream and De Montillac are one and the same?"

"As to that I have no doubt whatever. It must, however, be borne in mind that, had not the man in the first instance been strikingly different in some one point from the ordinary run of people, I should probably not have recognized him again. It was the fact of his being tattooed that first drew my attention to him in the Kursaal and then brought back to my recollection, one by one, the more minute traits of his appearance—the colour and expression of his eyes, his sharp aquiline nose with the mark of an old scar, a peculiar twitching of the under lip, and the same large ring set with brilliants which I saw in my dream."

"Granting for a moment," said I, "that De Montillac and the man you saw in your dream are the same, you do not, I suppose, imagine, as the remark in your diary would lead me to infer, that the man himself had a similar dream—that is to say, one in which he enacted the part of your assailant, at the same time that you had yours?"

"I am certainly inclined to believe that he had such a dream," answered Langholme, "although, even if we could question him on the point, it might be difficult to prove it; for he might have such a dream and yet on waking retain such a vague and confused impression of it that in the course of a few hours it would fade entirely from his memory, or, which I think quite as likely, he might have such a dream with all its seeming vivid reality and yet remember nothing whatever of it when he awoke."

"You are becoming charmingly obscure, my dear Langholme," I remarked. "Take care that you don't lose yourself among the clouds."

"The subject of dreams," resumed Langholme, without noticing my interruption, "is one that for me has always had a peculiar fascination, and one on which at times I have pondered deeply. I believe that dreams may, as a rule, be divided into two classes, which, for the purpose of illustration, we may term normal and abnormal ones. The latter are generally the result of extraneous circumstances, or may follow as the further unwinding of some thread of thought on which the brain has been busy during the day and now proceeds to take up again in a sort of wild tangle during sleep. Perhaps, indeed, it would be safe to put down all such dreams as the sequence of unhealthy action or over-excitement of the brain or stomach, producible by a hundred different causes, known and unknown. Of the other class of dreams, those I have termed normal ones, few in number as regards our recollection of them in comparison with those of the first-named class, I believe that we seldom retain any waking impression; with rare exceptions they pass away in the fumes of sleep and are forgotten. For I believe this, and it is the groundwork of my airy edifice—that we seldom sleep without dreaming. At the close of day, when brain and body are alike wearied, we retire to bed gratefully, to sleep and to gather up new vigour for the morrow; but while our earthly husk reposes, slumbers, is dead but for the mechanical action of certain pulses, the brain—or rather the busy unresting Ariel which tenants that strange domicile—is far away, gathering from fresh woods and pastures new, from the cloudy, illimitable realms of dreamland, stores of strength and elasticity to meet the dull earthly requirements of the morrow. We awake, and we know not that we have been visitants of a strange mysterious land, that we have been enacting a part in some fantastic drama wilder often than the daydreams of the maddest poet. In change, not in inaction, lie the elements of strength. Whenever, in a morning, I feel my mind to be more than usually clear and buoyant, I say to myself, 'Last night I had happy dreams.' Further, I hold with the old poetic dictum that 'All which seems is.' And this brings us back to the starting-point. According to my theory, in all cases of normal, healthy dreams, the actors in the visionary drama, however numerous they may be, all dream that they are filling the parts which the others in *their* dreams see them filling; thus De Montillac should have dreamt at the same time that I dreamt that he enacted the part of my assailant in our imaginary encounter. But, as I said before, to prove that such was the case would be next to impossible."

"What foundation," said I, "is there for supposing, or what proof have you to offer, that the theory you put forward is anything more than a wild flight of imagination on your part?"

"Alas! my friend," answered Langholme, "this is precisely one of those things which cannot be proved—at least, not by any rules of mental arithmetic at present known to us. My wild-goose theory has for its foundation nothing more substantial than certain remarkable coincidences which have come under my notice at different times, a few apparently authentic dream narratives which I have picked up in the course of much desultory reading, and some half-dozen dream stories told me by sundry friends and acquaintances on whose veracity I can rely. Beyond that it is indeed nothing more than a flight of imagination."

De Montillac and his wife were making their game as usual the following evening, and for three nights after that, winning largely on each occasion, but always leaving the table punctually as the clock struck ten.

On the morning of the fifth day of our sojourn, Victor and I left Kaiserbad for an excursion into the surrounding country. We were away nearly a week, and after a late dinner on the evening of our return we mechanically bent our steps towards the Kursaal. As before, we found the Frenchman, his wife, his valet, and his chair in front of one of the tables; only this evening, contrary to precedent, there was no little heap of winnings at the elbow of Madame; while De Montillac's hands trembled more than ever, and his former cynical smile was replaced by a thunderous frown as one rouleau after another was drawn from the velvet sachet.

Except the croupier, the only person at the table who seemed to be winning was a tall, thin, melancholy-looking young Italian of decidedly shabby appearance who sat directly opposite Madame. As usual, there was quite a crowd round the table, and it was amusing to hear the comments of some of the veteran gamblers upon the singular change of fortune which had befallen the Frenchman and his wife since the advent of the young Italian. They were now as unlucky as they had been fortunate before. On two points these ancient rooks were all agreed—that the melancholy-looking stranger was the *bête noire* who had brought ill-luck to the Frenchman, and that if the latter were wise he would quit Kaiserbad at once before the tide of ruin had set in too strongly.

For six consecutive evenings the Frenchman's run of ill-luck continued. The Italian always occupied the seat opposite Madame, silently constituting himself, as it were, her special antagonist; and every evening a hundred greedy eyes gazed enviously at the heap of gold, sometimes light, sometimes heavy, which he carried away at the end of his play. One evening he was later than usual in taking his seat at the table, and till he came fortune smiled brightly on De Montillac, only to desert him the moment his opponent began to play. On the sixth evening the agony of the Frenchman seemed to be culminating. Great drops of sweat stood on his brow as, in accordance with the exigencies of the game, he handed one rouleau after another to Madame and watched the croupier rake them one by one away; and when the clock pointed to ten he struck his clenched fist on the table and said with an oath, in French, "Another week of this work and I shall be a ruined man!"

"Fi donc, Henri!" said Madame reprovingly in low liquid tones. "Do not make a scene, I pray of you," and as she rose she flashed down on the Italian a swift venomous shaft of hatred that would have struck him dead on the spot had her power been equal to her will.

Early next morning Langholme and I set out for a drive, getting back just in time for the *table d'hôte*. The first news that greeted us was that the young Italian had been found dead in bed that morning under very mysterious circumstances, some people opining that he had committed suicide, while others averred that he had been robbed and murdered. But the doctors and the authorities had the case under investigation, and we should doubtless know more about it on the morrow.

III

I was so tired and good-for-nothing on the evening of our return from our excursion that I decided to stay indoors. So Langholme sallied out by himself when dinner was over, promising me that on his return he would furnish me with whatever particulars he might be able to pick up concerning the affair of the young Italian. It was late when he got back and I had gone off to bed, but he came to my room, and, finding I was not asleep, he sat down and proceeded to give me an account of what he had heard.

"Sure enough," said he, "the young Italian is dead—dead, too, under very singular circumstances. He arrived at Kaiserbad about nine days ago, and was, it seems, in the habit of depositing his winnings with the landlord of his hotel every night for safety. Last night, however, the landlord being ill had gone to bed before the Italian got back from the Kursaal. So the young fellow took the bag containing the money into his bedroom, saying with a laugh in the hearing of several people that he would make a pillow of his winnings, and so ensure golden dreams. He then went and smoked a cigar on the terrace, drank half a bottle of wine, asked for his candlestick, bade one or two casual acquaintances good-night, and retired to his room; and that was the last that was seen of him alive. On his arrival at Kaiserbad he complained to his landlord of an affection of the lungs, and got assigned to himself a bedroom on the ground floor, so as to avoid the labour of going upstairs. This bedroom, originally intended for a sitting-room, opened by means of two French windows on to a balcony on which were ranged a number of shrubs and evergreens. Both these windows were securely bolted by one of the servants just before the Italian retired for the night. When the servants knocked at the door this morning there was no reply, and after the scene usual on such occasions, the door was broken open, and the young man was found lying in bed, apparently in a pleasant sleep, but in reality stone dead. Near the bed was found a small empty phial, which gave rise to the rumour that he had poisoned himself, but all his winnings of last night had disappeared. A more minute examination showed that a square piece of glass had been cut out of one of the windows by means of a diamond, in such a position that any one from the outside by putting his hand through the aperture could at once draw back the bolt by which the window was secured. There seems to be no doubt that such was the method adopted for effecting an entrance, but whoever did it was cool enough to rebolt the window on leaving the room.

"There being no external marks of violence to account for death, the doctors have decided upon making a post-mortem examination of the body.

"For these and other particulars I am indebted to our obliging friend Herr Volckmann, who, as you are probably aware, is a Government functionary of high position.

"There are one or two points connected with the case respecting which I have not spoken to any one. Firstly, I discovered that the suite of apartments occupied by De Montillac and his wife are situated directly over the bedroom of the Italian. Secondly, the empty phial found near the dead man's bed is made of thick green cut glass and has a gold stopper—the very phial, in fact, seen by me in that dream with which our French friend was so signally mixed up, of which you read an account a few days ago in my diary. The phial, though empty, still retained a peculiar, faint, aromatic odour, very refreshing and delightful, the inhalation of which brought vividly to my mind every little half-forgotten incident connected with that visionary struggle among the ruins."

Next morning Langholme and I went to the hotel where the body of the Italian lay. The influence of Herr Volckmann procured me a sight of the phial, which was now in the hands of the police. It tallied exactly with the description given in my friend's diary.

"It has just been whispered to me," said Langholme on our way back, "that strong suspicions attach to the Frenchman and his wife, and that their rooms and effects are about to undergo a strict examination by the police."

"Do you intend to say anything to Volckmann respecting the phial in connection with your dream?" I asked.

Victor shook his head. "What I could tell would not be accepted as evidence by any one but a dreamer and visionary like myself. Volckmann would scout the idea of acting on such a suggestion. Besides, De Montillac is already under surveillance, and should the perquisition of the police bring to light nothing inculpatory, I don't think that I should be justified in endeavouring, on the mere strength of what you and I know, to build up an accusation against a man who may possibly be innocent, however much I myself may feel inclined to believe the contrary."

Next morning Langholme and I set out for Munich, and were away ten days. We had scarcely alighted at the hotel on our return to Kaiserbad before we encountered Volckmann. "What about the affair of the young Italian?" was Langholme's first question.

"Ah, bah! that bagatelle is hushed up and all but forgotten in our gay little pandemonium here," answered the lively Herr, with a lift of the shoulders that was quite as expressive as Lord Burleigh's historical nod could ever have been. "The result confirmed the opinion whispered by you at the first. There is no doubt that he died from the results of some strange poison, but by whom administered there was no evidence to show. That it was not his own act there can be no moral doubt; besides which, his winnings had disappeared. However, as the police could make nothing of the case, and as the doctors were puzzled and could not agree among themselves, and as on examination of the dead man's papers it was found that he was a nobody—merely the son of a Customs official at some petty Italian port—it was not thought advisable to make too much bother about a trifle, so the affair was allowed to lapse quietly into oblivion. For, as you are doubtless aware, it is the policy of a paternal Government as regards this favoured spot to imbue its visitors with the conviction that dining, flirtation, roulette, and rouge-et-noir are the sole ends worth living for."

"And De Montillac and his wife?"

"They left here several days ago," answered the German. "It did not suit them to have their effects examined, although nothing was discovered bearing on the case in hand, and the day after they were released from surveillance away they went to try their luck elsewhere. As for the Frenchman, it was proved by medical evidence that he was incapable of walking six yards except on crutches; and as regards Madame, in the first place it was not a likely deed for a woman to do, and, secondly, she was seen by two or three of the serv-ants to retire to her room shortly after eleven o'clock. Now, in order to effect an entrance into the Italian's room by way of the window she would have had to pass along a much-frequented corridor, down the principal staircase of the house, and out at the front door, round which there is generally a knot of young men smoking till a late hour, and after that the door is secured and left in charge of the night porter and could not possibly be opened by a stranger without attracting attention. But even supposing she reached the room without discov-ery, she would have to come the same way back. No, I don't see how it would be possible for her to do it and escape detection."

"Nevertheless," whispered Victor to me as we passed on into the hotel, "I for one believe that the secret of the young Italian's death rests between De Montillac and his wife, and nothing short of proof positive would convince me to the contrary."

"And that you are never likely to have in this world," said I.

A fortnight later my holiday came to an end, and after bidding Langholme a cordial farewell I set off for London and hard work, leaving my friend to pursue his tour alone.

IV

EXTRACT FROM A LETTER BY
VICTOR LANGHOLME, ESQ.

WASHINGTON, U.S.: DECEMBER 1862.

...I have already apprised you that I lately fell in with the ci-devant De Montillac while wandering in the neighbourhood of one of the many fields of slaughter which signalized McClellan's disastrous retreat from the Chickahominy to the Potomac, and I now proceed to give you some further particulars of our meeting. An announcement of my profession (you are aware that I hold a French diploma) procured me admission into places where as a mere stranger I should have been denied.

The moment I set eyes on him I knew him again. He was lying on a rude pallet in a corner of a large barn which for lack of a better place had been converted into a temporary hospital. You remember his appearance at Kaiserbad—his tattooed face, his jewellery, his invalid chair, his servant in livery, and his siren of a wife. Now, in a bundle by the side of his pallet, was tied up the uniform, torn and dirty, of a private in the Federal Army. He had been struck some days before by a splinter of a shell, and the doctors had given him up. His period of intense pain was over when I saw him; he suffered little now; it was a fatal sign, and he knew it. Firmly clutched in one hand he held a common horn box containing a little snuff, of which he inhaled a pinch occasionally with an air of thorough miserly enjoyment, his last earthly care evidently being to make his snuff last out till he should be past needing another pinch. I sat down on a rude plank by his side.

"Good-day, Monsieur de Montillac. How do you find yourself?" I said in French.

"How! Monsieur knew me during my *beaux jours*, and he recognizes me again—and here!" he exclaimed, turning on me with a momentary vivacity. "But Monsieur is English," he added, peering up curiously into my face, "and he must pardon me when I say that I do not remember ever having had the pleasure of meeting him in society." He gave a ghastly smirk, tapped his box, and peered into it as though debating with himself whether he could afford to offer me a pinch. Finally he decided that he could not.

"I encountered you at Kaiserbad some few summers ago," I said; "you and Madame de Montillac were there and had a great run of luck, if I remember rightly. May I venture to hope that Madame is well and happy?"

An evil light leapt into his eyes, and his lips tightened over his teeth as he muttered a string of execrations under his breath.

"And the young Italian," I said in a low voice, "the poor young man who died so mysteriously one night, after winning heavily at the tables?"

"What of him?" he asked. "Why do you speak to me about him?"

"Because you know the secret of his death," I whispered.

His lips turned livid, and a sudden terror looked at me out of his eyes. For a little while he lay without speaking.

"Well—yes—I do know the secret of his death," he answered after a time; "and if you are at all curious about it, I will tell you the story; though how you happen to know that I was in any way mixed up with the affair is more than I can imagine. However, that matters nothing now. A minute ago, when you spoke of the Italian, a sudden chill came over me. I forgot for the moment that I was past all earthly hopes and fears, that if I were the veriest murderer on earth, Justice could not touch me now, that if all the riches in the world were mine they would be as so much dust in my hands—to such a bitter strait have I come at last."

He lay still for a little while with shut eyes and a troubled look on his face. His thoughts were travelling back into the past; his memories were steeped in gall.

What follows was told me in a fragmentary way, in the course of the half-dozen visits I paid De Montillac before he died, and with many breaks and abrupt changes of subject between. I jotted down a few notes from time to time in the course of the recital, and now give you the narrative as nearly as possible in the man's own words.

"I am the son of one of the most eminent professors of the art of legerdemain which France has ever had the honour of producing. As a youth I wandered up and down the Continent with my father, assisting him in his performances and being gradually initiated into the mysteries of the profession. But I never took kindly to it. That, however, did not greatly matter, for my father's gains were large, I was his only son, and he indulged me in every way as though I were a young aristocrat.

"But when I was about twenty-two years old my father and I had a terrible quarrel. There was a *jupon* in the case, you may be sure.

Neither of us would give way to the other, and it ended by my father turning me out of doors. I borrowed a thousand francs from a friend and set out for England, a country which I had long wished to visit.

"But a thousand francs will not last for ever, and before long I saw starvation staring me in the face. Accordingly, I at once proceeded to furbish up my half-forgotten acquirements, designing, monsieur, to astonish your phlegmatic nation with a display of legerdemain such as they had never been privileged to witness before. Suddenly I saw the announcement of an exhibition by one of your great English wizards. I went to assist at it, and discovered to my dismay that the Englishman knew far more than I did, and that without long years of practice I could not hope to enter into competition with him.

"I will not weary you, monsieur, by dwelling on this part of my career. It is enough to say that I sank lower and lower, till at length I was glad to accept the offer of an eminent caravan proprietor to fill the post of New Zealand chief in his establishment, his last chief having lately died. The only condition was that I should allow myself to be tattooed. I was reckless and desperate, and acceded to the proposal. The operation was skilfully performed by an ex-sailor who had lived for years among a tribe of aborigines; and I then made my appearance before the public in the paint, feathers, and paraphernalia of a genuine Maori chief. It was a life that suited me well enough for a time; I had always a sufficiency of spare cash for absinthe and cigarettes.

"After a few years I was recalled to France by the death of my father. He had forgiven me at the last moment and had left me all his property. After airing my fortune in Paris for six months I set out on an extended tour. But I did not go alone.

"How or where I first met Elise Duvrier, it matters not to say. I knew nothing of her antecedents—know nothing of them to this day—and nothing I cared. I knew only that I loved her. Elise was wise; she loved no one but herself. I bought her a diamond bracelet, gave her ample proof that my fortune was a substantial reality, and she agreed to follow my fortunes.

"For two years we travelled from place to place as the caprices of Elise dictated. She was not without her little extravagances, and my fortune was slowly melting away; but I was powerless to help myself. After a time we grew tired of sight-seeing, and then Elise took to gambling; at first merely *pour passer le temps*, but after a time the passion grew upon her and became the one absorbing occupation of her life. As a rule she was wonderfully lucky, and for a time her winnings served to prop my tottering fortunes.

"After a time we came to Kaiserbad, and fortune befriended us as usual till the young Italian of whom you lately spoke appeared on the scene. But with his arrival everything changed, and before long I half began to believe in the theory of Elise that he had brought some diabolical influence to bear upon us. Elise, who was terribly superstitious, had indeed urged me to go away after the first night, but for once I decided contrary to her wishes and determined to remain. At the end of a week I found a frightful hole in my fast-decreasing resources, but Elise only laughed when I spoke of it, and said that I ought to have taken her warning in time.

"One night about eleven o'clock she came into my dressing-room and seated herself on a low stool at my feet. 'Henri,' she said, looking up and speaking very slowly and distinctly, 'Justine tells me that she heard our Italian friend say downstairs just now that he intended to make a pillow of his rouleaux tonight and so have golden dreams.'

"'What has that to do with us?'

"'Nothing—nothing at all. You like to hear the gossip of the place, so I thought I would tell you. But it is almost time for you to take your draught.'

"Shortly afterwards I went to bed. Elise brought me my custom-ary potion, after which I at once fell asleep, and did not awake again till aroused by the noise of some one effecting an entrance into my room by way of the window. Next moment I recognized the intruder as Elise. She was in male attire, having dressed herself for the occa-sion in a masquerade suit which formed a portion of her wardrobe, while a small black bag was slung by a strap from her shoulder. Having drawn up the rope-ladder by means of which she had both left and entered the room, she took off her slouched hat, wig, and mask, turned up the night-lamp, and came and sat down beside me.

"'Where have you been?' I asked, although I had already guessed the truth.

"'I have been paying our Italian friend a visit, and he has kindly made me a present of his last evening's winnings,' and she pointed carelessly to the bag.

"'You have robbed him!' I exclaimed. 'You are—'

"She laid her hand over my mouth. 'You forget, my Henri, that you are addressing yourself to a lady.'

"I stared at her, astounded by the audacity of the exploit.

"'You would like some particulars,' she said. 'Good; you shall have them. I put on my masquerade dress of Monsieur Smeeth the Englishman. I took the rope-ladder which you, in your foolish dread of fire, always keep by you wherever you go; I fixed the hooks in the window-frame, let down the ladder outside, and then descended with my empty bag as nimbly as a squirrel. After listening for a minute, I took my ring and cut neatly and deftly a little square out of one of the lower panes of the window. To unbolt the window, open it, and glide behind the curtains was the work of a few moments—then forward, into the room, step by step, till I stood by the bedside and bent silently over the sleeper. A night-lamp was burning on the chimney-piece.

"'Naturally, I may say unconsciously, my fingers strayed to his pillow. Yes—underneath it was certainly some hard substance—a bag of gold! But something disturbed him; he turned over, flung up one arm, muttered a few words, and seemed as if he were about to awake. What a predicament for your poor Elise! But thanks to you, my Henri, I had not come unprepared for such an emergency.'

"'Thanks to me! I do not understand you, Elise.'

"'I had the green phial concealed in the breast pocket of my coat.'

"I looked at her in astonishment. 'And pray who revealed to you the secret of the green phial?'

"'You yourself, dear friend; no one else.'

"'I had forgotten.'

"'Being, then, prepared, no sooner did my sleeper begin to grow restless than I applied the phial to his nostrils for a few seconds. It quieted him almost immediately. I then gently raised his head and drew the bag from under his pillow, together with a small box of very excellent *bon-bons* which I found there. Unfortunately as I was crossing the room the phial slipped from my fingers and rolled under the bed, but nobody will know it for yours when it is found. I re-fastened the window, climbed the ladder, and here I am. Signor l'Italiano will be rather astonished when he wakes in the morning and finds that his gold has taken to itself wings, and vanished for ever. Really these *bon-bons* are very nice.'

"Next morning, when the news spread through the hotel that the young Italian had been found dead in bed, even Elise paled for a time, and a deadly fear caused her to tremble in every limb. But she soon recovered her *sang-froid*. 'I never intended that it should end thus—never!' she asseverated, and I believed her.

"Probably, monsieur, you know as well as I how the affair ended. The police made a perquisition into our effects, but found nothing inculpatory—Elise was too wary for that—and as soon as we were free to do so, we left Kaiserbad for ever.

"From the night of the young Italian's death a cloud seemed to grow up between Elise and myself—an intangible something, easily felt, but difficult to describe. I loved her, and yet I feared her. I knew that if I should ever stand in the way of her interests she would sacrifice me with as little compunction as she had sacrificed the Italian, and yet I could not bear to part from her. It seemed to me, when I thought of such a thing, as if all the light and gladness of my life would be shut out for ever were she to leave me.

"After a time we found ourselves at Nice, where I fell ill of a fever. Elise was disconsolate. As soon as my wits began to wander she ordered me to be taken to the hospital; then she paid the hotel bill, packed up her trinkets, and fled away. And from that day to this I have never seen her again.

"How I gradually sunk in the world till I came to be what you see me now were a weary story for me to tell, and twice as weary for you, monsieur, to listen to. Enough that I am here, but not for long now—not for long!"

When De Montillac had ceased speaking, I said to him: "You made mention just now of a certain green phial, and seemed to attribute the death of the Italian to the inhalation of its contents. As a medical man I am interested in such matters. Can you give me any further particulars concerning the phial in question?"

"It was originally the property of my father," answered De Montillac, and descended to me, together with many other curious objects, at his decease. My father dabbled a good deal in toxicology, and professed, with what degree of truth I know not, to have discovered the secret of some of those subtle poisons of which such terrible use was made by the Borgias and other great Italian families during the middle ages. The green phial was supposed to be nothing more harmful than a tiny flask of perfume, but its properties were peculiar. It emitted a faint but delightful odour different from any other perfume with which I am acquainted. Inhale this odour for a quarter of a minute with the phial close to your nostrils, and the effect upon the system was refreshing and exhilarating in the highest degree, stimulating the brain, brightening the eyes, and causing the blood to course more generously through the veins—an effect delicious but transitory. Inhale the perfume of the phial for half a minute, and you would fall without warning into a profound lethargy lasting for several hours. Let some one hold the phial to your nostrils for sixty seconds, and you would never wake more on earth.

"I had kept this singular drug by me as a curiosity, never making further use of it—as, indeed, why should I?—than at rare intervals to take an exhilarating sniff, thinking sometimes that, should my troubles ever become greater than I could bear, I knew of an easy and pleasant mode of ending them for ever.

"When Elise made mention of the phial on the night of the Italian's death, there came into my mind the picture of a half-forgotten dream, in which, after overpowering a man—a stranger whom I had never seen before—I rendered him insensible by means of the phial and then robbed him of a box of precious stones which he had just dug out of the ruins of some old castle. I told the story laughingly to Elise over breakfast next morning, never thinking that she would ever call it to mind again or turn to such strange use in real life an incident based on nothing but a dream."

I had learned from De Montillac all I wanted to know.

He lay back in a state of exhaustion after he had finished his narrative, of which the latter part had been told in low, broken accents which showed how weak he was becoming. I administered a restorative and then rose to leave him, telling him that I would visit him again towards evening.

"You won't forget to come, doctor?" he said, his eyes gazing into mine with strange yearning wistfulness.

"I will not forget."

At five o'clock I went back to the hospital. De Montillac was lying with his face turned to the wall, his empty snuff-box firmly grasped in one hand. I thought he was asleep. I touched him. He was dead.

A MARKED MAN (1901)

W. W. Jacobs

William Wymark Jacobs (1863–1943) is renowned as the author of "The Monkey's Paw", a chilling gothic tale of a seemingly "ordinary little paw, dried to a mummy", which has a "spell put on it by an old fakir" to grant the owner three wishes, an alluring prospect that ultimately has dire consequences. Although the perennial popularity of this tale has made Jacobs' name synonymous with the macabre, he was also a successful writer of crime fiction (his work has been compared to the noir masterpieces of Raymond Chandler), and a notable comic author. To *The Times*, Jacobs was "one of the greatest masters of story construction, especially short story construction, in our language".

"A Marked Man", from the 1901 collection *Light Freights*, is a story in the comic mode that reflects Jacobs' close connection with the Thames as the son of a London river-man. The tale focuses on the sailor Ginger Dick who, unlike the majority of his shipmates, refuses as a matter of principle to get tattooed. His resolution fades, however, when two companions tempt him with a notable financial incentive. Jacobs draws here on the longstanding connection of tattoos with naval culture, a link which has had an ongoing influence on the iconography of traditional Euro-American tattooing. Ginger Dick's tattoo of a "full-rigged ship" remains, of course, an archetypal tattoo design.

"TATTOOING IS A GIFT," SAID THE NIGHT-WATCHMAN, firmly. "It 'as to be a gift, as you can well see. A man 'as to know wot 'e is going to tattoo an' 'ow to do it; there's no rubbing out or altering. It's a gift, an' it can't be learned. I knew a man once as used to tattoo a cabin-boy all over every v'y'ge trying to learn. 'E was a slow, painstaking sort o' man, and the langwidge those boys used to use while 'e was at work would 'ardly be believed, but 'e 'ad to give up trying arter about fifteen years and take to crochet-work instead.

"Some men won't be tattooed at all, being proud o' their skins or sich-like, and for a good many years Ginger Dick, a man I've spoke to you of before, was one o' that sort. Like many red-'aired men 'e 'ad a very white skin, which 'e was very proud of, but at last, owing to a unfortnit idea o' making 'is fortin, 'e let hisself be done.

"It come about in this way: Him and old Sam Small and Peter Russet 'ad been paid off from their ship and was 'aving a very 'appy, pleasant time ashore. They was careful men in a way, and they 'ad taken a room down East India Road way, and paid up the rent for a month. It came cheaper than a lodging-'ouse, besides being a bit more private and respectable, a thing old Sam was always very pertickler about.

"They 'ad been ashore about three weeks when one day old Sam and Peter went off alone becos Ginger said 'e wasn't going with 'em. He said a lot more things, too: 'ow 'e was going to see wot it felt like to be in bed without 'aving a fat old man groaning 'is 'eart out, and another one knocking on the mantelpiece all night with twopence and wanting to know why he wasn't being served.

"Ginger Dick fell into a quiet sleep arter they'd gone; then 'e woke up and 'ad a sip from the water-jug—he'd 'a had more, only somebody 'ad dropped the soap in it—and then dozed off agin. It was late in the afternoon when 'e woke, and then 'e see Sam and Peter Russet standing by the side o' the bed looking at 'im.

"'Where've you been?' ses Ginger, stretching hisself and yawning.

"'Bisness,' ses Sam, sitting down an' looking very important. 'While you've been laying on your back all day me an' Peter Russet 'as been doing a little 'ead-work.'

"'Oh!' ses Ginger. 'Wot with?'

"Sam coughed and Peter began to whistle, an' Ginger he laid still and smiled up at the ceiling, and began to feel good-tempered agin.

"'Well, wot's the bisness?' he ses, at last.

"Sam looked at Peter, but Peter shook 'is 'ead at him.

"'It's just a little bit o' bisness we 'appened to drop on,' ses Sam, at last, 'me an' Peter, and I think that, with luck and management, we're in a fair way to make our fortunes. Peter, 'ere, ain't given to looking on the cheerful side o' things, but 'e thinks so, too.'

"'I do,' ses Peter, 'but it won't be managed right if you go blabbing it to everybody.'

"'We must 'ave another man in it, Peter,' ses Sam; 'and, wot's more, 'e must 'ave ginger-coloured 'air. That being so, it's only right and proper that our dear old pal Ginger should 'ave the fust offer.'

"It wasn't often that Sam was so affeckshunate, and Ginger couldn't make it out at all. Ever since 'e'd known 'im the old man 'ad been full o' plans o' making money without earning it. Stupid plans they was, too, but the stupider they was the more old Sam liked 'em.

"'Well, wot is it?' asks Ginger, agin.

"Old Sam walked over to the door and shut it; then 'e sat down on the bed and spoke low so that Ginger could hardly 'ear 'im.

"'A little public-'ouse,' he ses, 'to say nothing of 'ouse property, and a red-'aired old landlady wot's a widder. As nice a old lady as any one could wish for, for a mother.'

"'For a mother!' ses Ginger, staring.

"'And a lovely barmaid with blue eyes and yellow 'air, wot ud be the red-'edded man's cousin,' ses Peter Russet.

"'Look 'ere,' ses Ginger, 'are you going to tell me in plain English wot it's all about, or are you not?'

"'We've been in a little pub down Bow way, me an' Peter,' ses Sam, 'and we'll tell you more about it if you promise to join us an' go shares. It's kep' by a widder woman whose on'y son—*red'-aired son*—went to sea twenty-three years ago, at the age o' fourteen, an' was never 'eard of arterwards. Seeing we was sailor-men, she told us all about it, an' 'ow she still 'opes for him to walk into 'er arms afore she dies.'

"'She dreamt a fortnit ago that 'e turned up safe and sound, with red whiskers,' ses Peter.

"Ginger Dick sat up and looked at 'em without a word; then 'e got up out o' bed, an' pushing old Sam out of the way began to dress, and at last 'e turned round and asked Sam whether he was drunk or only mad.

"'All right,' ses Sam; 'if you won't take it on we'll find somebody as will, that's all; there's no call to get huffy about it. You ain't the on'y red-'edded man in the world.'

"Ginger didn't answer 'im; he went on dressing, but every now and then 'e'd look at Sam and give a little larf wot made Sam's blood boil.

"'You've got nothin' to larf at, Ginger,' he ses, at last; 'the land-lady's boy 'ud be about the same age as wot you are now; 'e 'ad a scar over the left eyebrow same as wot you've got, though I don't

suppose *he* got it by fighting a chap three times 'is size. 'E 'ad bright
blue eyes, a small, well-shaped nose, and a nice mouth.'

"'Same as you, Ginger,' ses Peter, looking out of the winder.

"Ginger coughed and looked thoughtful.

"'It sounds all right, mates,' 'e ses, at last, 'but I don't see 'ow
we're to go to work. I don't want to get locked up for deceiving.'

"'You can't get locked up,' ses Sam; 'if you let 'er discover you
and claim you, 'ow can you get locked up for it? We shall go in an'
see her agin, and larn all there is to larn, especially about the tattoo
marks, and then—'

"'*Tattoo marks!*' ses Ginger.

"'That's the strong p'int,' ses Sam. "Er boy 'ad a sailor dancing
a 'ornpipe on 'is left wrist, an' a couple o' dolphins on his right.
On 'is chest 'e 'ad a full-rigged ship, and on 'is back between
'is shoulder-blades was the letters of 'is name—C.R.S.: Charles
Robert Smith.'

"'Well, you silly old fool,' ses Ginger, starting up in a temper,
'that spiles it all. I ain't got a mark on me.'

"Old Sam smiles at 'im and pats him on the shoulder. 'That's
where you show your want of intelleck, Ginger,' he ses, kindly. 'Why
don't you think afore you speak? Wot's easier than to 'ave 'em put on?'

"'*Wot?*' screams Ginger. 'Tattoo *me*! Spile my skin with a lot o'
beastly blue marks! Not me, not if I know it. I'd like to see anybody
try it, that's all.'

"He was that mad 'e wouldn't listen to reason, and, as old Sam
said, 'e couldn't have made more fuss if they'd offered to skin 'im
alive, an' Peter Russet tried to prove that a man's skin was made to
be tattooed on, or else there wouldn't be tattooers; same as a man
'ad been given two legs so as 'e could wear trousers. But reason was
chucked away on Ginger, an' 'e wouldn't listen to 'em.

"They started on 'im agin next day, but all Sam and Peter could say didn't move 'im, although Sam spoke so feeling about the joy of a pore widder woman getting 'er son back agin arter all these years that 'e nearly cried.

"They went down agin to the pub that evening, and Ginger, who said 'e was curious to see, wanted to go too. Sam, who still 'ad 'opes of 'im, wouldn't 'ear of it, but at last it was arranged that 'e wasn't to go inside, but should take a peep through the door. They got on a tram at Aldgate, and Ginger didn't like it becos Sam and Peter talked it over between theirselves in whispers and pointed out likely red-'aired men in the road.

"And 'e didn't like it when they got to the Blue Lion, and Sam and Peter went in and left 'im outside, peeping through the door. The landlady shook 'ands with them quite friendly, and the barmaid, a fine-looking girl, seemed to take a lot o' notice of Peter. Ginger waited about outside for nearly a couple of hours, and at last they came out, talking and larfing, with Peter wearing a white rose wot the barmaid 'ad given 'im.

"Ginger Dick 'ad a good bit to say about keeping 'im waiting all that time, but Sam said that they'd been getting valuable information, an' the more 'e could see of it the easier the job appeared to be, an' then him an' Peter wished for to bid Ginger good-bye, while they went and 'unted up a red-'aired friend o' Peter's named Charlie Bates.

"They all went in somewhere and 'ad a few drinks fust, though, and arter a time Ginger began to see things in a different light to wot 'e 'ad before, an' to be arf ashamed of 'is selfishness, and 'e called Sam's pot a loving-cup, an' kep' on drinking out of it to show there was no ill-feeling, although Sam kep' telling him there wasn't. Then Sam spoke up about tattooing agin, and Ginger said that every man in the country ought to be tattooed to prevent the smallpox. He got so excited about it that old Sam 'ad to promise 'im that he should be tattooed that very night, before he could pacify 'im.

"They all went off 'ome with their arms round each other's necks, but arter a time Ginger found that Sam's neck wasn't there, an' 'e stopped and spoke serious to Peter about it. Peter said 'e couldn't account for it, an' 'e had such a job to get Ginger 'ome that 'e thought they would never ha' got there. He got 'im to bed at last an' then 'e sat down and fell asleep waiting for Sam.

"Ginger was the last one to wake up in the morning, an' before 'e woke he kept making a moaning noise. His 'ead felt as though it was going to bust, 'is tongue felt like a brick, and 'is chest was so sore 'e could 'ardly breathe. Then at last 'e opened 'is eyes and looked up and saw Sam an' Peter and a little man with a black moustache.

"'Cheer up, Ginger,' ses Sam, in a kind voice, 'it's going on beautiful.'

"'My 'ead's splitting,' ses Ginger, with a groan, 'an' I've got pins an' needles all over my chest.'

"'Needles,' ses the man with the black moustache. 'I never use pins; they'd pison the flesh.'

"Ginger sat up in bed and stared at 'im; then 'e bent 'is 'ead down and squinted at 'is chest, and next moment 'e was out of bed and all three of 'em was holding 'im down on the floor to prevent 'im breaking the tattooer's neck which 'e'd set 'is 'eart upon doing, and explaining to 'im that the tattooer was at the top of 'is profession, and that it was only by a stroke of luck 'e had got 'im. And Sam reminded 'im of wot 'e 'ad said the night before, and said he'd live to thank 'im for it.

"''Ow much is there done?' ses Ginger, at last, in a desprit voice.

"Sam told 'im, and Ginger lay still and called the tattooer all the names he could think of; which took 'im some time.

"'It's no good going on like that, Ginger,' ses Sam. 'Your chest is quite spiled at present, but if you on'y let 'im finish it'll be a perfeck picter.'

"'I take pride in it,' ses the tattooer; 'working on your skin, mate, is like painting on a bit o' silk.'

"Ginger gave in at last, and told the man to go on with the job and finish it, and 'e even went so far as to do a little bit o' tattooing 'imself on Sam when he wasn't looking. 'E only made one mark, becos the needle broke off, and Sam made such a fuss that Ginger said any one would ha' thought 'e'd hurt 'im.

"It took three days to do Ginger altogether, and he was that sore 'e could 'ardly move or breathe, and all the time 'e was laying on 'is bed of pain Sam and Peter Russet was round at the Blue Lion enjoying theirselves and picking up information. The second day was the worst, owing to the tattooer being the worse for licker. Drink affects different people in different ways, and Ginger said the way it affected that chap was to make 'im think 'e was sewing buttons on instead o' tattooing.

"'Owever 'e was done at last; his chest and 'is arms and 'is shoulders, and he nearly broke down when Sam borrowed a bit o' looking-glass and let 'im see hisself. Then the tattooer rubbed in some stuff to make 'is skin soft agin, and some more stuff to make the marks look a bit old.

"Sam wanted to draw up an agreement, but Ginger Dick and Peter Russet wouldn't 'ear of it. They both said that that sort o' thing wouldn't look well in writing, not if anybody else happened to see it, that is; besides which Ginger said it was impossible for 'im to say 'ow much money he would 'ave the handling of. Once the tattooing was done 'e began to take a'most kindly to the plan, an' being an orfin, so far as 'e knew, he almost began to persuade hisself that the red-'aired landlady *was* 'is mother.

"'They 'ad a little call over in their room to see 'ow Ginger was to do it, and to discover the weak p'ints. Sam worked up a squeaky voice, and pretended to be the landlady, and Peter pretended to be the good-looking barmaid.

"'They went all through it over and over agin, the only unpleasantness being caused by Peter Russet letting off a screech every time Ginger alluded to 'is chest wot set 'is teeth on edge, and old Sam as the landlady offering Ginger pots o' beer which made 'is mouth water.

"''We shall go round tomorrow for the last time,' ses Sam, 'as we told 'er we're sailing the day arter. Of course me an' Peter, 'aving made your fortin, drop out altogether, but I dessay we shall look in agin in about six months' time, and then perhaps the landlady will interduce us to you.'

"''Meantime,' ses Peter Russet, 'you mustn't forget that you've got to send us Post Office money-orders every week.'

"Ginger said 'e wouldn't forget, and they shook 'ands all round and 'ad a drink together, and the next arternoon Sam and Peter went to the Blue Lion for a last visit.

"It was quite early when they came back. Ginger was surprised to see 'em, and he said so, but 'e was more surprised when 'e heard their reasons.

"''It come over us all at once as we'd bin doing wrong,' Sam ses, setting down with a sigh.

"''Come over us like a chill, it did,' ses Peter.

"''Doing wrong?' ses Ginger Dick, staring. 'Wot are you talking about?'

"''Something the landlady said showed us as we was doin' wrong,' ses old Sam, very solemn; 'it come over us in a flash.'

"''Like lightning,' ses Peter.

"'All of a sudden we see wot a cruel, 'ard thing it was to go and try and deceive a poor widder woman,' ses Sam, in a 'usky voice; 'we both see it at once.'

"Ginger Dick looks at 'em 'ard, 'e did, and then, 'e ses, jeering like:—

"'I s'pose you don't want any Post Office money-orders sent you, then?' he ses.

"'No,' says Sam and Peter, both together.

"'You may have 'em all,' ses Sam; 'but if you 'll be ruled by us, Ginger, you 'll give it up, same as wot we 'ave—you'll sleep the sweeter for it.'

"'Give it up!' shouts Ginger, dancing up an' down the room, 'arter being tattooed all over? Why, you must be crazy, Sam—wot's the matter with you?'

"'It ain't fair play agin a woman,' says old Sam, 'three strong men agin one poor old woman; that's wot we feel, Ginger.'

"'Well, *I* don't feel like it,' ses Ginger; 'you please yourself, and I'll please myself.'

"'E went off in a huff, an' next morning 'e was so disagreeable that Sam an' Peter went and signed on board a steamer called the *Penguin*, which was to sail the day arter. They parted bad friends all round, and Ginger Dick gave Peter a nasty black eye, and Sam said that when Ginger came to see things in a proper way agin he'd be sorry for wot 'e'd said. And 'e said that 'im and Peter never wanted to look on 'is face agin.

"Ginger Dick was a bit lonesome arter they'd gone, but 'e thought it better to let a few days go by afore 'e went and adopted the red-'aired landlady. He waited a week, and at last, unable to wait any longer, 'e went out and 'ad a shave and smartened hisself up, and went off to the Blue Lion.

"It was about three o'clock when 'e got there, and the little public-'ouse was empty except for two old men in the jug-and-bottle entrance. Ginger stopped outside a minute or two to try and stop 'is trembling, and then 'e walks into the private bar and raps on the counter.

"'Glass o' bitter, ma'am, please,' he ses to the old lady as she came out o' the little parlour at the back o' the bar.

"The old lady drew the beer, and then stood with one 'and holding the beer-pull and the other on the counter, looking at Ginger Dick in 'is new blue jersey and cloth cap.

"'Lovely weather, ma'am,' ses Ginger, putting his left arm on the counter and showing the sailor-boy dancing the hornpipe.

"'Very nice,' ses the landlady, catching sight of 'is wrist an' staring at it. 'I suppose you sailors like fine weather?'

"'Yes, ma'am,' ses Ginger, putting his elbows on the counter so that the tattoo marks on both wrists was showing. 'Fine weather an' a fair wind suits us.'

"'It's a 'ard life, the sea,' ses the old lady.

"She kept wiping down the counter in front of 'im over an' over agin, an' 'e could see 'er staring at 'is wrists as though she could 'ardly believe her eyes. Then she went back into the parlour, and Ginger 'eard her whispering, and by and by she came out agin with the blue-eyed barmaid.

"'Have you been at sea long?' ses the old lady.

"'Over twenty-three years, ma'am,' ses Ginger, avoiding the barmaid's eye wot was fixed on 'is wrists, 'and I've been shipwrecked four times; the fust time when I was a little nipper o' fourteen.'

"'Pore thing,' ses the landlady, shaking 'er 'ead. 'I can feel for you; my boy went to sea at that age, and I've never seen 'im since.'

"'I'm sorry to 'ear it, ma'am,' ses Ginger, very respectful-like. 'I suppose I've lost my mother, so I can feel for you.'

"'Suppose you've lost your mother!' ses the barmaid; 'don't you know whether you have?'

"'No,' ses Ginger Dick, very sad. 'When I was wrecked the fust time I was in a open boat for three weeks, and, wot with the exposure and 'ardly any food, I got brain-fever and lost my memory.'

"'Pore thing,' ses the landlady agin.

"'I might as well be a orfin,' ses Ginger, looking down; 'sometimes I seem to see a kind, 'andsome face bending over me, and fancy it's my mother's, but I can't remember 'er name, or my name, or anythink about 'er.'

"'You remind me o' my boy very much,' ses the landlady, shaking 'er 'ead; 'you've got the same coloured 'air, and, wot's extraordinary, you've got the same tattoo marks on your wrists. Sailor-boy dancing on one and a couple of dolphins on the other. And 'e 'ad a little scar on 'is eyebrow, much the same as yours.'

"'Good 'evins,' ses Ginger Dick, starting back and looking as though 'e was trying to remember something.

"'I s'pose they 're common among seafaring men?' ses the landlady, going off to attend to a customer.

"Ginger Dick would ha' liked to ha' seen 'er a bit more excited, but 'e ordered another glass o' bitter from the barmaid, and tried to think 'ow he was to bring out about the ship on his chest and the letters on 'is back. The landlady served a couple o' men, and by and by she came back and began talking agin.

"'I like sailors,' she ses; 'one thing is, my boy was a sailor; and another thing is, they've got such feelin' 'earts. There was two of 'em in 'ere the other day, who'd been in 'ere once or twice, and one of 'em was that kind 'earted I thought he would ha' 'ad a fit at something I told him.'

"'Ho,' ses Ginger, pricking up his ears, 'wot for?'

"'I was just talking to 'im about my boy, same as I might be to you,' ses the old lady, 'and I was just telling 'im about the poor child losing 'is finger—'

"'Losing 'is *wot?*' ses Ginger, turning pale and staggering back.

"'Finger,' ses the landlady. ''E was only ten years old at the time, and I'd sent 'im out to—Wot's the matter? Ain't you well?'

"Ginger didn't answer 'er a word; he couldn't. 'E went on going backwards until 'e got to the door, and then 'e suddenly fell through it into the street, and tried to think.

"Then 'e remembered Sam and Peter, and when 'e thought of them safe and sound aboard the *Penguin* he nearly broke down altogether, as 'e thought how lonesome he was.

"All 'e wanted was 'is arms round both their necks same as they was the night afore they 'ad 'im tattooed."

THE TATTOO (1909)

Mary Raymond Shipman Andrews

Mary Raymond Shipman Andrews (1860–1936) was a clergyman's daughter from Alabama who attained a degree of literary celebrity in 1906 for "The Perfect Tribute", a recreation of Abraham Lincoln's delivery of the Gettysburg Address which sold a remarkable 600,000 copies. Much of her writing is concerned with the American outdoors and she was an avid supporter of the scouting movement. Rather unusually for a woman of her generation, Andrews was also herself a big-game hunter. Contrastingly, she published a significant amount of sentimental, romantic fiction in American periodicals and it is to that world that "The Tattoo" belongs.

While the majority of fictional representations of tattooing in the late nineteenth and early twentieth centuries, on either side of the Atlantic, connect tattoos with the deviant, the primitive and the criminal, Andrews' story strikes a different tone. Set in Washington high society, the story in part reflects the increasing vogue for tattooing among the middle and upper classes around the turn of the century, although there is also a conventional naval back story here to explain the origins of the story's striking tattoo. The tattooed French Duke the tale presents is rich, worldly, and noble and shows the art of tattooing beginning to undergo a change in its cultural associations.

I T IS SELDOM THAT A PLOT HAPPENS IN REAL LIFE. DRAMATIC incidents are plenty, and people in general do not distinguish, yet there is the same difference as the difference between plum pudding and the fruits that go into it. One may find raisins and currents and citron lying on the kitchen table and at once have plum pudding suggested; but if these were served for dessert at Christmas, one would wonder why some one had not added flour and sugar and apples and mixed them as they should be mixed so that a pudding might have resulted. It is so with a story. The cook of tales may find the best ingredients ready to his hand, yet before he may serve it at that table where the guests are always hungry and always overfed there is much to do. He must go to his pantry and find flour to give it body, and sugar to give it sweetness, and spices to stir the palate, and must measure these carefully in the balance; above all, he must mix it honestly with the soul of him, else the taste is insipid.

A story is made so, mostly. A cupful of love, a spoonful of hero- ism; adventure and local colour—a pinch of humour to taste, stirred in through all; enough blood to make a good red colour; bake in an oven of enthusiasm—the honest cook of tales follows a recipe like the above. Sometimes the pudding is light and sometimes it is heavy, but always it is made with art and not by chance. Almost always. There is a tale which happened and which seems to me well-fashioned, yet because I was in it, I may not trust my own judgement, so I will tell the tale and let it be judged.

It began in Washington when my lad Philip was five years old; and such a handsome boy that I found myself conspicuous wherever I went with him. On a day I had him in a big shop, in the elevator, going down. He did not like the plunge and he clutched my hand while the machine slid, stopped, and dropped with a hideous suddenness. And then stopped, and dropped again. At length he thought it well to encourage himself by conversation. The passengers stood in crowded silence, and up to them floated this reflection:

"The elevator boy's very plucky, Mother; he doesn't have to hold anybody's hand," the lad said, and the elevator boy, jerked into publicity, blushed and a wave of laughter broke the solemnity.

Next to me stood a very tall woman who had come in at the last stop. I felt her stir as everyone looked toward us, and she bowed her head as a flower might bend on its stalk over Philip.

"The dear little soul!" she said.

Then I felt a quick movement and heard an exclamation, but I rather expected people to be startled by the good looks of my son. I simply checked off one more person of discrimination in my mind, and the boy and I left the elevator and hurried to our cab. I put the youngster in and stopped to give the driver an order, and at that moment there was a touch on my arm.

I turned quickly. There was the tall woman of the elevator. I saw her plainly in this clearer light and I realized at once that she was uncommon. She was tall beyond the measure of women—five feet eleven inches I knew afterwards—and she carried her height as unconsciously as a lily carries flowers, swaying a little, it seemed, as a lily might. She was not young—I think about sixty years old—and her hair was strong silver. Her eyes were grey and large; there was colour in her cheeks like a girl's bloom. The face was radiant. And about her was the quality which asserts itself without assertion—distinction. She was unmistakably "somebody".

I saw all this as I stood at the curbstone, Phil regarding us earnestly from the cab. There are many people in Washington today who, happening to read this, must recognize my tall woman, and they will know how I saw all this in five minutes, for everyone who met her did the same, because her personality was so vivid. I stood with one hand on the cab door and looked up to the beautiful face, surprised. Her voice came with the round cleanness of speech which those often have who speak several languages.

"I beg your pardon," she began, "but I couldn't let your little boy get away. It's such a big world—I might not have found him again. May I speak to him?" and she bent toward him. "Will you shake hands with me?" and Philip put out one hand with friendliness and pulled his cap over his left eye with the other—careful training and a chin elastic battling for the mastery.

A laugh rang out, which was astonishingly young and fascinating and delightful. I never heard a laugh so spontaneous, except in children. She turned to me with her eyes dancing.

"He's a charming person, this son of yours," she said eagerly. "And so like! It's a miracle! But I haven't told you—I am unpardonable. You will forgive an old woman." Her smile would have made me forgive real things. "The child is exactly like my own boy as he used to be—indeed it's not fancy—it's a resemblance. I saw it in the elevator, and then I thought I must have imagined it because Philip is always in my mind. So I have followed you to see. And it's a stronger likeness than I thought. It's like having my child little again to look at him."

"I'm very glad," I told her. "And it's strange, but this is a Philip, too."

"No!" she said. "Certainly Providence led me to that elevator." And then, after a second's pause: "You mustn't think I'm kidnapping you, but I feel as if I couldn't lose you and your boy. Won't you let me know you? I am Mrs. Gordon. I live in Washington. I hope you will let me show you my son's pictures and prove how extraordinarily your son is like him. Will you?"

Of course I said yes, and in a minute she had my address. For all her buoyancy she was a *"grande dame"*; so easily one that she might be eager. I fancy a queen does not trouble about her rank. I knew well enough that I was honoured, though I was new to Washington and had not heard her name. As my cab turned I saw a pair of horses stop before her, and a footman in handsome livery opened the door of a brougham, but the impressive establishment did not emphasize the certainty that I had been talking to a great lady.

"Who is Mrs. Gordon?" I asked at dinner that night. There were ten people at the table and they all happened to hear, and I think seven or eight answered with some variation of "You surely must know". And then my host gave me a short history of her.

Mrs. Gordon was a daughter of Nathaniel Emory Hewitt, who had been Governor of Delaware, Secretary of State, ambassador to France—a well-known man. The girl had visited in England and had met and married young Lord Herringstone, and a few years later he had died, leaving her, people said, not too unhappy, for apparently he was everything that a woman is well rid of—and with a child of three or four. A year or two later her father had been made minister to France, and, as Mrs. Hewitt was dead, she had gone to be at the head of his house. She lived there three years and at the end of that time her engagement was announced to Admiral Gordon, an Englishman and a distinguished officer, but a match at whom people wondered for the brilliant Lady Herringstone. Mr. TenEyck, my host, knew him. In his profession, he said, his name stood second or third in the Kingdom, and he had a splendid fighting record—but he was,

Mr. TenEyck said, the heaviest old hero who ever helped the British nation to a reputation for dullness.

"How she did it—that clever woman—I don't see," said Mr. Van Arden. "He had a great position. She met everybody English worth meeting. But—" he shook his head.

"I sometimes get curious," I told him, "to know the inside of such histories. No one ever does—all you can do is to reflect that the poorest man has two faces, one to meet the world with, and one to show his sweetheart."

"Well," commented Mr. Van Arden, "let's hope that the old boy's other face was quite different from the one we saw. He took it off to Heaven ten years ago—you can't satisfy your curiosity this side the grave, I'm afraid."

I smiled, not suspecting how that curiosity, redeemed from flippancy, was one day to be satisfied. "Likely not," I agreed.

I was glad to be at home the next afternoon when Mrs. Gordon came. While Philip explained the puppy in detail I watched the transparent, expressive face; a face more filled with youth than many of eighteen years. One could not think this woman old, as she called herself. I tried to fancy her in her brilliant prime, and I could not make her different to my mind. That the bright silver hair should be dark and the radiant face unlined seemed to leave her not different. The fire of youth was so much of her that the years had been burned as they passed.

"I see," she consulted with Phil earnestly, "the puppy can run faster because he has four legs and you have only two. But he hasn't any hands at all, or arms. Will you bring this charming person to lunch on Thursday?" she demanded, with an impulsiveness like a summer breeze, as unexpected as welcome. "And the puppy—it wouldn't be a real party without the puppy. Will you come, Café?" she addressed the whining lump, to Philip's gratification.

"He saysh he will." The lad followed her lead with a ponderous effort. "He saysh he hashn't got any imgagemem." And in laughter she was gone.

On Thursday, in the large house where she lived, it appeared to me that the rooms were filled with pictures of my boy. It was odd to see him looking at me from so many strange corners—Philip as a baby, as a toddler of two, as a strapping, square man of four, and again, with his legs beginning to lengthen, just as he was now—only all in unknown clothes. It was strangest to see him grown older—like a prophecy—at seven and nine and fifteen and twenty, a splendid broad-shouldered youth keeping his promise of beauty. The pictures culminated in the strong face, still with my lad's eyes, of Lord Herringstone at thirty-five, a good face which explained his mother's light-heartedness. The son had inherited from the right side; she was satisfied with him.

I looked at one likeness after another, and saw, as she showed them to me, that this son was the cornerstone of her life. Mr. TenEyck's account came to my mind, and I began to wonder, impertinently perhaps, if he had been the central fact always. It seemed unreasonable that a woman like this should go through life without a genuine love affair. The first marriage must have been simply two stages, delusion and disappointment; the second might have been convenience or ambition—even affection—anything but love. She was so intensely human that it was hard to think of her as missing any human joy, yet no more could one think of her with a tragic memory. It seemed likely that she had somehow come no closer to love than a bitterly ended infatuation.

Philip, when he had been extracted, lumpy and wedged, from his coat and entanglements, stalked to a table where stood a painting on ivory of a child. He regarded it with earnestness, and Mrs. Gordon and I waited. "That's me," he decided, and turned—the question being settled—to examine the room.

"Don't stop him—let him do what he chooses. No, I don't want him to be careful. I don't care what he breaks"—she threw at me, as I tried to guard priceless vases and carved pillars out of Florentine churches, and cobweb old embroideries, from the stumbling fingers. "It's a gift out of Heaven to see him. It's throwing off thirty years. Are you too young a woman to imagine how that seems to a woman?"

She was down on her knees by the boy with an arm about his white-linened figure.

"Philip—listen. I've lost my boy. He's across the ocean, and I can't have him all the time. Will you come often and play with Café here and let me pretend you're my boy? And whenever Mother will come we'll like that better. Will you?"

Philip looked straight in her eyes, considering. "Yesh, I will," he said at length. "If Café can come and my skin horshes, and sometimes Mother." His fat hand went up slowly, for he was a deliberate lad always, to her cheek. "I lovesh you," he said.

When he came out crumpled from Mrs. Gordon's arms she lifted her face and her eyes were dim. But Philip had no sentiment.

"Mother told me not to mush my bloush," he reproached her, and immediately inquired, "What's that picsher about? Is it a menagerie of snakes?" and he pointed to an old tapestry, where lovely but rather leggy angels sang in ranks.

It got to be a familiar event to see Philip driving off behind Mrs. Gordon's horses, sometimes decorously inside with his nurse, but oftener associating with the liveried gentlemen on the box—which he preferred. The beautiful woman's affection was wide enough to take me in, so that often I went with him, yet she certainly was happiest when she had him alone. The nurse reported that she was shipped to the servants' quarters at once, and "Madame *soignait le bebe toute seule*." More than once I met my small person driving in the city, with his foster-mother, and received, if he happened to be concerned with the horses, a preoccupied salute. It was so that affairs went on for three years, the tie becoming closer, until Mrs. Gordon counted for much in my life, and Philip at least for much in hers. It was understood that whenever we could let the boy go she wanted him, and he belonged to her as much as an adored only child might belong to anyone but his father and mother.

Two years after the encounter in the elevator Philip and I went to her one day for lunch. I sat at the piano, playing, after the meal, when through the chords I heard a crash, and I whirled towards where I had last seen Philip, for his freedom here was so insisted upon that I was always alert. He stood by a cabinet whose glass door he had opened; a dagger set with jewels was in his hand, and on the floor lay a vase or loving-cup, with three gold handles, broken. It had stood in the cabinet, and he had knocked it over in reaching for the knife.

"Oh, Phil!" I gasped. "I told you to be careful."

But Mrs. Gordon had flown to him. "You mustn't scold Philip," she objected. "It was my fault. I told him he could open any of the cabinets. He never does till he asks, and I trust him. I trust him as much as ever. We all have accidents; it isn't his fault."

The lad stood, his blond head white against the dark curtains, the knife in his hand, at his feet the broken, bright china, the gold handles glittering. He stared at me with wide eyes. I see the picture whenever I think of that day, and into it sweeps a radiant, tall presence protecting my boy.

"I'm so sorry," I gasped again. "I can't tell you how sorry—it's such a lovely cup."

"Don't be sorry," she said, and then I saw her look down at the pieces, and I saw her face change.

"Oh!" I cried. "It's something you care for a great deal!"

The big, dusky room was silent; Mrs. Gordon stood with Philip's yellow head against the long, black lines of her figure; her eyes did not lift from the wreckage. "Yes," she said, "I do care for it." Then the lovely grey eyes flashed up, and she smiled as wholeheartedly as sunlight.

"What it stood for can't be lost," she said. "It's only broken china—it's only a sign—Philip is a real thing." She bent and kissed his hair. "Come, laddie, we'll pick up the scraps." In a moment she had them on a table by a window, while Phil and I hovered anxiously.

It was a curious thing—a large loving-cup, of Sevres china, with three handles of Eastern-looking, very yellow gold. Across one side of it sprawled in orange colour a two-headed dragon; above this was a crown, and on either side of the crown a *fleur-de-lys*. The painting was done in small dots as if tattooed into the china. Mrs. Gordon's fingers fitted the pieces together, and I watched, quietly, my arm around guilty Philip.

"It can be put together; it's only three pieces and a jog," she decided. "Don't look so tragic. Philip will be afraid of me. You mustn't be frightened, Philip," she begged him. And then, "I shall like my cup better than before, because it will make me think of my American boy."

In five minutes the sinner was playing with a case of shells as contentedly as ever, but Mrs. Gordon knew that I was unhappy. Her face was flushed and I was sure that this "broken china" had some strong association and was valuable beyond its beauty. In the middle of a sentence her voice stopped; she rose from her chair and drifted to the table where the pieces lay, and looked down at them, and put her long hand lightly on them. She came back and sat down again and let her head fall against the cushions and gazed out of the window, where flakes of snow floated in vague warning of a storm. Philip, across the room, was absorbed in his shells; the fire crackled in an undertone. Mrs. Gordon's face had a look which I had not seen before, wistful yet not sad. Then her eyes met mine.

"That accident has brought back a great deal," she said. "Things that I like to remember, that I do remember always, yet which stir me too much for everyday living when they come vividly, as today. I've never told anyone," she went on, "and today I feel as if I wanted to." I kept very still, but she knew that she had my whole interest.

"Would you like to have me tell you a story?" she asked, hesitating.

"Would I?"

"It's a very personal story—about myself in my young days. Maybe it isn't so dramatic as I think it; maybe you wouldn't be interested."

A marvel about her was that she had no conceit, in spite of the charm which must have kept her breathing in devotion always. Perhaps the adorable people are the least conceited, because self in their case does not need to be asserted; moreover, carelessness of self helps to make one adorable.

"I'd love it, I'd love it," I said eagerly, and the great light eyes smiled.

"It's just the day," she considered. "Snow outside, fire inside, plenty of lazy time, and the lad over there to make me feel as if I were living it over. My Philip was his age. It was when I was with my father in Paris, thirty years ago, when you were a baby. Of course I met everybody—my father was our Minister to France

you know—and one of the first people I met was the Duc d'——.
No." She pulled herself up. "I won't tell you his name. You'd know
it, and I wouldn't be as free to tell the rest. I've said his title—I'm a
garrulous old person—so we'll just call him the Duke."

She drew a breath and clasped her long fingers behind her head.

"It's strange to be talking about him," she interrupted herself.
"I've never done it. He was the only man in the world. I never saw
anybody like him. He was everything—clever, good, beautiful—"
She stopped and glanced at me and laughed. "You'll think I'm a silly
old person; but you know everybody has a love affair once, and mine
missed the conventional ending. I never got over it."

From this most reserved and dignified person these words came
so quietly that I hardly wondered, even knowing her outside history,
and knowing that this had no place in it. It seemed inevitable and
essential the moment she had told me.

"He had plenty of faults," she went on, "but there was no fault
in him to me. He was head-strong and quick-tempered and likely
to do something irrevocable at a second's notice. But self-forgetting
always to absurdity—it was not in him to be small. It was perhaps
his bigness of all sorts which seemed so perfect to me—I'm so big
in one way myself. He towered like a giant among those small,
dark Frenchmen—unlike a Frenchman, six feet and massive and
blue-eyed—his mother had been Scotch. And he towered in other
ways, for he was a power. If he had lived he would have been a
great man—everybody in the world would have known him. I have
heard men say that who were statesmen—men who knew what
greatness meant.

"You are too young to remember," she went on, "but it was
at a confused time in French history, after the war with Germany.
The republic was struggling to its feet and there were factions

organized ready to push it over. The Bonapartists hoped to get back to power; the Orleanists waited with the Count of Paris ready to seize the throne; the Legitimists had the Duc of Chambord at their head; the undercurrent of French politics was a whirlpool. And in this whirlpool he was a strong swimmer, and a marked one, for he stood so close to one of these claimants to the throne that the succession itself was not impossible. He was important to his party and conspicuous in it, all the more because he was just far enough from the actual claimant to be conspicuous in Paris society, too. He was a warm friend of the President. His life was an obstacle in the way of a faction, and I trembled; but he laughed. His safety was the last thing he worried about. Yet—" she stopped. "That comes later. I mustn't jumble things.

"Well, my dear, he cared for me. He had difficulty in making me believe it; but about my own feeling I never had any doubt. He was instantly, as he has always stayed, the only man in the world. I had never—"

She stopped and considered, and turned her great eyes on me.

"I had never been in love," she went on, and left me to think what I might.

Then she was silent till I began to be afraid she would not tell me any more. After a long minute I ventured to speak.

"But," I began, "something happened."

Mrs. Gordon got up and went across with a light gait to Philip, now rattling his playthings ostentatiously. "Dear lamb," she smiled, amused. "He's bored to death with shells. Look, there's the carriage, and I don't want to drive and I won't let your mother. Run to Adèle and tell her to put you into a coat and take you out to Harrison. And tell Harrison you're to drive the horses with your own hands twice around the park. May he?" and I nodded, and the boy was gone.

Mrs. Gordon did not at once come back to her chair in the window. She moved about the room a minute, staring in the fire, going from one point to another, and at last she lifted the bits of the loving-cup and brought them back with her and sat down.

"He had this made for me," she said, and she put the orange dragon's broken back together. "It was like a tattoo done on his arm when he was a youngster in Japan. He went there on a war ship, and he and the other boy officers got themselves tattooed. He showed it to me. He rolled up his sleeves rowing on a lake at a country place, and I was fascinated. It was the first tattoo I had ever seen. I asked to see it once after. Then at a breakfast in the country, outside of Paris, which he gave for my father, my wine was put in this. He had had it made at the Sevres manufactory—the tattoo duplicated. The handles were taken from an old Japanese cup. You see it is curious gold." She smiled at the dragon reminiscently, her thoughts far from me. "How astonished I was! I thought simply that my wine glass had been forgotten; and then a footman placed this huge thing before me with a flourish. I remember how my father laughed and how the French servants stood smiling at me from a corner as I looked up. And the banks of violets on the table—and the trees and the sunlight outside—spring in France! I remember it like yesterday." I kept very still.

"That was in the brightest time, before words had crystal-lized what we felt. It was as bright and as evanescent then as a rainbow, light and brightness and colour—and not either right or wrong, because unsaid and undefined. That was my happiest time. Afterward, when he used all his strength to make me marry him; when he won over my father to help him, it was hard. My father thought I ought to marry him," she spoke as if to herself.

"But you did not," I burst forth. "How could you not?"

Mrs. Gordon's grey eyes turned on me. "How could I?" she asked. "I was engaged to the Admiral."

I was too eager now to be afraid. "To the Admiral!" I gasped. "Then?"

"Yes. He was off on a cruise—two years. We were to be married when he came home. It was not known because of his absence."

"But," I protested, "how could you stop for that? You weren't in love with the Admiral—you were with the Duke. It meant his happiness and yours—you two, young and full of vitality against an old man perhaps not capable of intense happiness. It meant giving up a great thing for a small one."

"Oh, no; oh, no, it didn't." The beautiful face showed no anger, but impetuous dissent. "It meant holding to the greatest thing, that I should keep my word. No real happiness comes from sacrificing others. And if it did, what is honour for if not to lead us through thick and thin? If we might step aside from the narrow road when we saw joy shining down another what would faith mean, how would my boy walk in the path if my footsteps weren't there? You see, my dear," her full tones rushed on as if saying words many times thought, and her face was lighted as if by fire. "You see it's a mountain-climbing affair for everybody, the road of perfect honour, and each woman owes it to her own soul, and to all the other souls of the world, that her footprints should widen the path a little and level it a little. I had promised the Admiral at a time when I thought nothing but my boy would ever matter. I did love him—he knew how—and he was satisfied. His life had been lonely and he trusted to Philip and me to bring into it at the end the good things that other men have all along. I was glad, when I promised, to have the chance to help a man so worth happiness. It seemed an anchor when I tossed in a sea of restlessness. I clung to it eagerly. Then, when I found that I was strong enough not merely to lie at anchor, but to sail, and love the winds and waves, should I throw it away because I was through with it? I couldn't do it. You and I are born with traditions, and bred to hold ourselves above broken faith. How will the world get better if we don't keep up the standard? That's the first rule in the book of '*noblesse oblige*', and it's about all of it, too."

As the voice of a brook in a forest seems always breaking, always making a song over the stones, so her voice lifted the words and linked them, and made them rhythm; and as the brook's undertone is lost when one turns a hill, so the cadence stopped.

I sighed, convinced perhaps, but unreconciled. "It may have been right," I said; "but I wouldn't have done it—ever. I think you're one of the martyrs."

Mrs. Gordon's shoulders and eyebrows joined in a movement with a touch of France in it.

"Hardly," she answered; and then "There are plenty of people more unhappy than the martyrs.

"But I want to tell you the rest. If I digress into morality this way I'll never get through. The Admiral came back and I married him and went away from Paris. Sometimes I was in England, sometimes in America—all over the world. He was Governor of Jamaica at the last and we were there for three years and he died there ten years ago. I think he was happy; it has been a joy to think I made him so. He was everything to Philip, and the boy loved him, and he helped to make my son the man he is."

Her eyes wandered contentedly to the last picture of Lord Herringstone on her desk. "I've never felt that I made a mistake," she said.

"But," I began, "did you never see *him* again—the Only Man? You spoke as if he were dead."

"Yes," she said. "I saw him once, in London. The Admiral met him at a club and brought him to dinner. We were dining alone, and in the evening my husband had an engagement and left us. Philip was there at first—he was eleven—but he went off to bed, and he and I were alone together. There wasn't a word spoken except commonplace till just as he went.

"'Good-bye,' he said, and he did not touch my hand; but we looked almost on a level as we were.

"'It's the last time in this world,' he said calmly.

"'*No.*' I threw at him, and he laughed because I was vehement. But I disliked having him speak so. 'We'll sometimes meet—you're likely to be in London with your—with the Prince. And I'm likely to be here.'

"His eyebrows drew together and he looked hard at me.

"'I may not be here. Things may happen,' he said thoughtfully. 'I heard today that the others want me out of the way particularly. Our party has been coming up and they give me credit. It would be convenient if I should make a sudden exit. I wouldn't be missed now, even by my own people, as things stand. I've done my work. So, if I drop out and leave not a ripple—' He saw that he was tearing my soul.

"Suddenly he threw out his hands with a gesture I knew. 'This life is not possible. To leave it is best.' As if he weighed each word he went on. 'As long as we have personalities we belong to each other. Since you will have us apart in this world I await another.' He gave me no chance to answer. Instantly, quietly, he said good-bye and was gone. I never saw him again; no one ever saw him again."

When she did not speak I asked, "What happened?"

"No one ever knew. It's supposed he was assassinated that night. The papers rang with his disappearance for days. There was a strong party in London of those whom he called 'the others', and he had grown so powerful that they saw in him their worst menace. Such a faction has always men ready to do murder. What he said seemed a premonition of that; it must have been that. He would not have taken his own life."

"How horrible!" I murmured, and then "How wonderful you are! You radiate happiness and yet you have that black shadow—" She turned on me.

"Shadow?" she repeated. "No, sunlight, brightness. You don't appreciate. It's enough for a life. No wonder I've been happy."

Suddenly her manner had flashed into everyday. She was on her feet and peering into the street, dim with fast-falling snow. "There comes the lad," she said. "Driving the horses—how well he manages them. Harrison says his hands are remarkable." Her handkerchief was waving and her face bright as the boy looked up, rosy and proud, from the box by Harrison.

A year later than this afternoon in February, Mrs. Gordon, her son, and his wife and their one child were drowned in a shipwreck which everyone will remember, one of the most wholesale accidents of these days of horrible accidents—the shipwreck of a huge trans-Atlantic liner. Two hundred lives were lost and several families besides this one whose loss touched me so closely were wiped out. We found some months later that Mrs. Gordon had remembered little Philip in her will, and at the same time there came to me from her lawyers a box which, when opened, I found to hold that Sevres loving-cup, the text of the story of the snowy afternoon, which I have tried to tell. I held it by its handles of yellow Eastern gold and looked again at the orange dragon painted in tiny dots like the other dragon, its prototype, gone long ago into dust. I looked at the crown above the dragon's head and at the flanking *fleur-de-lys*, and I saw plainly the old line of Philip's breakage. It was unlikely that I should forget this painting in any case, but the day when it came to be mine I learned each dot by heart. I knew them so well that I could go over the whole with my eyes shut. Nothing she could have given me could have seemed so like the touch of her hand as this. The cup holds her personality and I never look at it without feeling as if I could almost hear again the voice, and see the eyes, and feel the presence of the most wonderful person I have ever known.

As the boy had brought us together so it was he who happened last summer on the answer to my question about the Duke. "What happened?" I had asked her. And she had answered, "No one ever knew."

Through Philip I know. Truth is certainly bolder than fiction, even if it is seldom as well arranged, and I should have gone far afield in guessing before I guessed that a hermit monk of the Canadian forests would give me, without a word spoken, a full answer to that question, "What happened?"

It came about in this way: The boy, now eleven, but still a conspicuous youngster, still with the fair hair and brown eyes, which made him so like young Lord Herringstone—the boy and I went together last summer to Canada. His father was to join us later at Lake St. John, but in the mean time we were doing Montreal and Quebec together, till at last one morning we bobbed down the precipice roads of Quebec in a calêche, to take a train for Roberval. The little station was filled with voluble French-Canadians. A few sportsmen with rods and guns, a few citizens of the United States suggested that the road was not exclusively run for *habitants*, but carried members of the clubs which lie along it, and people like ourselves, travelling to that great northern sea of Lake St. John. We arrived into such a rush and bustle as the Central station in New York never achieves.

Everybody was dashing about and chattering, and the officials were the most excited of all. Sharp French voices ordered and wrangled in an accent not of Paris. With the habit of assorting people which one learns, Philip and I soon had the tumbling crowd ticketed.

"The nice man with the rod-case belongs to the boy with the gun," he assured me. "And I think the stylish lady's their mother—the boy's mother." He arranged the exhibits. "Look at that silly French bride. I should think they'd be ashamed to throw rice and giggle. Smarties, aren't they?" Suddenly he caught my hand. "Look, Mother, the wonderful priest."

I glanced up, startled, straight into the widely opened blue eyes of a tall man close to me—the priest. But he did not notice me. He was staring at Philip as if astounded by the child's face. The look flashed swiftly to me, and then it calmed to indifference. It was only a second. He passed on, and Philip and I both turned unconsciously and followed him with fascinated eyes. We had the day before been looking at pictures of different orders of priests in Canada, and at once I knew this striking and picturesque vision to be a monk of La Trappe, probably from the monastery which stands like a lonely sentinel beyond the farthest edge of civilization, far beyond Lake St. John, down the wild River Mistassini.

Again the monk passed. Anywhere, in any dress, the man would have been remarkable. His white gown flapped about his ankles a foot below the long black cape, and his big figure swung along with a vigour which made one think of soldiers and fighting more than of monks and monasteries. His great shoulders were deep and wide, and he had the thoroughbred air not of a greyhound or any slim beast, but of a huge, full-blooded mastiff—the type of man, perhaps, which, if all men could choose, most men would be. He carried his big, square head, as the saying is, like a prince. Yet the blue eyes were furtive with a shyness, like the eyes of a wild thing unused to people. It was impossible to guess his age. He might have been anywhere from forty to seventy.

In a few minutes he disappeared; but when at the last moment before the train started on its rattling way we went to our seats in the tumble-down parlour car, both of us were enchanted to find him seated in a chair across from our own. His strong, square-jawed face was impenetrable, his eyes were fixed on a book of prayers, but as we settled ourselves he suddenly lifted them and opened them wide on Philip and smiled a smile which transfigured his whole look with gentleness. I caught my breath in astonishment, for it seemed to reveal an individuality intense beyond my experience. The child turned to me in wonder.

The cars bumped along, creeping up mountains, through untouched forests, and past wild lakes, the only thread which ties the ancient French settlement of Roberval to the civilized world. As they bumped I tried not to stare at the splendid statue of black and white which sat opposite, motionless, withdrawn. A big yellow topaz ring which he wore drew my eyes like a magnet. Whatever I tried to do I found myself gazing at the stone. Why should he wear a ring, I wondered. His eyes hardly lifted from his prayer book for an hour, for two hours, but all at once he seemed to grow restless, and he picked up a folder of the railroad lying by him and read it here and there, and dropped it and sighed, and went back to his prayer book. Then he stopped reading and stared from the window, his massive face set into sad lines, the blue, clear eyes gazing unseeingly at depths of dark forests and steep mountains. What memories, I wondered, lay back of the face which had softened so extraordinarily to smile at Philip. What dramatic story was the beginning of this atrophied end of existence, the dead life which this man must lead? I recalled the account I had read of the Trappist monks, the most forbidding of all brotherhoods, how they may never speak even to one another, except with the grim greeting, "Remember death"; how they dig a part of their own graves every day. I shivered as I thought of these and other gruesome details.

Meanwhile the monk had gone back to the folder; he read it restlessly for half a page and tossed it from him. It was evident that he was in dire need of something that might help him to kill his thoughts. An impulse too quick for reason made me do a thing which I could not have done in cold blood. A magazine lay under my hand and I held it to him.

"Won't you have this?" I asked.

His eyes flashed to mine surprised, and then the wonderful smile changed the stern face again utterly. He was on his feet, and making me a courtly bow as he took it; no word, but the smile and the action were like words, and in two minutes he was devouring the pages like a starved man; it was as if an Earth citizen exiled to Mars should have the first news from his world. While he read, the joggling car tossed the folder at my feet, and I picked it up. It was an advertisement for the Quebec & Lake St. John Railway, and gave pictures and descriptions of places to be reached by the road. Turning the page I came on an account of the La Trappe monastery on the Mistassini River. I read it; it was bare enough, yet full of significance as I saw the hem of the white gown opposite; and facing the text, running lengthwise of the page, was a picture. I shifted the leaf and saw a group of white-robed men; and in the centre, the only one seated, was the priest who sat across the car reading my magazine. There was no mistaking the face or figure, and on his hand one could see plainly, even in the small photograph, the great yellow topaz. Under the picture I read "The Abbott and

Monks of the La Trappe Convent on the Mistassini". My monk was the Abbott.

In the mean time Philip was being a great nuisance. We were in the last car; and he insisted, with the winning and plausible manner which often quiets my reason, that the back platform was the only part of the train really fitted to carry him. Pleading with him to be careful, I weakly let him go there. The door was open. I watched him closely and he held to the rail as he promised, yet I was not comfortable. All this the Abbott knew—he did not look up, yet I knew he knew it. The car bounced on an especial boulder, and he lifted his head sharply and threw a glance at the boy, clinging enchanted outside; then he looked squarely over at me and shook his head. I should have ordered the youngster in, but I did not. I only smiled gratefully and went out, and saw that Philip was steady and braced with both hands and decided that he was safe, so I went back to the folder, and my conjectures as to who this "wonderful priest" might have been. Ten minutes later the train began to slow down heavily for a station. Then it backed, bumping harder. I saw the monk put down the magazine and go to the open door of the car where the boy stood. I saw him lay his hand on the light hair and I saw Philip look up and say a word in his friendly way; and the Abbott smiled back and shook his head with closed lips. Then suddenly, as if in a play, I saw him catch the boy in his arms and hurl him backward into the passage; the whole train shook and slid as our car plunged against some huge obstacle, and a flying mass of black and white shot through the air from the platform.

It was only five minutes, but it seemed an hour before the car stopped and I was kneeling in the track by the man who had offered his life for my boy's. The splendid figure lay there quiet, whether dead, or broken, or merely stunned I could not tell. Black robe and white were torn from one shoulder, and on the great arm flung out, bared, was tattooed an orange dragon, and above it a crown and yellow *fleur-de-lys*.

THE TATTOOER (1910)

Jun'ichirō Tanizaki

Jun'ichirō Tanizaki (1886–1965) was a Nobel-nominated novelist and short story writer who was one of the most significant figures of twentieth-century Japanese literature. He is also an author who has provoked a good deal of controversy. The dark, lyrical eroticism of his prose and his consistent interest in forms of "perversion" (particularly sadomasochism and foot fetishism) saw his work deemed "injurious to public morals" in Japan and he was prevented from publishing during the Second World War. Despite the censure of conservative readers (and indeed some radical readers who saw his writing as decadent), Tanizaki's work has drawn considerable interest from literary critics, especially those interested in depictions of gender, sexuality, and violence. Tanizaki drew extensively on Japanese literary and cultural traditions, but was also influenced by Western writers, notably Edgar Allan Poe, Charles Baudelaire, and Oscar Wilde.

"The Tattooer" is Tanizaki's earliest story and was first published in English in 1917, translated by Yone Noguchi, himself a significant Japanese writer. The tale is set in the late Edo period which dates it to the middle of the nineteenth century. The narrative focuses on a young tattooer, Seikichi, who derives unusual pleasure from the pain his art inflicts on his clients. Seikichi becomes enthralled by a woman's foot he sees poking out from a palanquin and a tale of obsession and cruelty unfolds. Tanizaki's story is evidently gauged to be disturbing as he blends lush literary style with a complex account of male fantasy.

I T WAS AN AGE WHEN MEN HONOURED THE NOBLE VIRTUE OF frivolity, when life was not such a harsh struggle as it is today. It was a leisurely age, an age when professional wits could make an excellent livelihood by keeping rich or wellborn young gentlemen in a cloudless good humour and seeing to it that the laughter of Court ladies and geisha was never stilled. In the illustrated romantic novels of the day, in the Kabuki theatre, where rough masculine heroes like Sadakuro and Jiraiya were transformed into women—everywhere beauty and strength were one. People did all they could to beautify themselves, some even having pigments injected into their precious skins. Gaudy patterns of line and colour danced over men's bodies.

Visitors to the pleasure quarters of Edo preferred to hire palanquin bearers who were splendidly tattooed; courtesans of the Yoshiwara and the Tatsumi quarter fell in love with tattooed men. Among those so adorned were not only gamblers, firemen, and the like, but members of the merchant class and even samurai. Exhibitions were held from time to time; and the participants, stripped to show off their filigreed bodies, would pat themselves proudly, boast of their own novel designs, and criticize each other's merits.

There was an exceptionally skillful young tattooer named Seikichi. He was praised on all sides as a master the equal of Charibun or Yatsuhei, and the skins of dozens of men had been offered as the silk for his brush. Much of the work admired at the tattoo exhibitions was his. Others might be more noted for their shading, or their use of cinnabar, but Seikichi was famous for the unrivalled boldness and sensual charm of his art.

Seikichi had formerly earned his living as an ukiyoye painter of the school of Toyokuni and Kunisada, a background which, in spite of his decline to the status of a tattooer, was evident from his artistic conscience and sensitivity. No one whose skin or whose physique failed to interest him could buy his services. The clients he did accept had to leave the design and cost entirely to his discretion—and to endure for one or even two months the excruciating pain of his needles.

Deep in his heart the young tattooer concealed a secret pleasure, and a secret desire. His pleasure lay in the agony men felt as he drove his needles into them, torturing their swollen, blood-red flesh; and the louder they groaned, the keener was Seikichi's strange delight. Shading and vermilioning—these are said to be especially painful—were the techniques he most enjoyed.

When a man had been pricked five or six hundred times in the course of an average day's treatment and had then soaked himself in a hot bath to bring out the colours, he would collapse at Seikichi's feet half dead. But Seikichi would look down at him coolly. "I dare say that hurts," he would remark with an air of satisfaction.

Whenever a spineless man howled in torment or clenched his teeth and twisted his mouth as if he were dying, Seikichi told him: "Don't act like a child. Pull yourself together—you have hardly begun to feel my needles!" And he would go on tattooing, as unperturbed as ever, with an occasional sidelong glance at the man's tearful face.

But sometimes a man of immense fortitude set his jaw and bore up stoically, not even allowing himself to frown. Then Seikichi would smile and say: "Ah, you are a stubborn one! But wait. Soon your body will begin to throb with pain. I doubt if you will be able to stand it…"

★

For a long time Seikichi had cherished the desire to create a master-piece on the skin of a beautiful woman. Such a woman had to meet various qualifications of character as well as appearance. A lovely face and a fine body were not enough to satisfy him. Though he inspected all the reigning beauties of the Edo gay quarters he found none who met his exacting demands. Several years had passed without success, and yet the face and figure of the perfect woman continued to obsess his thoughts. He refused to abandon hope.

One summer evening during the fourth year of his search Seikichi happened to be passing the Hirasei Restaurant in the Fukagawa district of Edo, not far from his own house, when he noticed a woman's bare milk-white foot peeping out beneath the curtains of a departing palanquin. To his sharp eye, a human foot was as expres-sive as a face. This one was sheer perfection. Exquisitely chiselled toes, nails like the iridescent shells along the shore at Enoshima, a pearl-like rounded heel, skin so lustrous that it seemed bathed in the limpid waters of a mountain spring—this, indeed, was a foot to be nourished by men's blood, a foot to trample on their bodies. Surely this was the foot of the unique woman who had so long eluded him. Eager to catch a glimpse of her face, Seikichi began to follow the palanquin. But after pursuing it down several lanes and alleys he lost sight of it altogether.

Seikichi's long-held desire turned into passionate love. One morning late the next spring he was standing on the bamboo-floored veranda of his home in Fukagawa, gazing at a pot of *omoto* lilies, when he heard someone at the garden gate. Around the corner of the inner fence appeared a young girl. She had come on an errand for a friend of his, a geisha of the nearby Tatsumi quarter.

"My mistress asked me to deliver this cloak, and she wondered if you would be so good as to decorate its lining," the girl said. She untied a saffron-coloured cloth parcel and took out a woman's silk cloak (wrapped in a sheet of thick paper bearing a portrait of the actor Tojaku) and a letter.

The letter repeated his friend's request and went on to say that its bearer would soon begin a career as a geisha under her protection. She hoped that, while not forgetting old ties, he would also extend his patronage to this girl.

"I thought I had never seen you before," said Seikichi, scrutinizing her intently. She seemed only fifteen or sixteen, but her face had a strangely ripe beauty, a look of experience, as if she had already spent years in the gay quarter and had fascinated innumerable men. Her beauty mirrored the dreams of the generations of glamorous men and women who had lived and died in this vast capital, where the nation's sins and wealth were concentrated.

Seikichi had her sit on the veranda, and he studied her delicate feet, which were bare except for elegant straw sandals. "You left the Hirasei by palanquin one night last July, did you not?" he inquired.

"I suppose so," she replied, smiling at the odd question. "My father was still alive then, and he often took me there."

"I have waited five years for you. This is the first time I have seen your face, but I remember your foot... Come in for a moment, I have something to show you."

She had risen to leave, but he took her by the hand and led her upstairs to his studio overlooking the broad river. Then he brought out two picture scrolls and unrolled one of them before her.

It was a painting of a Chinese princess, the favourite of the cruel Emperor Chou of the Shang Dynasty. She was leaning on a balustrade in a languorous pose, the long skirt of her figured brocade robe trailing halfway down a flight of stairs, her slender body barely able to support the weight of her gold crown studded with coral and lapis lazuli. In her right hand she held a large wine cup, tilting it to her lips as she gazed down at a man who was about to be tortured in the garden below. He was chained hand and foot to a hollow copper pillar in which a fire would be lighted. Both the princess and her victim—his head bowed before her, his eyes closed, ready to meet his fate—were portrayed with terrifying vividness.

As the girl stared at this bizarre picture her lips trembled and her eyes began to sparkle. Gradually her face took on a curious resemblance to that of the princess. In the picture she discovered her secret self.

"Your own feelings are revealed here," Seikichi told her with pleasure as he watched her face.

"Why are you showing me this horrible thing?" the girl asked, looking up at him. She had turned pale.

"The woman is yourself. Her blood flows in your veins." Then he spread out the other scroll.

This was a painting called "The Victims". In the middle of it a young woman stood leaning against the trunk of a cherry tree: she was gloating over a heap of men's corpses lying at her feet. Little birds fluttered about her, singing in triumph; her eyes radiated pride and joy. Was it a battlefield or a garden in spring? In this picture the girl felt that she had found something long hidden in the darkness of her own heart.

"This painting shows your future," Seikichi said, pointing to the woman under the cherry tree—the very image of the young girl. "All these men will ruin their lives for you."

"Please, I beg of you to put it away!" She turned her back as if to escape its tantalizing lure and prostrated herself before him, trembling. At last she spoke again. "Yes, I admit that you are right about me—I *am* like that woman… So please, please take it away."

"Don't talk like a coward," Seikichi told her, with his malicious smile. "Look at it more closely. You won't be squeamish long."

But the girl refused to lift her head. Still prostrate, her face buried in her sleeves, she repeated over and over that she was afraid and wanted to leave.

"No, you must stay—I will make you a real beauty," he said, moving closer to her. Under his kimono was a vial of anaesthetic which he had obtained some time ago from a Dutch physician.

The morning sun glittered on the river, setting the eight-mat studio ablaze with light. Rays reflected from the water sketched rippling golden waves on the paper sliding screens and on the face of the girl, who was fast asleep. Seikichi had closed the doors and taken up his tattooing instruments, but for a while he only sat there entranced, savouring to the full her uncanny beauty. He thought that he would never tire of contemplating her serene mask-like face. Just as the ancient Egyptians had embellished their magnificent land with pyramids and sphinxes, he was about to embellish the pure skin of this girl.

Presently he raised the brush which was gripped between the thumb and last two fingers of his left hand, applied its tip to the girl's back, and, with the needle which he held in his right hand, began pricking out a design. He felt his spirit dissolve into the charcoal-black ink that stained her skin. Each drop of Ryukyu cinnabar that he mixed with alcohol and thrust in was a drop of his lifeblood. He saw in his pigments the hues of his own passions.

Soon it was afternoon, and then the tranquil spring day drew toward its close. But Seikichi never paused in his work, nor was the girl's sleep broken. When a servant came from the geisha house to inquire about her, Seikichi turned him away, saying that she had left long ago. And hours later, when the moon hung over the mansion across the river, bathing the houses along the bank in a dreamlike radiance, the tattoo was not yet half done. Seikichi worked on by candlelight.

Even to insert a single drop of colour was no easy task. At every thrust of his needle Seikichi gave a heavy sigh and felt as if he had stabbed his own heart. Little by little the tattoo marks began to take on the form of a huge black-widow spider; and by the time the night sky was paling into dawn this weird, malevolent creature had stretched its eight legs to embrace the whole of the girl's back.

In the full light of the spring dawn boats were being rowed up and down the river, their oars creaking in the morning quiet; roof tiles glistened in the sun, and the haze began to thin out over white sails swelling in the early breeze. Finally Seikichi put down his brush and looked at the tattooed spider. This work of art had been the supreme effort of his life. Now that he had finished it his heart was drained of emotion.

The two figures remained still for some time. Then Seikichi's low, hoarse voice echoed quaveringly from the walls of the room:

"To make you truly beautiful I have poured my soul into this tattoo. Today there is no woman in Japan to compare with you. Your old fears are gone. All men will be your victims."

As if in response to these words a faint moan came from the girl's lips. Slowly she began to recover her senses. With each shuddering breath, the spider's legs stirred as if they were alive.

"You must be suffering. The spider has you in its clutches."

At this she opened her eyes slightly, in a dull stare. Her gaze steadily brightened, as the moon brightens in the evening, until it shone dazzlingly into his face.

"Let me see the tattoo," she said, speaking as if in a dream but with an edge of authority to her voice. "Giving me your soul must have made me very beautiful."

"First you must bathe to bring out the colours," whispered Seikichi compassionately. "I am afraid it will hurt, but be brave a little longer."

"I can bear anything for the sake of beauty." Despite the pain that was coursing through her body, she smiled.

"How the water stings!... Leave me alone—wait in the other room! I hate to have a man see me suffer like this!"

As she left the tub, too weak to dry herself, the girl pushed aside the sympathetic hand Seikichi offered her, and sank to the floor in agony, moaning as if in a nightmare. Her dishevelled hair hung over her face in a wild tangle. The white soles of her feet were reflected in the mirror behind her.

Seikichi was amazed at the change that had come over the timid, yielding girl of yesterday, but he did as he was told and went to wait in his studio. About an hour later she came back, carefully dressed, her damp, sleekly combed hair hanging down over her shoulders. Leaning on the veranda rail, she looked up into the faintly hazy sky. Her eyes were brilliant; there was not a trace of pain in them.

"I wish to give you these pictures too," said Seikichi, placing the scrolls before her. "Take them and go."

"All my old fears have been swept away—and you are my first victim!" She darted a glance at him as bright as a sword. A song of triumph was ringing in her ears.

"Let me see your tattoo once more," Seikichi begged.

Silently the girl nodded and slipped the kimono off her shoulders. Just then her resplendently tattooed back caught a ray of sunlight and the spider was wreathed in flames.

THE BACKGROUND (1911)

Saki

Saki was the penname of H. H. Munro (1870–1916) one of the twentieth century's most accomplished exponents of the English short story. His fiction is marked by a stylistic perfection and a dark humour that is often turned scathingly towards the British upper-middle class. Despite the social criticism his writing often performs, politically Munro was a profoundly conservative figure: scathing of the movement for women's right to vote, patriotic to the point of jingoism and fiercely supportive of the British Empire, he served in Burma as a young man. Although he was much too old to enlist when the First World War broke out, enlist he did and the manner of his death in the trenches reads like a bleakly ironic scene from one of his own stories. Noticing a comrade enjoying a smoke at night, Munro yelled "Put that bloody cigarette out", words which turned out to be his last as he was promptly shot and killed by a sniper.

"The Background" is presented as a story narrated by a journal-ist to Clovis Sangrail, a recurrent character in Saki's fiction who takes a wry perspective on the foibles of Edwardian society. Henri Deplis, the focus of the journalist's tale, is a commercial traveller from Luxembourg who, coming into a modest legacy, decides to get what would now be called a backpiece from Italy's finest tattoo master. "The Background" is somewhat unusual in its treatment of tattooing in the period for the prominence it gives to the tattoo as a legitimate form of artistic expression (though it is precisely this that causes Henri all manner of troubles).

"THAT WOMAN'S ART-JARGON TIRES ME," SAID CLOVIS TO his journalist friend. "She's so fond of talking of certain pictures as 'growing on one', as though they were a sort of fungus."

"That reminds me," said the journalist, "of the story of Henri Deplis. Have I ever told it you?"

Clovis shook his head.

"Henri Deplis was by birth a native of the Grand Duchy of Luxemburg. On maturer reflection he became a commercial traveller. His business activities frequently took him beyond the limits of the Grand Duchy, and he was stopping in a small town of Northern Italy when news reached him from home that a legacy from a distant and deceased relative had fallen to his share.

"It was not a large legacy, even from the modest standpoint of Henri Deplis, but it impelled him towards some seemingly harmless extravagances. In particular it led him to patronize local art as represented by the tattoo-needles of Signor Andreas Pincini. Signor Pincini was, perhaps, the most brilliant master of tattoo craft that Italy had ever known, but his circumstances were decidedly impoverished, and for the sum of six hundred francs he gladly undertook to cover his client's back, from the collar-bone down to the waist-line, with a glowing representation of the Fall of Icarus. The design, when finally developed, was a slight disappointment to Monsieur Deplis, who had suspected Icarus of being a fortress taken by Wallenstein in the Thirty Years' War, but he was more than satisfied with the execution of the work, which was acclaimed by all who had the privilege of seeing it as Pincini's masterpiece.

"It was his greatest effort, and his last. Without even waiting to be paid, the illustrious craftsman departed this life, and was buried under an ornate tombstone, whose winged cherubs would have afforded singularly little scope for the exercise of his favourite art. There remained, however, the widow Pincini, to whom the six hundred francs were due. And thereupon arose the great crisis in the life of Henri Deplis, traveller of commerce. The legacy, under the stress of numerous little calls on its substance, had dwindled to very insignificant proportions, and when a pressing wine bill and sundry other current accounts had been paid, there remained little more than 430 francs to offer to the widow. The lady was properly indignant, not wholly, as she volubly explained, on account of the suggested writing-off of 170 francs, but also at the attempt to depreciate the value of her late husband's acknowledged master-piece. In a week's time Deplis was obliged to reduce his offer to 405 francs, which circumstance fanned the widow's indignation into a fury. She cancelled the sale of the work of art, and a few days later Deplis learned with a sense of consternation that she had presented it to the municipality of Bergamo, which had gratefully accepted it. He left the neighbourhood as unobtrusively as possible, and was genuinely relieved when his business commands took him to Rome, where he hoped his identity and that of the famous picture might be lost sight of.

"But he bore on his back the burden of the dead man's genius. On presenting himself one day in the steaming corridor of a vapour bath, he was at once hustled back into his clothes by the proprie-tor, who was a North Italian, and who emphatically refused to allow the celebrated Fall of Icarus to be publicly on view without the permission of the municipality of Bergamo. Public interest and official vigilance increased as the matter became more widely known, and Deplis was unable to take a simple dip in the sea or river on the hottest afternoon unless clothed up to the collar-bone in a substantial bathing garment. Later on the authorities of Bergamo conceived the idea that salt water might be injurious to the master-piece, and a perpetual injunction was obtained which debarred the muchly harassed commercial traveller from sea bathing under any circumstances. Altogether, he was fervently thankful when his firm of employers found him a new range of activities in the neighbour-hood of Bordeaux. His thankfulness, however, ceased abruptly at the Franco-Italian frontier. An imposing array of official force barred his departure, and he was sternly reminded of the stringent law which forbids the exportation of Italian works of art.

"A diplomatic parley ensued between the Luxemburgian and Italian Governments, and at one time the European situation became overcast with the possibilities of trouble. But the Italian Government stood firm; it declined to concern itself in the least with the fortunes or even the existence of Henri Deplis, commercial traveller, but was immovable in its decision that the Fall of Icarus (by the late Pincini, Andreas) at present the property of the municipality of Bergamo, should not leave the country.

"The excitement died down in time, but the unfortunate Deplis, who was of a constitutionally retiring disposition, found himself a few months later once more the storm-centre of a furious contro-versy. A certain German art expert, who had obtained from the municipality of Bergamo permission to inspect the famous master-piece, declared it to be a spurious Pincini, probably the work of some pupil whom he had employed in his declining years. The evidence of Deplis on the subject was obviously worthless, as he had been under the influence of the customary narcotics during the long process of pricking in the design. The editor of an Italian art journal refuted the contentions of the German expert and undertook to prove that his private life did not conform to any modern standard of decency. The whole of Italy and Germany were drawn into the dispute, and the rest of Europe was soon involved in the quarrel. There were stormy scenes in the Spanish Parliament, and the University of Copenhagen bestowed a gold medal on the German expert (afterwards sending a commission to examine his proofs on the spot), while two Polish schoolboys in Paris committed suicide to show what *they* thought of the matter.

"Meanwhile, the unhappy human background fared no better than before, and it was not surprising that he drifted into the ranks of Italian anarchists. Four times at least he was escorted to the frontier as a dangerous and undesirable foreigner, but he was always brought back as the Fall of Icarus (attributed to Pincini, Andreas, early twentieth century). And then one day, at an anarchist congress at Genoa, a fellow-worker, in the heat of debate, broke a phial full of corrosive liquid over his back. The red shirt that he was wearing mitigated the effects, but the Icarus was ruined beyond recognition. His assailant was severely reprimanded for assaulting a fellow-anarchist and received seven years' imprisonment for defacing a national art treasure As soon as he was able to leave the hospital Henri Deplis was put across the frontier as an undesirable alien.

"In the quieter streets of Paris, especially in the neighbourhood of the Ministry of Fine Arts, you may sometimes meet a depressed, anxious-looking man, who, if you pass him the time of day, will answer you with a slight Luxemburgian accent. He nurses the illusion that he is one of the lost arms of the Venus de Milo, and hopes that the French Government may be persuaded to buy him. On all other subjects I believe he is tolerably sane."

THE TATTOOED LEG (1919)

John Chilton

"The Tattooed Leg" appears to be John Chilton's only published story. It appeared in 1919 in *Overland Monthly*, a literary magazine based in San Francisco and edited by the noted short-story writer Bret Harte. *Overland* was for a time one of the most significant publications of its kind in the U.S. and featured work by some of America's most acclaimed authors, including Mark Twain and Jack London. It is probable therefore that Chilton was an American, and the story suggests (though this is pure speculation) that he had recently returned from military service in the Great War.

The 1914–1918 war left hundreds of thousands of young men with lost limbs. Official statistics show 240,000 British soldiers alone had arms or legs amputated. "The Tattooed Leg" begins with an amputation and, though the cause of the injury is vaguely described as a "wreck", the atmosphere of trauma and the "smell of anti-septics" that pervades the story's opening would surely have been painfully evocative for homecoming servicemen and women. The tale can certainly be read as an account of post-traumatic stress disorder as the story's wounded hero endeavours, not particularly successfully at first, to adapt to a new life following his injury. When he discovers the appearance of some unexpected and undesired body art, it is worth recalling that gunshot wounds can at times result in the tattooing of the skin around the bullet's entry point.

"The Tattooed Leg" is a strange tale, somewhat in the vein of Mary Shelley's *Frankenstein*, and one which represents a singular contribution to tattoo literature.

TWO SCENES SEEMED TO LIVE THEMSELVES OVER AND OVER in his mind as he lay outstretched on the narrow hospital bed—one his good-bye to Bess, and somehow he seemed to be taking the kisses he had not quite dared to take, Bess was always so standoffish. He saw her face and figure quite clearly against a black background. Bess was distractingly pretty, but always she faded away and he saw himself lying on a roughly improvised table in a freight shed struggling with a keen-eyed, thin-lipped man who pressed a wet towel over his face—and everything was blotted out; yet, even as life faded he heard a voice say:

"It is the chance I have prayed for and I shall take it—he can only die!"

Then one morning he woke up. He was lying in a small room where everything was white and clean and smelled strongly of antisceptics, and a strange woman, a nurse in white cap and apron, was sitting by an open window rolling bandages. He tried to roll over and found he could not move. The woman looked up:

"Oh, you're all right again," she said, laying down her work and rising.

"I want to get up," he said shakily in a voice faraway and quite unlike his own.

"You must be patient and get strong first."

The nurse placed her cool, firm hand lightly on his head and smiled. "Just a little while and you will be quite well. I am glad to see you conscious."

"Tell me—"

"Drink this."

And then he slept, this time dreamlessly and like a child, and awakened refreshed and clear-headed, and life began again.

Then came long, happy days of convalescence, and the great day of days when he sat up for the first time. He felt strong with renewed life and vigour as he threw his limbs over the edge of the bed and laughed up at his nurse for her assisting arm.

"You can bet I'm not sorry to get out of that plaster and on my pins again."

"You've been a wonderfully fortunate young man, and that girl who has been haunting the hospital is waiting down stairs to tell you so," answered the nurse.

Just then he glanced down at his legs protruding from the bed covers.

"Gee! What's the matter with my legs? What's that blue mark? Who's been tattooing me? Good Lord! Why, that isn't my leg—what is it?"

He glared wildly up into the serene face above him.

"You lost your leg in the wreck, and Dr. Amsden, the great surgeon, has successfully grafted on another. It is the most wonderful piece of work that was ever done, and—"

"Whose leg have I got?" he asked faintly, his face whitening.

"There, there, brace up—be brave, you haven't anything to worry about now; it's all over and you are going to be as good as new."

Then he weakened and fell back on the pillow sick with the horror of the thing and not daring to ask further, his still weakened mind unable to grasp what had happened while he cried over and over childishly:

"I want by leg—Give me my leg!" until the nurse was obliged to give him a quieting powder and put him back to bed.

It took several days of care before he could reconcile himself to a certain nervous horror that seemed to pervade his being whenever he thought of what had happened to him and then Bess came and he talked it all over with her. She was a girl among a thousand, with a wealth of good common sense, and whatever she thought in her heart she loved him enough to dissemble and encourage him, and so he came out from the fear and horror and gradually grew strong until the time came when he left the hospital and took up his old life, with only a slight limp to remind his friends of his accident.

Then came his marriage to Bess, and in his new happiness he almost forgot the strange blue marks that had so puzzled him at first, and yet sometimes, when rubbing himself down after a bath, he would pause and endeavour to decipher the meaning of the crosses and circles and the long, straight mark between.

Then a strange thing happened to him which he did not tell Bess for very shame. He was walking down a side street in a not very respectable part of the town, making a short-cut to the ferry, when he passed a low corner groggery, a sinister sort of place with a half door of faded, dirty green lattice, when, without volition on his part he found himself pushing through the lattice in an endeavour to enter. Horrified, he turned with visible effort and almost ran down the street. If anyone had seen him—a prominent member of the Y.M.C.A.! A few days afterward he found himself following a common, bedraggled, painted creature down an alley, and only turned back by the greatest effort.

After several like experiences he went to a specialist for treatment. He was so ashamed of it all that it affected his manner at home, and Bess noticed it and questioned him. Finding him reticent, she resented it, and a coolness came between them. The medicine the doctor gave him did no special good. Perhaps it might have been that he controlled his inclinations a bit more easily for a while, but the effect wore away and it was all worse than ever. He began to be obsessed by a craving for strong drink, and found himself inventing excuses for going out at night at late hours. Then Bess and he quarrelled outright. She cried, and told him she never would have believed a man could change so, and then he broke down and told her all, and with her usual common sense she went right to the root of the matter and wondered why they hadn't thought of it before. It was the strange leg beyond the shadow of a doubt. The man from whom it had been taken was a bad man, and the influence had grown and the blood, the vicious blood, had simply poisoned her dear, true-hearted, honest husband, and if not treated properly would ruin him mentally and physically. The first thing to do was to go to the best blood specialist they could find and be thoroughly cleansed, and if that were not efficacious, then they, as a last resort, could have the leg amputated again. But, after all, would that be a cure? Wasn't the whole system of the man so permeated that nothing save a seven-years' course of treatment could help him. Poor things! They worried and fretted until Bess had gotten him ready, and they set out to discover a certain Dr. Everett, who was of great repute.

The learned man was delighted with the case, but, being in consultation with a very great and celebrated detective over a criminal case of much importance, could only make an appointment with them for the following morning, and so it came about that as they wandered through a small park on their way to the ferry they met with an adventure that changed everything for them.

Bess was carrying one of those fancy gold meshed bags so much affected by young women, one of her wedding gifts of which she was very fond, when a small, mean-looking man jostled her and she felt it suddenly jerked from her hand. She turned with a cry and saw him running around a corner—gave chase, followed by her husband, who went blindly, only sensing the fact that something had happened. Bess was an athletic young woman, and at first gained on the thief, but he got among the crowd of people on the streeet and eluded her. She stopped as a crowd gathered, and a policeman came hurrying up for explanation, and half crying over her loss, gave a description of the man who had robbed her, as well as a close description of the contents of the bag.

They took a short-cut through a by-street, and walking slowly along close together, hand in hand, as each sought to comfort the other, they saw a crowd gathered about a fallen man. As they passed, Bess looked.

"There he is!" she cried, dashing through and catching hold of the fallen man: "Oh, aren't you ashamed of yourself to steal my bag! If you are hurt, it serves you right."

Everyone looked at Bess, and her husband tried to draw her away.

"No, I will not come till I have given him in charge. Why doesn't a policeman come?"

"The man's hurt, Miss," said a rough-looking bystander. "He was hit by an automobile as he was running across the street, an' I guess he's pretty bad for he hasn't spoke a word since. We're waiting for an ambulance—here it comes!"

They took a car to the hospital and arriving there found that the man was seriously injured, also that Bess's bag had been found in his pocket. They would not give it up at first, but on her proving the property finally said they would risk it, after taking the address and asking innumerable questions.

As they were leaving, a nurse came hurrying after them.

"Good morning," she said, "perhaps you don't remember me, but I used to help watch when you were here. How's your leg?"

Bess recalled the woman, though her husband did not.

"That poor man that was run down by a motor," she explained, "is conscious. He cannot live, and I promised to bring you. He wants to see you."

"Wants to see me," cried Bess. "I don't want to see him. He stole my pretty bag, and I never want to see him again. Of course I'm sorry he's not going to get well—" then as a sense of what it really meant came over her, she said, shamefacedly: "Oh, I didn't really mean to be so thoughtless; come, let us go to him at once and see if there is anything we can do."

Her husband smiled a little sadly. He was so filled with his own trouble that he had little thought for anything else just then, but the nurse electrified him into the present.

"He is the man that—the man, you know, whose leg they took—he didn't die—"

"What? Good God! Come—take me to him at once—let us hurry!"

The man lay white and sunken among the pillows. His eyes gleamed strangely from his pinched face.

"I'm glad she got you," he said faintly. "I guess I'm all in this time, all right. It's all the fault of that damned cork leg—it played out on me just when I needed it most. Well—you know me, don't you? I know you—I've followed you long enough to get your points down pretty fine—an' I've had my fun with you all right—you ain't such a bad subject when it comes to hypnotizin', an' I'd got you If it hadn't been for her—" he laughed, a rattling, mirthless, cackling laugh that chilled his hearers. "Say, you nurse, how long have I got? There's a lot to tell—"

"You mustn't excite yourself, try and keep calm," said the nurse, moistening his lips with a bit of cotton after dipping it in liquid, "there, is that better?"

He did not answer her, but kept his fading eyes fixed on his visitors by turns.

"I don't know what I'm tellng you for—I guess because of her, she always looked good to me, an' she sure always was lookin' out for you—or I'd have got my leg back long ago—" he mumbled a bit to himself, and then his voice came clearer. "It's a long story, an' I ain't got time for it all, so I'll cut it short an' say as my pal was run out of Colorado a couple o' years ago an' by fate as he was footin' it over the hills he stumbled on the richest lead as he ever saw. The gold stuck out in regular chunks. He covered it up after takin' the bearings of it so's he could locate it if he wanted to come back, but when we got together he thought it'd be safer to send me, an' so he give me a paper with a plan o' the location on it, an' for safety he tattooed the same on my leg. If I lost the paper or had it swiped from me I could follow my leg, see?" The voice trailed off and the eager listeners feared the end had come.

"Oh, give him something, quick," cried Bess; "you don't know what this means; it is more than life to my husband; do, do something—"

As if in answer to her pleading the dying man opened his closing eyes and began speaking again:

"I was on my way out to Colorado when I got caught in that wreck and that damned doctor, thinking I was dead—oh, he knew I wasn't, all right—all he wanted was his damned experiment, I'd like to live long enough to get him— Well, you got my leg all right, though I s'pose it wasn't your fault. It put me back, and I've had the devil's luck ever since with one thing after another, an' I haven't got out to that gold mine—an' now I never shall, so's I'm goin' to give you the chance. It's for her, for her," his eyes rested on Bess with a sort of dog-like devotion that seemed somehow to dignify the meanness of the poor creature.

"It's to pay you for takin' that bag. I didn't go for to steal it—I was takin' it for luck—an' I meant all the time to give you part of the mine when I got it, I did, so help me—"

They hung breathless on his broken words, not daring to question, but the man who listened felt the load of horror lifted from his soul and knew himself free from the hideous bond.

"The circles are the big boulders at the north edge of the town—listen close—I'm goin' now—the straight line runs north one mile on the county road—the crosses—oh, God!—thirty feet—west."

"The town?" cried Bess breathlessly.

There was only a hideous gurgle as he tried to answer, and then his jaw dropped as his last breath sighed forth.

BRANDED (1919)

Albert Payson Terhune

Albert Payson Terhune (1872–1942) was a journalist, amateur boxer, and writer of fiction who carved out an unusual niche for himself in American literature as an author of dog stories. The most celebrated of these is the 1919 *Lad: A Dog*, a collection of short stories based on the life of the author's own collie which went on to sell over a million copies. As he continued to publish dog tales by the dozen, Terhune also made a name for himself as a dog-breeder. There is more to Terhune than dogs, however. He produced fiction on a diverse array of topics, often in the vein of historical or adventure fiction.

"Branded" follows the plot of the straight-laced lawyer Jim Ross trying to prevent his brother Walton marrying the beautiful but penniless Helen Ward, a mission that unfolds during a country-house party in upstate New York. Arriving at the party, Jim discovers that his hostess has employed a Japanese "drawing room entertainer" stereotypically named Cherry San to "sing in costume and tattoo" the guests. The story addresses the so-called tattoo craze of the early twentieth century while articulating social anxieties about tattooed women and the cross-cultural exchanges associated with tattooing, particularly between America and Japan. Cherry San is an intriguing figure. Described generically as "the Jap" (a term which would become a racial pejorative during the Second World War—before the war it was more neutrally descriptive), her representation forms a key part of the story's satirical perspective on the conservative attitudes Jim Ross embodies.

I F HELEN WARD NUMBERED FIVE HUNDRED MEN IN HER HERE-
and-there acquaintance, it was fairly safe to catalogue the thousand in this order:

One hundred of them were either in love with her or else waited
but the spark of hope to make them so. Three hundred and ninety-
nine of the remainder liked her better than almost any other girl
they knew; and the wedded contingent among them wished furtively
that their wives could make a personal study of her. (Helen was the
kind of girl one marries.)

This accounts for all of the five hundred—with a single exception.
That exception was Jim Ross. And Jim Ross neither loved Helen nor
so much as liked her. He detested her. He hated her more consistently
than ever in his morose career he had been able to hate any one else.

He had begun disliking her on general principles. Perhaps on the
same theory that made the Athenians banish Aristides, because they
were tired of hearing him called "the Just". As a born and bred and
expert lawyer, Jim invariably refused to take anything for granted.
Hearing Helen's praises sung in a myriad different keys, he had
sought to verify or confute the praise. And, naturally, he had ended
by confuting it. To him, Helen Ward was a butterfly—a female drone
in life's hive. She served no good end. And she did not put herself
out to be cringingly agreeable to his important self.

Not until Helen's engagement to Ross's younger brother, Walton,
was made known did Jim sweep from impersonal dislike for her into
active and resentful hatred. He told himself that it was because Walt
was throwing himself away on such a girl. He told many people so.

No one but his own timid little wife could have proved otherwise. And Marcia Ross was too much in chronic terror of her aggressive husband to criticize him—even to herself.

Jim Ross had dreamed a dream. From his standpoint, it had been a beautiful dream. Because it had been about money. He had married Marcia two months before the death of her supposedly ultra-rich father. The father had died all but insolvent. And the blow had come close to breaking Jim's pure heart. He had never been able quite to forgive Marcia for her sire's poverty. True, he needed no more money than he and his brother had inherited at their parents' death, and he was making a good livelihood at the law. But that a man of his acumen should have saddled himself with a penniless bride was an endless grief to him.

Then into his ken and his guardianship recently had flapped a flat-chested and dish-faced damsel who, in her own right, possessed something like two million dollars. And Jim, straightway, had enlisted Marcia's feeble aid in throwing the heiress and Walt together at all times and places. Walt had rewarded this brotherly effort by engaging himself to Helen Ward—a girl with barely enough money to dress on. And just as the two-million maiden had begun to show a keen interest in Walt's society, too!

Still, Jim did not give up all hope. An engagement is not a marriage. Much may happen between the merging of those two blissful states. So he fought on.

Jim Ross used to say the chief difference between a night at Mrs. Greaves's country house and a night in a cell was that in jail there are no servants to tip.

It was Jim Ross's pleasing way to say a thing like that. It was on a par with his wonted view of life, and of those who sought to make it pleasant for him and for Marcia.

Mrs. Greaves, of course, heard of his sneer at her house-parties. And it vexed her not at all. She did not so much as bother to stop inviting Jim to Restmere. Her parties were too jolly and worth-while to be hurt by Jim's slurs or even by his presence.

"Some one has to ask the poor man somewhere," she used to say. "Every one else has stopped inviting him. So now it's more exclusive to have him as a guest than not to. Besides, there's his poor wife. I like Marcia. I'd like her better if I didn't have to be sorry for her."

The "jail" resemblance at Restmere, to which Ross referred, was the quaint dormitory system. Restmere, two hundred years earlier, had been built with a view to the entertaining of hordes of guests. Wherefore, on either side of the rambling house was a huge room, some fifty by a hundred feet. And along the sides of these two rooms were airy little alcoves—to hold a bed, a chair, and a dresser.

The alcoves all connected with the main dormitory-room, which was blended lounge and assembly-hall.

In Colonial days (when men and women used to sit at opposite sides of a church and so forth), the eastern dormitory had been set apart for women guests and the western for men. And, ever since, the odd old custom had been kept up. Such of the Greaves's guests as did not like the arrangement were not forced to accept the hostess's invitation. But few of them objected. Even Jim Ross, despite his comparison between his alcove bedroom and a cell, continued, unprotesting, to occupy such a "cell" whenever he was asked to Restmere.

One of these rare invitations came to him and to his wife a fortnight after Jim heard of the engagement of his brother and Helen Ward. It was a weekend party for which Mrs. Greaves sent forth a dozen invitations, and for which she received, at once, precisely twelve acceptances.

Besides the Jim Rosses and Helen Ward, the guest list included Jim's law partner, Barry Cahill—a hard-headed and taciturn man, who was one of the few living mortals whereof Jim wholly approved—and, naturally, Jim's aforesaid younger brother, Walton.

Jim and Mrs. Jim arrived at the Greaves's home late on Saturday afternoon. They were the last guests to reach Restmere. They found their fellow revellers all assembled in the wide entrance-hall at tea. On a fat sofa-pillow at the hostess's feet sat a tiny cross-legged figure in kimono and obi, plucking daintily away at a samisen's strings and crooning sweet little queer songs in a queer little sweet voice. The other guests, teacups in hand, were grouped interestedly round the singer.

To Jim, the scene's central figure was puzzling. To Marcia, his wife, there was nothing perplexing about it. Mrs. Ross gained her few glimpses of social pleasure by going to various people's houses while her husband was at his office. And several times before she had met this mite of a Japanese woman.

Cherry San, as she chose to call herself, was a society fad that year, and was coining a fortune as a drawing-room entertainer. From house to house she was bidden, at fabulous sums, to sing in costume and to tattoo. One of the recurrent tattoo crazes was at its height. And many a New York woman was willing to pay insane prices for the privilege of having her white flesh disfigured by one of Cherry San's minutely small artistic designs.

Mrs. Greaves had summoned the Jap to Restmere for the amusement of her weekend guests. And the pleasure with which her songs were now received and encored proved the experiment a success. Cherry San, today, sang sometimes in Japanese, sometimes in English.

"And now for the tattooing—*please!*" called Helen Ward, as the singer at last laid aside her samisen and got to her feet.

"Please *not!*" begged Cherry San, flexing her little yellow hands. "Not yet. Unless you wish very bad art in tattooing, please! When I play for so long, my fingers get what you call cramp and stiff. If I use the needles before my fingers have an hour to rest them, then my hand wiggles, and I spoil my art. After dinner, by gracious leave, yes?"

"After dinner, then," assented Mrs. Greaves. "But it will have to be very soon after dinner. I'm asking twenty or thirty neighbourhood people over for a dance this evening. And you know how it is in the country. People begin drifting in the minute they finish their own dinners. I want you all to come out and look at my new Italian garden before you dress. If you've finished tea, suppose we go now."

The guests followed her through the wide doorway out to the veranda and across the lawn. Walton Ross, to his brother's disgust, manœuvred not only for a place at Helen Ward's side in the irregular procession, but also managed to detach her from the bulk of the party. Jim was glumly relieved to see Barry Cahill leave the rest and join the two lovers. Oblivious of Walton's lack of enthusiasm, Cahill proceeded to monopolize as much of Helen's attention as he could.

This unusual expansion on the part of his taciturn partner surprised Jim almost as much as it pleased him. He turned to his wife, who, as usual, was pattering along meekly at his side.

"Look there, Marcia," he grunted joyfully, under his breath. "See Cahill trying to cut Walt out? I hope to the Lord he succeeds! She doesn't seem to object, either. See? I wonder if there's a chance—"

"But Jim," timidly protested his wife, "it would make poor Walt so unhappy if—"

"'Unhappy!'" snorted Jim, in the tone that always wilted his scared wife into silence. "'Unhappy?' It makes a man unhappy to have his vaccination take. But it saves him from smallpox. Not a chance, though, I suppose. Walt's got twice the money Cahill will ever have. The Ward girl knows which side her bread's buttered on. Still—" He grunted again, and fell silent.

Dinner was late. And, as usual on the first night of a house-party, it was a long-continued meal. When the women trooped out of the dining-room into the broad hall, they found Cherry San standing patiently beside a table on which was arrayed her tattoo-kit.

They flocked round her—Helen Ward most interested of all the six. The Jap answered their idle questions as best she could, the while taking out and arranging on the table her divers jars of tattooing fluid and her case of assorted needles. From the bottom of the kit she produced a roll of thin Japanese vellum on which were printed a host of coloured designs.

The women were still looking over this chart when the men joined them and augmented the group round Cherry San. Jim Ross, whose dinner was already beginning to disagree with him, viewed the gay-hued vellum with no favour at all. Presently he broke upon the lively chatter by thrusting out a thick finger and tapping with disapproval one of the charted designs.

"Rare Japanese art, hey?" he scoffed jarringly. "That pattern, for one, is startlingly new and Oriental! A heart transfixed by an arrow! Was Saint Valentine a Samurai?"

"No," calmly intervened Helen Ward. "Tradition says he was the patron saint of thieves—and lawyers."

"But Mr. James Ross is right," shyly affirmed the tattooer, unvexed by the man's rudeness and not comprehending Helen's rebuke of it. "He is right as to the bad taste of that design. It is not art. It is not new. It is not even ancient. It has a—what you call a savour—of the sailorman and the dock-worker. Not of the social world. It is bad art. I do not like to have it with my good designs. Yet I must. For some folk—lovers and the like—prefer it to—well, to this exquisite and blooming branch of flowering peach blossoms or this best-of-all rainbow-moth. You see—"

Her exposition was interrupted. The first carful of dance-guests was at the door. With a sigh of an artist whose work is temporarily shelved for less worthy matters, Cherry San proceeded to efface herself from the foreground.

Jim Ross was not in the least interested in the new arrivals, since he did not dance and did not care to talk. He stood where he was as the others gradually moved away. And, aimlessly, he began to play with the tattoo-kit. He picked up one or two of the shining needles, examining their ice-bright points, dipping them inquisitively into one or another of the open jars of liquid pigment, and smearing the resultant ink drops on a bit of paper to sample their colours.

Tiring, presently, of this tame sport, Jim left the table and stood for a while in a doorway, watching the dancers. Watching people dance is, for a non-dancer, perhaps the stupidest way to spend an evening. But Jim was not bored. For he fell to following the progress of Helen Ward.

She was dancing with Walton when Jim first caught sight of her in the swirl. But, five minutes later, he saw her fox-trotting with Barry Cahill. And life, for Jim, began to resume its charm. He caught her dancing with Cahill a second time a little later. He studied the swaying couples as though they represented an abstrusely fascinating law case.

Jim shifted his observation base to a black-shadowed niche of the veranda close to one of the open windows. He had noticed that couple after couple came to the window from time to time to cool off. The niche was a fine natural vantage-point. For example:

In another half-hour, Helen and Walton paused there, between dances. They were talking animatedly. And at once Jim was able to verify an aged proverb as to the kind of things listeners are likely to hear about themselves.

"Dear, I tell you he hates me!" Helen was saying, her guarded voice barely reaching the listener. "Honestly, he does. And you know it. Why, he looks at me as if I were a blend of the Kaiser and the man who invented the income-tax! I don't know why. For I always tried to be nice to him—just for your sake and poor Marcia's—as long as he'd let me. I suppose it's because you had the bad taste to ask me to marry you."

"Nonsense!" laughed Walton. "You're all wrong about old Jim. He dislikes most people on general principles. It's his nature. I suppose it's partly because his law work has shown him such a lot of the seamy side. But when he knows you better, he'll be dead sure to fall in love with you. Nobody could help it. Don't bother your glorious self about Jim."

"I don't," Helen assured him. "If I did, I'd get to wondering all sorts of horrible things about family traits. And then, perhaps, I'd begin looking at you the way he looks at me. Walt—do something for me?"

"Anything!" he promised.

"Dance with Marcia," she commanded. "The poor little thing is sitting over there, trying to smile and look festive. And, all the time, she is afraid Jim will appear from somewhere and scold her or glower at her. I know she is. He's so jealous she dare not dance with any other man, I suppose, for fear of a row with him. But you're her brother-in-law. So Jim can't be very jealous of *you*."

Walton Ross laughed indulgently.

"All right!" he agreed. "Only, you're wrong about Jim, sweetheart. If he's jealous of Marcia, it's only because he loves her. I guess that's

one of the manifestations of love—in some chaps. I'd be as jealous
as the very deuce—if you ever gave me cause."

"Marcia never gave him cause to be jealous," denied Helen. "You
know that as well as I do. She worships him. And he bullies her to
death. As for *your* being jealous—why, you wouldn't know how to
be. And I love you for not knowing how. Now run along to Marcia,"
she ended abruptly.

The obedient Walton took his departure, leaving her standing
there, half shielded by the window-curtain. Jim Ross fought back
a yearning to shake his fist at the girl and to bellow forth a retort
to her frank opinion of him. He hated her tenfold more than ever.
His moody eyes followed Walton's course through the room toward
the corner where Marcia was sitting alone, a deprecatory little smile
on her face.

Then, all at once, Jim's muscles stiffened. A man had hurried up
to Helen Ward, and was bending close to her as he said something
in so low a voice that Ross could not catch the words. The man was
Barry Cahill.

Jim leaned perilously far forward and strained his ears. He heard
the words: "Italian garden", in Barry's rumbling voice. He saw Helen
step forward at Cahill's side as if to leave the room. Then he saw
Mrs. Greaves bearing down on her, with a newly arrived man in
tow. And he heard Helen whisper to her escort a word that sounded
like "Later".

Jim Ross stayed not upon the order of his going. He sped from
the veranda and across the lawn to a cypress-lined pathway leading to
the patch of greensward which Mrs. Greaves had recently converted
into a formal Italian garden.

The night was moonlit, with an occasional spring cloud blowing
over the soft glow and shading it. There was plenty of illumination

whereby Jim could find his way to the evergreen-surrounded Italian garden, and could choose a good listening-post there.

In the garden's centre was a lily-pool bordered with flowering iris. At one side of this was a carven stone bench—an ideal seat for spooning couples. Set deep in the shrubbery, twenty feet farther on and facing the house, was a second stone seat. To this second seat repaired Jim Ross.

Lounging upon it, half sitting, half lying, he was concealed from any but the keenest sight, and, in that position, his head would not show on the sky-line above the clipped evergreens. He commanded a full view, not only of the opposite bench in the open but of the broad path itself and of the distant veranda and front doorway.

As a strategic position for eavesdropping, it could not have been improved on. Luck, assuredly, was with the solicitous elder brother this night! All he need do was to remain there until Helen and Cahill should keep their moonlight tryst in the garden.

Then it ought to be the simplest thing in the world to collect evidence enough to convince Walton of his sweetheart's unworthiness. A single kiss—nay, even the suffering of Cahill's arm to steal about her waist—an unconsidered love-word from her. Jim knew Walton would take his word for what he had seen and heard. Jim was truthful. And Walton knew it.

All that remained was to get indisputable evidence—evidence to which, if need be, Jim could swear. And Ross waited, grimly triumphant, for the furnishers of that evidence to come in sight.

The evening wore on. The dance-music reached Jim fitfully through the stillness. Now and again a woman in white and a man in black would stray across his vision, as some couple chose to stroll on the moonlit lawn instead of dancing in a hot room. At sight of these occasional promenaders, Ross would invariably crouch lower, in keen expectation. But none of them came so far afield as the Italian garden.

Once, between dances, he heard Cherry San's reedy-sweet voice singing to the tinkle of her samisen. And diverted by the haunting melody, he recognized an air from the *Chinese Child's Day*. He even made out a fragment of the quaintly accented words:

> Many things I sing—
> Of the cherry blossoms blooming in the spring.
> Of the bird that is homeward winging.
> Of the temple-bell a-swinging—
> You can almost hear it ringing.

Then, one after another, the cars that had brought the dance guests came whirring up the drive to the veranda. And voices and laughter from departing neighbours told that the dance was at an end. After the last car had gone, several of the house guests stood chatting on the veranda for a few minutes.

One by one they went back into the house, bound for bed. Jim, by the glow of the veranda lamps, could recognize some of them as they passed in through the double doorway. He discovered his wife and Walton and a few others as they moved indoors.

Then the veranda lights were switched off, and he heard the front doors closed. The shaded windows of the two huge dormitories gleamed into vision against the house's dark background. And still Jim Ross stayed at his post.

He had staked everything on those two scraps of overheard talk: "Italian garden", and "Later". They meant—if they meant anything—a secret moonlight rendezvous in the garden at the first free moment. And, with the dumb stubbornness which had won him so many cases, Jim Ross was staying on.

But Jim had had a hard week. The silence and the coolness and his half-reclining posture—all had wooed him to drowsiness.

He never knew whether he slept a minute or a half-hour. But, suddenly, he started up, blinking and bewildered—awakened from his doze by the uncontrolled sobbing of a woman not twenty feet away from him.

Dazed, not yet realizing where he was nor why he was there, Jim looked about him in the elusive moonlight.

Directly in front of him, and on the far side of the lily-pool, stood a woman and a man. They were close-locked in each other's arms. The woman's head was on the man's breast, and she was weeping. Her back was towards Ross.

The man, however, was facing him. And, as he raised his head for an instant, Jim saw him distinctly. It was Barry Cahill.

Jim Ross was always slow to collect his senses on awakening. And now he stared in owlish dullness at the couple, wondering where he was and what was happening. Only subconsciously did his mind focus on the scene before him.

Cahill was murmuring to the woman in his arms, and was seeking to soothe her hysterical grief. Jim heard her cry out brokenly, her voice sob-strangled past all recognition:

"Oh, I can't stand it any longer! I *can't*! He—"

And, at that point, Jim Ross remembered why he himself had come hither. His furtive task was accomplished. He had succeeded beyond his wildest hopes.

Here, in Barry Cahill's arms, wept Helen Ward! And she was bewailing her lot! Presumably her lot in being engaged to

Walton Ross! Jim had evidence aplenty for the breaking of the engagement.

A thrill of triumph swept away the last of the sleep-mists from Ross's brain. He was himself again—vigilant, crafty, eager. And he comprehended that one move alone remained to make his victory complete. He must see Helen Ward's face, that he might be able to swear it was she he had found in Cahill's arms.

All intent on this final proof, he jumped to his feet. As though by a signal, a cloud, whose feathery edges had been dimming the moon's full glare, swirled its dark centre athwart the face of the orb. Jim's leap from the shrubbery brought the two lovers spinning round to confront him. Then, in almost the same motion, they wheeled and fled at top speed up the path toward the house.

In Ross's mind was a fierce chagrin. Thanks to the dim light, he had not yet seen Helen's face. It had been a whitish blur. He could not swear to her identity, morally certain of it as he was. Losing control of himself, as he saw his prey escaping, he roared after the fugitives:

"Take your time, Miss Ward! There's no hurry!"

As he spoke, he hurled his body forward in pursuit. But the others had gained too good a start for him to overtake them. As he ran, the moon shook off its grimy cloud and shone out again in dazzling radiance.

By the gleam, Ross could see the lovers gain the veranda steps. The man held open the front door for his companion. As she glided into the house, he stooped and kissed her. Then he slammed shut the door behind her and dashed round the veranda to the side entrance of the men's dormitory.

Jim Ross paid no heed to his vanishing law partner. He was after Helen, not Cahill. Feverishly he craved to catch her before she could traverse the long hall and reach the entrance to the women's dormitory. Up the low steps he sprang and across the deep veranda. As he flung open the front door, he saw a gleam of white showing triangular against the outer panel near the floor. And his heart gave a savage throb of joy.

For Cahill, in his loverly haste to close the door on his *inamorata*, had shut it a fraction of a second too soon. And the hem of her fluffy skirt had been caught between portal and jamb. She was a prisoner!

Jim, with one hand, swung wide the door. With the other, he made a lunging clutch at the newly freed white figure which fled before him. His outflung fingers closed round a cold little wrist just as the front door blew shut behind him.

In the pitch-black hallway the woman fought mutely to free herself. Jim thrust his unused hand into his waistcoat pocket in search of his match-box. It was not there. He did not know where to look elsewhere for matches to give him the brief glimpse he needed of his wriggling captive's face. Nor did he know the location of the light-switch.

There was something of the noiselessly desperate trapped beast in the woman's wild struggles to free herself. Panting sobs punctuated her writhings as she sought to tear away her wrist from the pursuer's sweating grip. So violently did she tug that, at one moment, Jim Ross all but lost his balance. He threw out his other hand to steady himself.

Down came his waving hand on a corner of the hall table. And something pricked him so sharply as to wring a grunt of pain from his twisting lips. His palm had come into contact with one of the tattoo-needles he had left strewn there. The pain bred a clever inspiration.

Bracing himself, and tightening his left hand's hold on the dumb prisoner's wrist, he picked up the needle with his right hand and groped for the nearest jar of pigment. Into this jar he plunged the needle to the full depth.

Brandishing the suffused point of steel, he turned back to the woman.

"Miss Ward," he said coolly, "light isn't the only way of identifying people. A tattoo-mark will serve just as well."

Pulling her hand nearer to him, he drove the needle into the soft flesh just where the palm joins the wrist.

Three times he jabbed the needle into the shrinking wrist—deep, slanting, ragged jabs. He had no time for a fourth stab. Whimpering with agony and fright, the woman struck out in blind horror with her other fist. The random blow smote Jim Ross heavily across the bridge of the nose.

Anguish at the impact added to the surprise of the attack. Instinctively, Jim slackened his hold on the branded wrist. And the prisoner took quick advantage of her chance.

Next morning, Jim Ross was the first man to enter the hall, where the guests always assembled for breakfast. One by one, the other men joined him there. But not a woman appeared. Even Helen Ward—a notoriously early riser—had not yet come from the dormitory. Jim waited her advent with quiet anticipation. As he waited, he strolled over to Walton.

"Walt," he said cryptically, "when the women come in, watch for one with a smudge or a sore or a bunch of scratches on the inside of her right wrist. Look sharp for it. And then remember I told you about it beforehand."

"What's the main idea?" asked Walton, puzzled.

Before Jim could reply, Mrs. Greaves came into the hall full of apologies for her own lateness and with word that the other women would be with them in a minute or so. Jim Ross did not hear a syllable of her salutation. His eyes were glued to her outstretched wrist as she shook hands with Walton.

His glance focussed on a saffron smudge nestling in the crease between wrist and palm. And his jaw drooped in crass amaze.

It was not Helen Ward, then—it was this stately, gracious, lofty-souled hostess, this ideal wife and mother whom he had seen clinging so adoringly to Barry Cahill, there in the moonlit garden, when all her guests were supposedly in their dormitories!

A closer covert look at the hostess's wrist, as she shook hands with a man still nearer to him revealed to Jim that the supposed smudge was a cleverly wrought bit of tattooing. On a space no larger than a girl's little finger nail was pricked a tiny saffron heart transfixed by a rosy arrow.

A second woman was coming into the hall from the dormitory—a buxom and noisy damsel named Polly Armytage. She was nursing her right hand in the cupped palm of the left, and looking down solicitously at her wrist as if it hurt her.

As Miss Armytage brushed past Jim, in her progress toward Mrs. Greaves, he saw that the wrist which she was so worriedly scanning bore, in its juncture-crease, an arrow-transfixed heart of the same size and hue as the hostess's. And his head began to swim.

A moment afterward, Helen Ward entered. Glowing with youth and health, she gave the impression of a sweep of mountain air in a hot room. Walton Ross hurried across to greet her. Jim, moving like a sleep-walker, tagged at his brother's heels. And, by so doing, he saw something that escaped Walton's loverly gaze. Walton was looking into his sweetheart's laughing eyes. Jim was studying the wrist of the hand she had extended to his brother. And on that wrist he discerned a replica of the heart and arrow.

The three remaining women came in together. Jim Ross, hypnotized, ambled across the long hall to greet them—an act of effusive courtesy that astonished them all, especially his own wondering wife, who was last of the trio. On all three right wrists—even on Marcia's—he saw the tiny saffron heart and its pink arrow.

With a warning scowl, he stayed Marcia's further progress into the hall. Calling her away from the rest, Jim pointed dramatically to his frightened wife's wrist. Growling the words from deep down in his throat, he demanded:

"What's the meaning of this? What's the meaning of it? Speak up!"

"Please, Jim," she protested, shrinking back from her vehement spouse: "please! People are looking. Please don't growl like that, dear, or glower at me so, when every one is here. And it—it frightens me to—"

"I'll speak and look as I choose!" he cut in, too angry to heed her almost tearful plea. "Tell me what all you women mean by tattooing yourselves like that! *Tell* me!"

"Oh!" quavered Marcia. "The hearts on our wrists? I—I didn't know you'd mind. Last evening you seemed so interested in the pictures, and—"

"Tell me!" he interrupted harshly.

"Why," she faltered, trying not to cry as his accusing glare summoned her to answer, "why, there's nothing much to tell. Cherry San did it. This morning. That's what made us late. We—we thought it would be a lark and—and a pretty souvenir of this visit—if—if we all six had the same little design put on our wrists. We—I didn't think you'd mind, Jim. Honestly—"

"Who suggested the idea?" demanded Jim, his legal instincts abristle. "Whose idea was it for you all to be tattooed with the same design—and in the same spot? Hey? Whose?"

"Why—why—I think—that is—why, it was Helen Ward," replied
Marcia. "She suggested it only for—for a lark, Jim," pleaded the
unhappy woman. "She didn't mean any harm. Oh, *please* don't let
it make you dislike her any more than you do! She's a dear. And—"

"She's a—" began Jim hotly, only to be cut short by the signal
for breakfast.

As the guests trooped into the sunny breakfast-room, Jim found
a chance to whisper to Marcia:

"Did you happen to notice Miss Ward's wrist before it was tattooed—or while it was being done? Did you?"

"Why," bleated Marcia, "I didn't. I was so—"

"Yes," grunted Jim. "You always are."

Sullenly he sat down to breakfast. As he made pretence of eating,
he gave grudging tribute to Helen Ward's alert wit. Yes; he bowed in
glum resignation to her genius. Humbly, if ungraciously, he realized
that she had beaten him.

Yet, even the cleverest witnesses may be swept off their feet by
sudden attack. Jim's court-room experience had taught him that.
And it had taught him how best to make such attack. Wherefore,
as they arose from the table, he succeeded in drawing Helen Ward
to one side in a niche of the veranda.

"Miss Ward," he began abruptly, "I stood here, last evening, while
the dance was going on. I heard Barry Cahill arrange to go to the
Italian garden with you. Something interfered, and you said you'd
go later. He—"

"You heard remarkably well, Mr. Ross—for an eavesdropper," she
made answer, her level gaze steadily upon his. "But even the most
accomplished eavesdropper can't hear everything. Mr. Cahill brought
me a message from Walt, whom I had sent to dance with Marcia.
Walt wanted me to save him the next dance, so he could sit it out

in the Italian garden. Just then, Mrs. Greaves brought up a man to dance with me. So I sent word to Walt that we must wait till later. As a matter of fact, we didn't go there at all. There were so many—"

"Pardon me," Jim broke in on her glib recital. "You did go there. Two hours later. Not with Walt. With Barry. You were—"

"Mr. Ross," was the sweet reply, "I have learned—when I am anywhere near you—to establish a continuous *alibi*. I was in the house or on the veranda—as plenty of people can prove—till after the last dance-guests went away. Then I went to the dormitory. Mrs. Greaves and Marcia and Polly Armytage went there at the same time. Any of the three can so testify. I was there until an hour ago. We didn't go to bed till three o'clock. Marcia and I sat and talked till then. My presence, every minute, can be accounted for by competent witnesses, you see. Now, if the cross-examination is quite ended—"

She finished the sentence by moving away to where Walton Ross was emerging from the hall in search of her.

Jim stared dully after the daintily stepping girl. In his heart of hearts, he knew this pat series of *alibis* had been framed by her in anticipation of just such a charge as he had been about to make. She had rattled it off with an ease that spelled rehearsal.

More than ever he was convinced of her guilt. But he was finally thoroughly convinced that she had beaten him—and could continue to beat him—at every turn. With a sigh of genuine misery he surrendered.

At the doorway, fifty feet distant. Mrs. Greaves was saying good-bye to Cherry San. Jim was not near enough to have heard their parting words, had he cared to. Which was rather a pity. For those words were worth his hearing.

"We all thank you so much!" Mrs. Greaves finished her valedictory. "Your songs were charming. So was your tattoo-work. It—"

"No, no!" disclaimed Cherry San, her smilingly upturned face clouding. "Not the tattoo-work, *madame*! Not that! That was very bad—very hasty—very poor. And no true artist would use that foolish heart-arrow design. But what could I do?"—with a despairing outspread of the yellow little fingers. "What else *was* there to do? There was no other design that was shaped right to hide those three hideous slanting marks on Mrs. Ross's wrist!"

THE TATTOOED EYE (1920)

Arthur P. Hankins

Arthur Preston Hankins (1880–1932) was a one-time hobo who tried his hand at a huge array of jobs across America—from cowboy, to sailor, to soldier, to tombstone seller, and orange farmer—before finally making a living as a pulp fiction author, sometimes under the pseudonym Emart Kinsburn which combines his name with his wife's. He also worked in the movies as a scriptwriter for silent films and finally achieved some success as a novelist, who wrote mainly in the Western genre.

"The Tattooed Eye" is one of a number of American detective stories published in the heyday of hard-boiled fiction in the 1920s and 30s that revolves around the subject of tattooing. Rather unusually for the time, Hankins, like Terhune in "Branded", represents a female tattooer. Madame Nan Sundy is no back-street scratcher but a high-end artist who "caters to the fancies and whims of the rich" in San Francisco. She finds herself caught up in the criminal machinations of a secret society along with the story's down-on-his-luck hero, Tyler Lake. As Nan helps Tyler unravel the story's mystery, the tattoo appears poised between its conventional association with criminality and its emerging status as a fashion item.

CHAPTER I
BECAUSE OF THE BUTLER

T O RECORD THE PARTICULARS OF HOW IT CAME ABOUT THAT
Tyler Lake found himself in a strange city, hungry, friendless,
and without a penny to his name is scarcely necessary to this narrative. An adventuresome spirit was at the bottom of it all; and the
fact that he was well educated and came of a good family made his
predicament all the more embarrassing.

San Francisco was the city, and a freight train had deposited
him there. His suit of clothes, of dark blue serge, fortunately
was presentable, as were hat and shoes. But before he dared seek
employment commensurate with his abilities, the four days' growth
of black beard must be shaved from his face, and he must have
clean linen.

Where and how to procure these requisites of a presentable
appearance was a pressing problem, to say nothing of that other difficulty of supplying the inner man with the food his rugged system
so ravenously craved.

Tyler Lake was not a tramp, and never had been meant to become
one. Just now, though, so depressed were his spirits because of the
lack of food that it is difficult to state to what lengths he might not
have gone in order to regain his hope and self-respect.

It was a little after noon when he hurried from railroad property
to the Clay Street employment offices. It seemed, after half an hour's
reading of the employment offices' announcements, that there was
no hope for him in this section. Two dallars was the least that any

of the agencies would accept before revealing their well-kept secrets as to where jobs might be secured. He was about to leave Munsen & Reed's, the largest of these institutions, when a well-dressed man of about his own build, and with hair and eyes as black as his own, walked in a bit unsteadily and leaned through a window opening into the inner sanctum.

"Shay," he said thickly. "I wanta get a butler. Want 'im quick an' ain't—ain't particular, see? Got one?"

"I'm afraid not, sir—not today," said the clerk, smiling. "Have you tried Selden & Moore? They supply a great deal of domestic help. We deal mostly in construction labourers, you know."

"Selden & Moore no good," remarked the other, tilting his imported crush hat to a comical angle over one eye. "They can't get nushin'. Shay"—he wheeled suddenly—"whassa matter this fella here?" He levelled a finger unsteadily at Tyler Lake. "He ain't any labourer. Looks like butler. Wanta gota work?" He addressed Tyler. "Good pay—easy—cinch. What-tayshay?"

Tyler Lake smiled. "I'm afraid not," he said quietly. "I'm not familiar with a butler's duties; and besides—well, I need work, but I can't bring myself to accept employment of that kind."

The clerk frowned and shrugged as he left the window. The applicant swept his crusher over the other eye, hipped his fists, and, teetering unsteadily, nodded his head sagaciously at Tyler.

"I get you," he announced. "Gemman, an' all that, eh? I'm gemman m'self. Been down an' out, though, just like you. Don't blame you a bit. No job for a gemman. Shay, my name's Kiley— Austin Kiley. Been down an' out m'self—'preciate your fix. As one gemman to another, c'n—c'n I help you any? Don't be offended— gemman m'self, y'know. Little under the weather ri' now"—he lowered his voice to a confidential key—"but—but gemman just th' same. C'm on—le' me show you I know how tish when gemman gets down 'n' out—tem-temp'-rarily, o' coursh."

So saying he stepped totteringly to Tyler Lake and linked his arm in his.

"Like your looks," he confided as he led the other out. "Gonta do to you jush what I'd want you to do to me if I was in your fix. Don't get sore. C'm on with me. Took a fancy to you—thash all."

A handsome automobile awaited Mr. Austin Kiley at the curb. With great solemnity Mr. Kiley endeavoured to assist his only half willing guest into the tonneau.

"Kirkmyre, Jones," he ordered his chauffeur when they were seated.

"Wife sent me outta get a butler," he confided as the car purred away, "an' I got cuckooed. Hirin' a butler'll make any man get cuckooed."

"Really, Mr. Kiley—" Tyler began.

"Really nushin'!" interrupted the other. "Took a fancy to you. Been down an' out m'self before I made my pile. Gonta show you time o' your young life jush—jush f'r luck."

When a man is really hungry—Well, Tyler Lake had eaten nothing for forty-eight hours, and Mr. Kiley was taking him to one of the most renowned restaurants in the West. So Tyler Lake said nothing.

The fatal sixteenth of January was still a week distant, and it appeared that Mr. Austin Kiley had a private stock of liquors at the Kirkmyre. He had had recourse to it nine times that morning he confidentially told his guest as an obsequious waiter seated them in the spacious dining room—all because of that butler.

"Now I'm gonta letta butler go to dickens," he said, "an' you an' me's gonta have one good time all by ourselves."

Tyler Lake never will forget that meal. When at last he leaned back he was a new man again. Mr. Kiley had continued garrulous throughout their lunch, but Tyler had been much too busy to pay serious attention to him. Now, with black coffee and a cigar before him, he was ready to listen to any one, for he felt warm and comfortable and happy as a clam.

"What d'ye weigh, Mr.—Mr.—I lost that name again."

"Lake," prompted Tyler for the fourth time. "Why, ordinarily I weigh about a hundred and seventy pounds."

"Thash me—hundred an' seventy to a hundred an' eighty. Stranger inna city, eh?"

"Yes," replied Tyler.

Mr. Kiley seemed to have reached that stage of insobriety wherein the most sophisticated of men glory in their fancied physical superiority. "Betcha I'm taller'n you, though," he challenged.

"I think not," said Tyler, smiling. "I'm six feet one."

"Then I gotcha beat! Stand up an' we'll put our backs together, and th' waiter'll decide."

Mr. Kiley started to suit the action to the word.

"Oh, not here in the café," laughingly protested Tyler.

"Wouldn't look right, would it? Then you come with me. I know where there's a s'loon—usta be s'loon—where they got a measurin' business an' scales an' ever'thing. C'm on, Rivers! I'm gonta have a time today! T'dickens with butler! I took fancy to you. You're jush 'bout same man's I am every way. We'll have anusher drink an' go measure ourselves atta s'loon—usta be s'loon, anyway."

"Mr. Kiley," said Tyler, greatly embarrassed. "I can't impose any further on your hospitality. I—I—"

"Forget it, ol' man! Been there m'self. Have a good time with me t'-day; I give you a job t'-morrow."

"Can you do that?"

"Sure I can! Here—read thash!" He fumbled in a vest pocket and brought forth a gold card case. Clumsily extracting a card, he tossed it across the snowy linen to his guest.

Tyler read:

AUSTIN KILEY
Real Estate—Oil Lands—Investments
Suite 416
Manners Building   San Francisco

"Give you job in my office!" he cried loudly. "You're gemman—you're no butler. Leave it to me, Rivers."

"Lake," corrected Tyler with a sigh.

Could he depend on this man to keep his word when he was sober again? It was too great an opportunity to lose. Common sense advised him to humour the jovial Bacchanalian until he could see what might come of it.

From an imposing roll of bills Mr. Kiley detached a twenty and handed it to the waiter, recklessly telling him to keep the change.

"Now, c'm on, Waters, an' I'll show you th' town!" he said, grinning as he struggled to his feet. "We'll tend to thish job o' yours t'-morrow. Confoun' thash butler—I'm cuckooed! Stick with me—er—whash yer name again? Cain't remember thash name t' save m' life, ol' man!"

CHAPTER II
THOU ART THE MAN

The happy jag of the eminent Mr. Austin Kiley caused him to experience many strange twists of the mind that afternoon. He insisted on having his chauffeur drive him and his newfound bosom friend to the "usta-be s'loon", where were slot-machine scales, measuring apparatus, and a contrivance, with a leather pillow in evidence, designed for the testing of one's striking powers.

It developed that Mr. Kiley weighed a few pounds more than Tyler, over which he crowed triumphantly. Tyler, albeit, was nearly half an inch the taller, and Mr. Kiley moped over this. But when his guest allowed him to register the greater strength on the striking machine his spirits rose amazingly. So much so that he proposed another trip to the Kirkmyre and the private stock.

After this he insisted on going to a matinée; but he became disgusted at the tardiness in the rising of the curtain and led the way out, loudly asserting that never in his life would he enter that particular theatre again. He nursed himself back to good humour again at the Kirkmyre.

"Rivers," he said, as they entered the car once more, "I gotta sober up. Ol' lady'll bounce somethin' off m' bean if I don't. Jones"—to the driver—"take us to good Turkish bath. I gotta sober up an' get thash butler. Stick with me, Lakes—you gotta sober up, too. Go to thash Turkish bath on Jones Street, driver."

He would hear to nothing else, so Tyler rode with him to the bath house, which was conducted in connection with a barber shop. Here nothing would do but that "Waters" should likewise indulge in the luxury of a steam bath; and soon the two were stripped but for the thick, coarse towels about their waists, and were conducted by an attendant to the steaming rooms beyond.

"By golly, Rivers, you're pretty good man!" commented Mr. Kiley, gazing with drunken admiration at Tyler's handsome body. "But I'm pretty good man m'self, hey? Huh! We're jush 'bout same build, Rivers."

"Just about," agreed Tyler, smiling at the attendant, who was rather worriedly testing Mr. Kiley's pulse as the perspiration streamed from that gentleman's pink body.

On Kiley's left forearm Tyler noticed a small tattoo mark in blue, but did not get close enough to make out the design.

"He's all right," the attendant whispered to Tyler a moment later. "I'll send him home fine and dandy in a couple of hours."

The bibulous one did indeed seem almost sober when, about an hour later, he left the slab where the attendant had been punishing him and padded to a sleeping booth. Tyler Lake scarcely knew what to do with himself now, but decided to forego a sleep and wait for the man who had agreed to give him work. Just then Kiley called from behind his curtain.

"I'm getting fixed up fine," he said as Tyler looked in. "An hour's sleep will put me on my feet. Now, look here, Lake—I wasn't talking through my hat this afternoon. I told you I'd give you office work, and I'll keep my promise. Tell that attendant to bring me my trousers, will you, please?"

With his trousers in his hand Mr. Kiley sat on the edge of his bunk and dived into a pocket. He passed Tyler a ten-dollar bill. Once more Tyler saw the small blue tattoo mark on his left forearm; but as the arm was in motion he failed again to discover what it represented.

"Don't feel offended," Kiley said. "Go get a hair cut and a shave, and fix yourself up generally. Get a room some place, and come around to the office about eleven tomorrow morning. Don't thank me—been there myself. Do that, now, Lake—and good-bye till then. I'll be home in an hour, and everything will be O.K. Not a word now. Beat it, if you want to be my friend!"

As Tyler Lake sat in a barber chair at the front of the building a little later a customer entered and removed his coat, preparatory to getting into another chair. Tyler noticed casually that the stranger's coat resembled his own in that it was a blue serge. He noticed, too, that it had been hung on the hook next to the one that held his. At this moment the barber who was working on him finished cutting his hair, and lowered the chair to begin shaving him.

He was drowsy from the Turkish bath, warm, content. Half heedingly he heard the man who had hung the blue-serge coat beside his own complain to his barber that a package in his hip pocket felt uncomfortable.

"Just slip it in a pocket of that blue-serge coat, there on the hook—that's the one," Tyler heard him say; then he dozed.

A massage followed the shave, and when at last he left the chair Tyler saw only one blue-serge coat—his own—hanging against the wall, the owner of the other having had his shave and gone. Tyler paid what he owed, put on collar, tie, and coat, and sauntered out into the now lighted streets to look for a haberdashery and a lodging place for the night.

In a store near by he selected collars and shirts and ties. The collars were wrapped up separately, and as he put the small package in his coat pocket he felt another package already there. Wonderingly he took it out and gazed at it.

It was thin and rectangular, and just fitted his pocket. It was rather loosely wrapped, and on the paper appeared the words: "Mr. Cass Starr, 1921 Cedarview Avenue, City. RUSH!"

In a flash he realized what had occurred. The barber had placed the package of Tyler's fellow customer in a pocket of the wrong blue serge coat.

With it in his hand he hurried back to the barber shop, to find it now closed for the day. He looked at the parcel again. "Rush!" he read.

"I guess that means me," he said, laughing; and, inquiring the direction, he boarded a street car to deliver the package that so strangely had been intrusted to him.

With excusable curiosity he took it again from his pocket when he was settled in the street car. The paper gaped open now, because of the loose string. Through the crack he saw that the paper covered a small, thin volume bound in limp leather. A word of the title in gold letters blinked out at him: "Thou."

With a half guilty conscience he spread the crack wider, and now read this: "*Thou Art the Man*, by Edgar Johnson."

Tyler Lake was a lover of Johnson, the famous author, and never before had he seen this popular short story in book form. As the book would have to be rewrapped, anyway, he made bold to remove it, and skipped through the thick, wide-margined pages. And in the middle of the volume, at the top of a page, he came across something pasted to the paper that caused him to sit erect and blink in wonder.

It was an oval piece of paper about an inch in length by three-fourths of an inch the other way. In the centre of it was the photograph of a human eye.

CHAPTER III
1921 CEDARVIEW AVENUE

As the street car clattered along Tyler Lake sat looking at the life-size, elliptical photograph of the human eye. In his mind was the hazy idea that he recently had seen something of about the same shape and size of this photograph, but he could not recall what it was.

He thumbed the pages of the thin book from first to last, but nothing else of a foreign nature appeared on any of them. He rewrapped the book and put it into his pocket.

Tyler wondered why anybody should send this work to anybody else with "Rush" marked upon it. All that occurred to him in this connection was the possibility that some literary society was to convene at the address indicated on the wrapper, and that this book was necessary to a possible lecturer's discourse.

Anyway, it had been unceremoniously thrust upon him. He could not afford to hire a messenger to deliver it; his purchases and his immediate needs precluded that. The mail service or an express company would not take it to 1921 Cedarview Avenue before next morning. It was marked "Rush". Tyler Lake was too thorough a gentleman, too considerate of the welfare of others—even complete strangers—to think of any course but to comply with the instructions on the wrapper.

Cedarview Avenue proved to be a street of some importance, a residential thoroughfare given over exclusively to private houses. Number 1921 was dark as he ascended the steps, but an electric light flashed above his head as he pushed the bell button.

The door opened to frame a handsome, rounded blonde woman in a blue silk-and-lace evening gown. She raised inquisitive eyebrows at the caller.

Tyler Lake lifted his hat. "I beg your pardon," he said, holding out the book. "Through a rather strange mistake this package came into my possession. It is marked 'Rush', and, as I had no idea who should have delivered it, there seemed nothing for me to do but bring it along myself."

She took the package slowly, a jewelled bracelet glittering on her white, round arm.

"Why, how odd!" she murmured. "'Came into your possession through a rather strange mistake?' I—I don't believe I understand."

Tyler began to tell the details, when she interrupted with:

"How rude of me! Do come in until I can understand this matter. I expected a package—or Mr. Starr did—but I don't know you. Won't you explain?"

She stood back, smiling distantly, the parcel in her hand. He entered the lighted hall. She closed the door and carried the book to a stand lamp on a little table. Her red lips moved as she read the inscription on the paper.

"This is the book we were expecting," she said, as she unwrapped it and swiftly fluttered the leaves. "But I can't understand. Do be seated, won't you, and finish telling me how you came to bring this book to me?"

But two chairs were in the hall. As she spoke she seated herself in the one at the side of the table, and turned large, expectant, blue eyes on Tyler. The remaining chair stood with its back to a stairway. Tyler sat in it and began his explanation again.

As he progressed he detected a strange look in the expressive blue eyes. The white, bejewelled hand that lay at rest on one of the woman's silk-covered knees trembled slightly. For a moment he put this down to a mild excitement over the strange occurrence that he was relating; then suddenly some unknown sense warned him of impending calamity.

Try as he would he could not shake off this feeling of nervousness that was altogether foreign to his nature. In spite of himself tiny beads of cold perspiration oozed out on his forehead. It was but a momentary flash of her eyelashes that he saw now, but he realized that her glance quickly had travelled up the stairway at his back. Then, just as she leaned swiftly forward in sudden excitement and half rose, Tyler Lake knew that danger lurked behind him.

He sprang to his feet, and had halfway whirled about, when there came a resounding rap on the lower part of the stair railing at his back. A low, smothered scream came from the woman as he spun on his toes, to confront a man leaning over the banister. One of his hands was lowered, and in it was a leather-covered blackjack.

As if it had been printed for him to read Tyler Lake knew that this man had stolen down the stairway and aimed a blow at the back of his head as he sat there. Just in time some sixth sense had warned him, and he had sprung to his feet a fraction of a second ahead of the cowardly stroke. The weapon had hit the hardwood staircase just back of where his head had been.

For a brief instant the eyes of the two men flashed fire; then with a low oath Tyler sprang upward, clutching at his assailant's throat. His grasping fingers caught the man's tie and a handful of shirt-front; and, with a growl of anger, he heaved and pulled the other head first over the banister and into his arms. Next moment they were locked in a fierce encounter.

Tyler's antagonist was a smaller man than he, but strong and quick as lightning. From his right wrist dangled the blackjack, held there by a thong. As Tyler struggled to down him and sit upon him the blackjack whipped about and beat him in the face and on the back of the head. His opponent fought to free the arm from which the weapon dangled so that he might administer the knockout blow which had been postponed.

They wheeled about, stepping on loose rugs which covered a polished hardwood floor. It was a wrestling match pure and simple, for so entangled were their arms—neither daring to release his hold on the other—that no blows could be struck.

In one of their gyrations, which threatened the lamp that stood on the table, Tyler saw the woman, half crouched, slinking about after them. Something gleamed in her right hand.

Now they danced over the floor, crowding her into a corner. There came a low scream, and the bright object flashed again in her hand as the two bore down upon her. It flashed before Tyler's eyes. She held a tiny penknife. He saw the blackjack drop from the other's wrist, heard it thud on the hardwood floor. The woman stooped for it; he saw it grasped firmly in her hand.

With a mighty heave he swung the man, who clung to him so tenaciously, between himself and the woman. Her lips were now set, and a cold menace gleamed in her blue eyes. Still crouching, she followed them about, the hand holding the weapon drawn back for a vicious blow at Tyler's head when opportunity offered.

But he contrived always to keep the man between her and him. No matter how quickly she would dart behind him, his great muscles would swing his antagonist between them. Not a word had any of them spoken since the fight began; and, considering the fierceness of the struggle, they made little noise.

Of a sudden the man released all holds on Tyler and sank to the floor. He grasped him about the knees and heaved back and forth to topple him over, hiding his face against Tyler's legs and receiving without a yell of pain a volley of vicious fisticuffs on his skull. Tyler realized that this would give the blonde her chance, and he reached down and entwined his fingers in the man's hair to torture him into releasing his deadly leghold.

The man endured the punishment and continued to wrench back and forth in a supreme effort to throw Tyler. The woman was leaping forward now, her eyes agleam, the blackjack drawn back. Tyler lost his balance and fell backward. With a grunt the man crawled upon him and grasped at his throat.

A mighty heave of Tyler's torso sent the fellow sprawling. Tyler felt the wind of the long impending blackjack blow as he sprang after the man on hands and knees.

Both in this position they came together. With a swift movement Tyler grasped the man's right wrist, twisted the arm to the small of the man's back, and hurled his weight upon him.

The man toppled over backward, pitching against the woman's knees. She lost her balance and staggered forward. The man's back struck the floor, his arm beneath it. There came a sickening crack and a high-pitched scream of pain.

Tyler bounded to his feet. The man lay writhing from the torture of a broken arm. The woman's tight skirt for the moment kept her on hands and knees. One leap and Tyler was at the door.

But as he grasped at the knob the door opened suddenly, and for one fleeting instant he glared into the eyes of the newcomer. Next moment there came a swish, a thud, white, darting lights, and black oblivion.

Tyler Lake crumpled in the doorway. Over the unconscious victim of his brass knuckles, chuckling throatily, bent Mr. Austin Kiley.

CHAPTER IV

WANTED: AN ARTIST

Miss Nan Sundy was an artist. She told herself she was an artist; her friends told her that she was an artist; her instructors told her that she was an artist. In fact, everybody with whom she came in contact told her the same, with the exception of people who are ordained to draw cheques for artists. This callous crew is comprised of art lovers with the funds to buy, and art editors with the power to buy.

Her financial condition, since the art school had set her adrift to make a name and fortune for herslf, had gone from bad to worse. No one who would pay a reasonable amount for her work would buy. Post-card manufacturers had kept her from starving while the necessities of life remained at normal prices; but when these prices began to soar it seemed that pay for work rose accordingly, with the exception of remuneration for post-card drawings.

Work along many other lines the pretty Miss Nan Sundy could have obtained; but she determinedly maintained that she was an artist, and she would live by art alone or starve.

She nearly starved.

But starvation breeds original ideas. An item which Nan chanced to see in a newspaper set her to thinking. Among the many foibles and fancies and fads which have helped along the hysteria of the past year or two, the item mentioned London society's sudden craze for tattooing.

Nan craftily reasoned that New York society quickly would ape London in this new fad, and that San Francisco would as surely ape New York. Tattooing was art—could be made an art, at any rate. *Ergo*, she would tattoo the pampered flesh of society until art editors got ready to awake from their long, untroubled nap.

She borrowed money from a sceptical relative, handbagged her pride, and opened "The Bon Ton Tattooing Studio" on Grant Avenue. In the three months or more that followed this original venture she raised tattooing to the dignity of art, paid the relative who was no longer sceptical, went regularly to the bank, and declined with thanks the repeated requests of post-card manufacturers to send them more drawings. She charged fabulous fees and gloated over her nerve to do so. And society was content to pay the price.

It was nine o'clock at night. Nan was just preparing to close her little Orientally furnished hole-in-the-wall on Grant Avenue. A chubby society matron had insisted on having the green serpent, which was being wound about her puffy ankle by "Madame Nan Sundy", completed before another day had dawned. She had paid double price for after-hours' work, and Nan had been obliged to humour her.

She had just been driven away in her shining car, snake, pain, and all, when the door opened suddenly on Nan's closing-up operations, and a man in a heavy, fur-lined overcoat and a silk hat came in.

He lifted his hat politely. "Madame Nan Sundy, the artist?" he asked.

She bowed and smiled a professional smile.

"Madame Sundy," he said, "I want to impose upon your good nature by making a very peculiar request. It is undoubtedly a strange hour of the twenty-four in which to call upon a lady to go with one and help one out. But very peculiar circumstances demand that I do just that. To be brief, I have come to get you to do a small piece of tattooing tonight. I—"

"Impossible," she returned coldly. "It is nine o'clock. I usually close at five. Besides, I do no work whatever for gentlemen. There are men tattoo artists in the city, who keep open to a late hour. Surely—"

"Bah! Artists!" he cried. "Do you imagine I wish a battleship or a spread eagle with flags tattooed on my chest? I am not a deep-sea sailor, Madame Sundy. Besides, it is a woman who is to be tattooed. And it must be done tonight. I can explain. Just a moment. You may see the lady herself."

He stepped outside, and now Nan noticed a closed car drawn up before the studio, with a liveried driver at the steering wheel. Through her Oriental silk curtains she saw him step to the car and assist to the pavement a fur-coated woman who had striking blonde hair.

"My name is Austin Kiley," he said, entering again. "Permit me to present Mrs. Kiley, Madame Sundy. My card, Madame Sundy."

On the thick white pasteboard which he handed to her Nan read, in embossed letters:

AUSTIN KILEY

Real Estate—Oil Lands—Investment

Suite 416

Manners Building   San Francisco

"Now, please permit me to explain my rather peculiar request," he continued. "I cannot go into details, for it is more or less a secret matter. I am a member of a select secret society, and Mrs. Kiley here is to be initiated as a member tonight. It has been the unalterable custom of this society that, at the initiation of a new member, the secret design of the order shall be tattooed on his or her arm in the presence of the older members. This is part and parcel of the initiation, I may say.

"One of the members of this order is an artist like yourself, Madame Sundy—a real artist. He has been accustomed to tattooing the designs on the arms of the members of our little society. Unfortunately, however, he chanced to break his arm this evening, shortly before Mrs. Kiley was to present herself for initiation.

"Everything is now in readiness for the ceermony. Postponement would cause a needless loss of money and render valueless certain intricate and carefully planned preparations. So, after a consultation with society members who were present, I have come to ask you to help us out. Money is no object, Madame Sundy. The design is not complicated, and our artist is in the habit of completing it on a member's arm in less than half an hour, by hand. It must be done by hand, Madame Sundy, instead of with electric apparatus. This is another unalterable rule. Now, name your price, please." He took out a fat roll of bills. "I assure you that my car will set you down at any address you may name in an hour's time."

Nan's dark eyes looked quizzically from one to the other of them.

"Oh, do help us out, Madame Sundy!" pleaded the woman, her lips pouting. "If only you knew how much this means to me."

"Do indeed!" added her husband. "Come now—here's a hundred dollars. Surely such an amount will make it worth your while. We must have some one who is an artist. Now that our friend has suffered this accident nobody in San Francisco save yourself can fill his place."

It had become Nan Sundy's business in life to cater to the fancies and whims of the rich, and a hundred dollars for a half-hour's work was not to be despised. She secured the kit that she used when working outside the studio, locked the door, and was helped courteously into the closed car by Austin Kiley.

The limousine had rolled along for perhaps twenty blocks when the man asked Nan:

"Do you know what part of the city you are passing through now, Madame Sundy?"

"I have only a vague idea of where we are," she told him.

"If you have even a vague idea," he said, laughing softly, "it won't do at all. Please don't be alarmed if I lower the side curtains. Secret societies, you know—but then, perhaps you don't know much about them, after all."

Accordingly he started to lower the shades. They had been riding in darkness, which Nan had thought rather odd. One of the shades proved obstinate, and Mr. Kiley flashed an electric spotlight. With his left hand outstretched toward the curtain, his wrist and a part of his forearm protruded from the sleeve of his fur-lined coat. On the forearm, in blue tattooing, Nan saw the life-sized reproduction of a human eye.

The curtain came down, and the light was snapped off. They sat in total darkness as the car purred along. It turned corners frequently now, Nan was positive. She felt just a trifle nervous.

"Don't be worried," said Kiley assuringly. "We take our little secret order quite seriously, no matter what others may think. It would not be proper for you to know the location of the house where we meet tonight."

A little after this the car stopped gently, and Mr. Kiley assisted the women out into the night. At once the machine left the curb. The three walked up a set of granite steps, and Mr. Kiley pushed a bell button.

Nan Sundy looked about and along the street. She now had no idea of what part of San Francisco she had invaded.

Just then a light, operated from within, flashed over her head. Quickly she looked over the front of the building, at the door, and over the door, but could find no number.

The door was being cautiously opened as she completed her scrutiny. She instinctively drew back.

"Oh, I—I don't want to go in!" she cried. "I—I think I'm afraid."

"Nonsense!" said Kiley, laughing as he grasped her arm.

CHAPTER V

A RAPID ORGANIZATION

When Tyler Lake recovered consciousness he was being half dragged, half carried, through the hall which had been the scene of his struggle with the blonde woman and her companion. Instantly he became aware that only a few moments had elapsed between the blow that had struck him down at the door and now. There was a ringing in his ears, and a burning, sickening pain throbbed at his temples.

Now his assailants were three to one; and, worn out from the fight, sick and dizzy as he was, he wisely decided that to resist would be useless. Therefore he kept his eyes closed as they bore him along, having decided to feign unconsciousness for the time being, in the hope thus of bettering his chances for winning in the end.

He was dragged through a door, and a moment afterward thrown unconcernedly on a bed.

"You must have handed him a beautiful crack, Kile," came the voice of the blonde woman. "You certainly reached the door just in time. He's a regular bull for strength. Poor Cass! He's all done up. This fellow would have made his get-away clean but for you."

"I did tap him pretty briskly, Wyn," remarked Mr. Austin Kiley, chuckling. "He'll be out for an hour, I'll bet."

"You don't think he's—he's dead, do you? Hadn't you better examine him, Kile? If you've bumped him off—heavens!"

Tyler kept his eyes closed as Kiley bent over him and laid an ear against his heart.

"He's all O.K.," was the decision. "Heart's beating fine. Just stunned. Well, this is a devil of a mess—Cass with a broken arm! Who's going to do the tattooing, I'd like to know."

"Let's see what we can do for Cass," the woman called Wyn suggested. "Maybe his wing's not broken, after all."

There came a metallic *snick*, and the door closed. The man on the bed heard the click of a key.

He opened his eyes, to find that he might just as well have kept them closed, because he was in total darkness. The *snick* that he had heard accompanied the turning off of an electric light. However, Tyler rose silently and, reeling a little, groped towards the door.

Light shining through the keyhole made a tiny beacon to guide him, and soon he was stooping and looking through into another room.

He saw only Mr. Austin Kiley, standing with his hands on his hips; but, hearing voices, he flattened his ear against the keyhole to listen.

"Oh, it's broken, all right," came in grumbling tones. "Go get a doctor right away, Kile. And for Heaven's sake give me a shot of booze!"

"A fine piece of business!" growled Kiley. "With your right arm on the bum you won't be able to do that tattooing for weeks. And we don't want to be hanging about Frisco forever. That tattooing must be done at once, so it can get to healing as soon as possible."

"Confound the tattooing!" moaned the other masculine voice. "Get a doctor!"

"Yes, do that, Kile," put in the woman's tones. "Phone for a doctor right away. I've a plan to get us out of the tattooing difficulty."

Grumbling still, Kiley was heard to leave the room. Soon his distant voice indicated that he was telephoning. When he returned he said:

"Doctor's coming right out. Grit your teeth, Cass. Well, Wyn, what's your big scheme?"

"We've simply got to get another tattooer," replied the blonde. There's one—"

"And give everything away! Fine idea, I must say!"

"Not necessarily," she retorted. "Give me a chance to explain, please."

"And no water-front sailor can do the artistic job that we require," again expostulated Kiley.

"Will you allow me to talk, or not?" the woman snapped.

"Go ahead—go ahead," was Kiley's grudging invitation.

"Well, then, listen here: Down on Grant Avenue there's a woman who calls herself Madame Something-or-other, who does tattooing for society folks. Though I've never seen any of her work, it's a safe bet it's not slovenly, considering the class she caters to. I've seen her place open quite late at night. Chances are, if we go right away we'll find her in. Give her a big fee, and she'll take a chance on coming out here."

"Yes, and she'll leave us with her brain bursting with information, and hunt up some dick to—"

"Listen! Listen, can't you! I've thought it all out. We can tell her we're members of a secret society, and that this bum you found and I are to be initiated tonight. A part of the initiation, we'll say, consists of the new members having the society emblem tattooed on their arms. And this must be done in the presence of the other members, we'll say. We can make it all very mysterious, you know; and when she's tattooing me I'll lie down and keep my eyes closed and pretend to be in a trance, or something foolish like that. We'll say it's a test, maybe—that if the party being initiated opens her eyes, or shows pain, she's in bad with the society, or something. Then when we bring in this bum for her to work on, he'll already be knocked out, and she'll think he's just acting, as I was."

"But—"

"Oh, we can chloroform him before bringing him in, if there's any danger of the pricking of the needle bringing him to from the rap you gave him. We can fix it so she won't even know where she is. The metal letters of the street number out beside the door can be pried off with a screwdriver. Say, it's a cinch, boys! Slip her a century, and she'll break her neck to please."

"Yes, slip her a century!" growled Kiley. "Believe me, Wyn Godfrey, you're some little century-slipper. You handle money as if a fellow were able to draw it from a faucet, and has nothing to do but turn off the flow when he has enough for immediate needs. Maybe you don't know that I dropped a good-sized wad in finding out about this fellow and getting him here today. I had to buy him a bang-up lunch, take him to a matinée, and get him stripped in a Turkish bath before I could make sure he was enough like me to play the part we've outlined for him. Then I handed him a ten to go to a barber, so Billy the Bung could drift in after him and have the book slipped into his coat pocket. I didn't dare steer him out here myself. It would have looked too raw. He's no fool. So I had to make it appear as if the thing that made it necessary for him to beat it out here was the unconscious work of somebody not connected with me at all. I'd played drunk too long, and was overdoing it. I thought he was getting suspicious. I pasted my eye in the book so you'd know I sent him. I wonder if he opened the book and saw it. Or if he read the title, *Thou Art the Man*.

"Your fool dramatics will queer us some day, Kile," remarked the woman.

"Born in me," said Kiley, laughing. "Where's the zest in the game if a fellow can't be a bit dramatic now and then? But just the same, Wyn," he continued, "there's something in your idea. All that I can see against it is the fact that there are only the three of us here, and three won't make much of a society to spring on the Jane that's to do the tattooing."

"Oh, you know a dozen underworld characters out at the Barbary Coast. Call 'em up and have 'em put on their glad rags and beat it out here ahead of her. They can pose as society members, and needn't know any of the particulars of our business. Just slip 'em five apiece, and they'll help on any good work, blindly and faithfully."

"Slip 'em five!" groaned Kiley. "Five times twelve is sixty. Say, woman, d'ye think I'm Santa Claus?"

"Show me a better plan, then," she said coldly.

"You can't beat it, Kile," put in, between groans, the man whose arm Tyler Lake had snapped. "That work ought to be done at once, so it can get to healing. When the doctor comes you and Wyn beat it for this tattoo artist. And right now you'd better—oh, heavens, how that arm hurts!—better call up your crooks and get 'em out here."

"Billy the Bung, for one, will look fine as a member of a select secret society," snorted Austin Kiley. "That blue-black bulldog jaw of his—"

"Mask 'em! Mask the bunch of 'em!" cried Wyn Godfrey. "We'll all be masked. Make the initiation more mysterious, you know. I can cut holes in old silk stockings and make masks for fifty. Oh, she'll fall for it, all right, and never suspect it's anything but a bunch of stupid society folks trying to be bright. Kid her up about her superior work, and all that. Go call up the gang. There's the doorbell—the doctor, I guess. I'll let him in."

There was silence for a time, then a new, brusque, kindly voice spoke to the crippled man. Soon the doctor was at work setting the arm of the man called Cass, and groans were the only sounds to be heard. Wyn and Kiley did not again return to their friend.

When the physician had taken his leave there was not a sound. Tyler found a match, and in its light he explored the room. It was empty but for the bed, and seemed to be an inside room. The door was the only opening he could find. He was effectually imprisoned.

He returned to his kneeling posture at the keyhole, through which light still shone. For nearly an hour, now, silence reigned throughout the building. Then at intervals the doorbell rang, and Tyler heard the groaning of Cass each time he went to admit whoever had pushed the button. Several low voices, some of them feminine, were now audible in the room beyond, and still the doorbell rang at intervals.

"Society's gathering for my initiation," said Tyler grimly. "Well, as the convict who was to be hanged next morning said to the sheriff, 'I'll be there.'"

There came a signal ring at the doorbell.

"That's Kiley and Wyn," said the voice of Cass, in the midst of the hush that followed in the other room. "Get through that door, there, you folks, and keep still till you're told what to do. Bung, you put on this mask and let Kiley in. Keep your trap closed, now—do whatever Kiley says."

CHAPTER VI
THE DESIGN TO BE TATTOOED

Nan Sundy, not without strange misgivings, entered a lighted hallway ahead of Mr. Austin Kiley and the fur-cloaked blonde. She shrank back with a little scream as she found herself confronted by a man over whose face was stretched a black mask.

Kiley chuckled. "Don't be alarmed, Madame Sundy," he said assuringly. "Remember you are now in the meeting place of a secret society, and that masks and such things are necessary. No cause to worry. Pemit me to help you out of your coat."

The wraps of the trio were draped from the arm of the silent masked figure who had admitted them.

"Come this way, please," said Kiley and escorted Nan through a door in the left-hand wall of the hall.

They entered a room well but not lavishly furnished. Electric lights were aglow, but no one was there to meet them.

"Wyn, dear, please make our guest feel at home," said Austin Kiley. "And excuse me for a short time, Madame Sundy. I'll notify the society that you are here and ready to help us out, and shall try to expedite matters as much as possible for your sake."

The blonde woman, whom Nan now noticed was in evening dress, chattered childishly while Mr. Kiley was absent, and Nan listened politely but unheedingly. The vague impression that all was not as it should be had settled upon her. Now that she was able to see "Mrs. Kiley" better she did not like her looks. She was a pretty woman in a doll-like way, but her beauty was not augmented by any evidences of character.

Kiley returned, stood before Nan, and made a wry face.

"I'm afraid, Madame Sundy," he said, "that I shall be obliged to try and intrude further upon your good nature. While we were away, the doctor arrived and set our friend's broken arm. He said that the accident would prevent him from doing any work as delicate as tattooing for perhaps months to come.

"This being the case, another prospective member of our society has been pitched into the depths of despair. He intended joining us in about two weeks, expecting by that time to have fulfilled the requirements which are necessary before one may present himself or herself for initiation. Now he must wait for an indefinite time, unless you can see your way to stretch your generosity a point further.

"It develops that he already has fulfilled our strict requirements—two weeks ahead of time. And while Mrs. Kiley and I were away tonight he presented himself for initiation, only to learn of our artist's accident. Madame Sundy, can you—will you—" He coughed in an embarrassed manner. "In short, would it be asking too much of you to request you to tattoo this man's arm also tonight? It will take very little more of your time; and we are willing to pay."

"Oh, do agree to help us out, Madame Sundy!" said the blonde in enforced intonations. "You don't know how much it means to us, or what one is missing when he or she is obliged to wait."

Nan Sundy pondered, frowning slightly, now more mistrustful than ever.

"You won't even be obliged to see this gentleman's face," added Kiley. "You see, the face of one going through our initiation is covered, as will be the faces of all of us. He will not speak to you, or make a move. This is one of the peculiarities of our initiation, and to explain the significance of it would be to reveal well guarded secrets of the order."

Nan bowed silently. She was in it now, she reasoned, and might as well see it to the end. In her was a streak of adventure, and she was curious, as are all women.

She refused additional pay, considering that she already had received more than the work called for. Mr. Kiley again left her and the other woman. But he returned presently and beckoned them into an adjoining apartment.

"Now, if you will excuse Mrs. Kiley and me," he said, seating his guest, "we shall go in to the meeting and get through with the preliminaries. You may get your paraphernalia ready—if you will permit me to suggest—and in a short time you will be at work."

The two left her forthwith. She opened her small case and busied herself with inks and needles, all the time listening to a dull rumble of voices from beyond the door through which the two had passed.

When everything was in readiness, and still her patrons did not return, Nan idly picked up a thin volume lying on the table beside her kit. She noted with interest that it was a copy of Johnson's well-known story, *Thou Art the Man*. Allowing the leaves to ripple through her fingers, she ceased the movement suddenly, turned back a few pages, and looked bewilderedly at a curious photograph pasted on one of them.

It was the life-sized photograph of a human eye; and, strangely enough, it seemed to her that she ought to know the owner of that eye—that somewhere recently she had seen the face of which it was a part.

She closed the book as the doorknob turned. Kiley, now masked, entered softly and mysteriously. He picked up a chair and carried it beside a leather-covered couch.

"If you will sit here with your tools and inks, Madame Sundy," he said, "all will be ready in a moment's time. The gentleman of whom I spoke will be your first subject."

She arose and went to the chair beside the couch. Kiley stepped to the closed door by which he had entered, and administered a peculiar series of taps on a panel. Then he stood at one side.

The door opened soon, and about a dozen masked men and

women filed gravely into the room. They silently formed a half circle about Nan and the couch. Then came four masked men bearing a fifth, also masked and covered by a sheet, on a sort of litter, covered likewise.

They deposited this silent, immovable figure on the couch at Nan's side and stepped back.

From under the sheet the man's bare left arm protruded. On the inside of it, halfway between the elbow and the hand, was a tiny inked X.

Kiley stepped to Nan's side. "The X on his arm indicates the exact spot where you are to tattoo the design," he whispered. "Here's the design. Please make a reproduction as accurate as possible."

He handed her a small oval photograph of a human eye.

For an instant Nan stared at it in amazement. Once again it seemed that she should know to whom that eye belonged. The eye was not the same that she had seen in the book. Though an artist, she never had painted portraits, and did not then realize the great extent to which the eye is responsible for the entire expression of the human face.

Where had she seen this eye? She was nervous as she asked that a portable electric lamp be brought closer, and that a glass of water be supplied, while she made ready with her tiny instruments of torture. Whose eye was it?

Ah! Now she knew. She had looked into it only a few minutes before.

It was a photograph of the left eye of the blonde woman called Wyn. Austin Kiley had introduced Wyn as his wife. Yet now, with her husband's consent, the likeness of her left eye was to be tattooed on the arm of another man!

CHAPTER VII

SIGNALS

When the man with the broken arm—the Cass Starr whose name had been written on the package—announced to the fictitious society that Kiley and the blonde woman were at the door, Tyler Lake left his post at the keyhole and groped his way back to the bed. The return of Starr's fellow conspirators meant that whatever was to be done to Tyler was now imminent; and he decided again to feign unconsciousness in order, if possible, to surprise them and gain the upper hand.

Voices came to him now only mumblingly. He lay in total darkness, waiting for he knew not what. That they had resolved on chloroforming him, though, he was aware; and he raked his brain to find some way of frustrating this.

He was not given long to plan, for soon the door opened softly and the light was turned on again.

Though he kept his eyes closed Tyler was aware that two persons had entered the shut-in room. Directly their guarded voices told him that he had to deal only with Austin Kiley and the woman Wyn. They stepped to his bedside, and Tyler struggled to keep his face expressionless as he felt their questioning eyes on him.

"He's still out," Wyn remarked. "You sure slipped him a peach, Kile!"

Kiley chuckled. "Just the same," he told her, "when the needles begin pricking his arm he's likely to come out of it. Too bad we couldn't have had this girl use her electric apparatus; it's not nearly so painful and might not rouse him. But there is a vast difference between tattooing done by hand and what is done by electricity. And as my design is hand-work his must be the same. We don't want to leave any loopholes for some expert to see through."

"You think it's not safe, then, to take him out as he is?"

"I'm afraid not. I'll put him to sleep with chloroform, then she can dig into him to her heart's content, and he'll never know the difference."

There was a space of silence, and afterward came the squeaky sound of a cork being pulled. Tyler Lake braced himself for an ordeal.

Now came the sounds of liquid gurgling from a bottle, followed by the pungent odour of chloroform, gaining in strength as it permeated the atmosphere of the unventilated room.

"That'll fix 'im," announced the man.

Whereupon Tyler cautiously deflated his chest and forced every breath of air from his lungs. Then slowly he drew in fresh air till he felt that his chest could hold no more. He ceased the long draught, and clapped his tongue to the roof of his mouth just as Kiley spread a towel, saturated with chloroform, over his face.

Tyler Lake was an expert swimmer and diver, and when a boy he had held the record for remaining under water longer than any of his playmates. If Kiley and Wyn failed to notice that his breast was not rising and falling he felt that he could keep from inhaling the potent fumes for a length of time which, if the two knew about it, would surprise them. Everything depended upon how soon they would decide that the cloth could safely be removed. They were in more or less of a hurry, he imagined, and his hope held out.

Seeing that he made no move, they walked away from the bed, talking in lowered tones. Tyler was suffering not at all as yet, but he knew that soon his lungs would seem to be bursting from the strain. He could not smell the drug at all, and knew that its fumes were as yet not entering his system to deaden his senses.

Moments seemed like minutes, minutes like hours. Bright sparks now were darting like flashes of lightning before his eyes; but as they were closed, he knew it to be only a hallucination. Time dragged on, and still he held his breath.

It seemd at last that his chest and head were splitting, and the pain of his bruise began throbbing anew. In a moment or two he knew he must breathe or burst a blood vessel.

Then the thought of a new subterfuge came to him. He moaned aloud, tossed his head, and contrived to displace the wet cloth as he did so. This gave him the chance to carefully allow the air to hiss through his nostrils; and by the time Kiley had hurried to him he was drawing in fresh, sweet air as a starving man eats food.

"Don't like it, eh, old boy?" chuckled Kiley, replacing the cloth once more over Tyler's nostrils. "That'll be about all from him, though," he told Wyn reassuringly. "They usually pitch about a little just before they succumb."

For only a short time now he allowed the cloth to lie clammily over his victim's face. And Tyler, having a fresh supply of air, was ready for another siege. Presently Kiley shook him, easily at first, then vigorously.

"Dead to the world," was his verdict as he whipped off the cloth. "Get a couple of the boys, Wyn, and we'll lug him out for his initiation."

Tyler breathed slowly, and before the woman had returned with the men his respirations were nearly normal.

With them the men brought a door, or a shutter, or some form of impromptu litter. They dragged him from the bed and stripped the bed of its sheets. One they draped over the litter to hide its makeshift appearance from the tattoo artist. Lifting Tyler's inert form they laid it on the sheet and cast the remaining sheet over it. Kiley drew Tyler's left arm from under the sheet, rolled up the sleeves, and, with his fountain pen, indicated the place where the design was to be tattooed.

Two of them now lifted the litter and its burden, and, with the woman giggling, they marched out of the room, unconsciously bearing a man as alert of mind as in any previous moment of his life.

In another room they lifted his head while the woman affixed a mask over his eyes. Then they solemnly bore him through a second door and gently lifted him from the litter to a soft, springy couch.

Kiley spoke in low tones to some one—the tattoo artist, Tyler supposed. Lights were carried closer. So close and so bright were they that, even through closed lids, they hurt his eyes.

Silence reigned for a time, then a soft, warm hand touched his. A moment more and the fingers grasped his forearm, stretching the skin over the under side. There was a moment's wait, then a soft, cold, wet something—a tiny camel's hair brush, he imagined—began tickling his flesh.

He knew this "Madame Somebody-or-other", as the blonde woman had called her, was not in league with the others in the room. He dared not open his eyes, even though the mask shadowed them, for some of the conspirators might be standing directly over him. How could he let this woman know that he needed her help? That he was an unwilling subject, scheduled to play a part in some ghastly farce the nature of which he had no knowledge?

The under side of his arm was turned uppermost, and strong, warm fingers gripped the arm from beneath. The other hand of the artist plied the brush in the preliminary execution of whatever design was to be tattooed under his skin. He reasoned that if he could elevate his fingers without being observed by the conspirators, he might touch the arm with which she was outlining the work.

Slowly, cautiously, blindly, he began putting this into execution. He feared that before his fingers had touched her arm she might remove it, as she reached to dip her brush in the ink again. This would leave his hand exposed in the midst of an upward movement, with the fingers outstretched. So he took a bold chance, reached up swiftly, and touched a soft, smooth forearm.

The tickling of the brush ceased immediately, then it began again. She doubtless thought his movement involuntary. He had not lowered his hand; and now his fingers sought out the smooth arm once more, and this time, when they touched it, they pinched it softly.

No sooner had he done this than the fear seized Tyler that she would misinterpret. He had forgotten that she did not know he was an unwilling subject for her needles. She might think him a flirtatious male, who, not so serious in the solemn initiation as his fellow society members supposed, was taking advantage of the situation to act in an ungentlemanly manner toward her. So he quickly changed his signal and began tapping rapidly with his forefinger against her skin.

To his great relief and delight there was only a momentary cessation of the tickling. Then she was at work again, while he continued to tap her arm.

A great wave of hope surged over him as he now felt her left hand, which held his arm steady for the work, signalling back to him. Softly the fingers squeezed again and again, so there could be no mistake.

Then said a clear contralto voice, quite close:

"Pardon me, please—but so many of you standing about and looking on makes me decidedly nervous. I am accustomed to have no spectators near me when I am at work. I don't wish to spoil this design. But my hand trembles; I must request that you all withdraw a little."

Tyler pinched her arm again to indicate that he interpreted her tactics; she squeezed his arm in reply.

A shuffling of feet sounded as the "society" politely withdrew to a respectful distance.

The girl now raised Tyler's arm as if to study her work closer to the lights. Still holding it, she rose to her feet. As she reseated herself he knew that she was leaning over him, for he felt her warm breath on his eyelids.

"Open your eyes," she whispered.

He did so, slowly, guardedly. For a moment the strong white lights blinded him; then he saw that no one but a beautiful girl with brown hair and eyes was near him. Her lips were parted, and her face was white and worried.

At once the expressive brown eyes flashed a message to his. Then long dark lashes covered them, and once again the tiny brush began tickling his skin.

In a little while, however, she raised his arm, as before, studying her work at closer range. She half rose, twisting the arm towards the light. It came within the range of his vision. On its white surface, under the outlines of a human eye, he saw words painted with the little brush and the India ink:

Are you in trouble?

He blinked his eyelids rapidly to indicate "Yes". With her eyes she returned this signal. She lowered the arm again, and he felt a cold wet sponge erasing the painted words. For a time she gave her attention to the design, then the tickling sensation began wandering about over his arm, even down to his wrist.

It ceased abruptly. Once more she raised his arm so that he could see, while she pretended to be studying her work. He read:

I will place an inked brush in your left hand. Write on my arm what you wish to tell me.

A little later the handle of a small brush crept into his hand. As she bent over her work again his fingers sought her bare forearm, found it, and clumsily, blindly, printed this:

Help!

Five minutes later he read the following on his own arm, once more elevated:

Close your eyes again. I can help you, and will. Trust me.

He closed his eyes and sighed. The words were sponged away again, and a moment later he winced as a cluster of sharp needles began pricking his flesh.

But instead of torturing, the pain somehow seemed to sooth him. Even with his eyes closed he still could see the dewy brown eyes of the girl who plied the tiny needles and had promised aid.

CHAPTER VIII
THE SECOND EYE

Nan Sundy worked feverishly at her tattooing, dully trying to reason it all out in her mind. She was confident now that the man under her needles was a prisoner and needed help. Also she was able to name the strange odour which she had noticed when he was first carried in to her. It was the odour of chloroform. Again, before she had finished the design on his arm, she caught sight of a crimson clot in the black hair over his left temple. Something was wrong—that she knew.

In a little over half an hour she had finished tattooing the eye on his arm and was well satisfied with her work, considering the difficulties under which it had been accomplished.

Kiley studied the design closely at a word from her, smiled his approval, and nodded for the litter bearers to carry the man out.

They did so when Nan had covered her work with antiseptic bandages. Soon they returned with the blonde woman, likewise covered by a sheet, likewise masked and silent. Her bare left arm protruded, ready for embellishment.

Kiley returned to Nan's side, took up the tiny photograph which she had reproduced so accurately on the man's arm, and handed her a similar one.

A glance convinced her that this was the photograph of another person's eye. Promptly came the realization that this one was the same as the one she had discovered in the book on the table. Then swiftly she knew. This and the one in the book were photographs of the eye of Austin Kiley himself.

Silently she began her work, insisting, as before, that the spectators stand back. But she demanded this for an entirely new reason now. Ranged about the walls, silent, the masked observers were not close enough to her to interpret the meaning of certain operations of hers. They did not see, when she had finished outlining the eye with her brush, that she spooned from a squat bottle in her kit a thick, colourless substance, which she mixed with the India ink with which the tattooing was to be done. If they had seen they probably would have suspected nothing at the time.

The woman winced as the needles pierced her white skin for the first time. Knowing that this lisping blonde was one of the number who were holding her first subject against his will, Nan did not put herself out to use her instrument with a gentle hand.

Another silent half hour passed, then she leaned back with a little sigh, her task completed.

"Very fine indeed," commented Kiley, bending over "Wyn, dear."

Again he gave the signal, and the woman was borne out. The other masked men and women, all but Kiley, filed out after the litter in solemn procession.

"We certainly have appreciated this, Madame Sundy," said Kiley as the door closed. "I'll call the car now, and we'll have you home in no time."

"You will wish me to return, I suppose," remarked Nan demurely, collecting her paraphernalia and taking it to the table on which she had left her carrying case.

"Oh, no," said Kiley, smiling. "Why do you think that?"

Nan opened her case and began placing inks, brushes, and instruments in their proper places within it.

"Why," she told him, "I have only accomplished the preliminaries, one might say. After the wounds have healed and the skin is firm once more the work should be gone over carefully a second time—retouched, you know—and any defects corrected."

"Oh, I see. Yes, I know that is usually done. But it won't be necessary in this instance, Madame Sundy. By the time your work is ready for retouching, our regular tattoo artist will be about again, and he can attend to it himself."

She bowed with apparent unconcern.

"I'll call the car now," he said again and left the room.

The door had no sooner closed than Nan snatched up the little book, which still lay beside her case. Desperately she thumbed the leaves, and at last came to the page to which the photographed eye was pasted. Her moist sponge descended upon it, and with her tiny spatula she worked around the edges, lifting them and squeezing moisture underneath. In a surprisingly short time the paster was free. She closed the book, and, hastily drying her prize, tossed it into her case and was snapping the lid as Austin Kiley reappeared.

"The car is ready," he announced, standing at the door.

She bowed and walked to him.

Once more the curtains were drawn in the limousine, and the machine twisted in and about and turned many corners. When at length Nan was assisted courteously to the pavement before the entrance to her own apartment house she had not the slightest conception of where she had been that night—no idea of the location of the mysterious house without a number.

CHAPTER IX
JEFFERSON MERCER

Next morning Nan Sundy called on one of the most astute criminologists in the West, Detective Jefferson Mercer, to tell him what she had discovered the night before.

Jefferson Mercer was a big, strong, healthy individual, with a keen zest in life and deep love for an obstruse criminal problem. With sparkling eyes he listened to the pretty tattoo artist's breathlessly told account and rubbed his hands with delight as she concluded and sat with lips parted awaiting his comment.

"By George!" he cried. "And you say, Madame Sundy, that you contrived to swipe the eye that you found pasted in the book?"

She opened her hand bag and placed on his desk the small oval photograph.

Eagerly Mercer scooped it up, turned on a strong white light, and studied the picture through a lens.

"Please call me Miss Sundy," said Nan. "When I'm with real people 'madame' gets on my nerves."

"I thank you for the implied compliment," he said with a laugh. "Well, Miss Sundy, I am particularly interested in the human eye in its application to criminology. A little case that I cleaned up a short time ago revolved about certain people's eyes hand-painted on ivory cuff buttons. For clews I had only paintings of one eye of each of the actors in the little drama, yet I was able to solve the mystery and bring a murderer into court.

"That case gave me my start, and since then I have given no little thought and study to the human eye. Portrait painters, above all people, know how decidedly the human eye is accountable for the entire expression of a person's face. Given photographs of nothing more than a man's two eyes, one famous miniature artist claims that he can reconstruct a recognizable likeness of the man's face. Truly the eye is 'the window of the soul'.

"In mulling over this matter I came upon certain old police records which tell of a certain secret semi-criminal, semi-political ring, the members of which used photographs of their eyes for identification. When they were together they were always masked, and it was claimed that no one of them had ever seen the faces of the others. Each was known to the rest by his eyes, showing through the holes in his mask. In sending written communications a photograph of the writer's eye was pasted at the bottom of the letter, and took the place of his signature. One glance was sufficient to tell the recipient of a letter who had written it. Unique, eh?

"But this is getting us nowhere. Right now we must give our undivided attention to freeing this man, finding out why the tattooing was done, and why he is held prisoner.

"The fact that you found this eye pasted in a book leads me to the belief that this old ring that I spoke about is again operating, or that their custom has been copied by others. The eye pasted in that book suggests to me that the volume was the property of the owner of the eye, and that he took this means of so informing the rest. Did you notice the title of the book?"

"It was *Thou Art the Man*, by Edgar Johnson."

Mercer leaned back suddenly from his study of the photograph. "*Thou Art the Man*, eh? That sounds mighty significant, when one has considered the other points you have mentioned. M'm-m! Now, you say this Austin Kiley had a human eye tattooed on his arm, and that this eye here which you took from the book is a photograph of his?"

"Yes."

"And on the prisoner's arm you tattooed the woman's eye? And on her arm you tattooed Kiley's?"

"Exactly."

"Can you say whose eye was tattooed on Kiley's arm?"

"No, I cannot. I saw it only momentarily as he was darkening the interior of the limousine."

"I see. Well, I have no doubt at all but that it is this woman's eye that is tattooed on his arm. Can you describe the prisoner?"

"Not very well," she said musingly. "He was covered by a sheet, you know, and his face was masked. But the outlines of his figure convinced me that he is probably a tall, well-built, strong man. His hair is coal-black."

"Austin Kiley's is, too, I believe you said."

"Yes."

"And can you say that you consider the prisoner and Kiley of about the same height and build?"

"Yes, I would say that," Nan replied thoughtfully.

"*Thou Art the Man*," Mercer repeated sonorously.

Nan looked at him with comprehension.

"That's obviously the answer," he told her. "This imprisoned man has been chosen to impersonate Kiley in some manner, and for some distinct reason. To make this similarity stronger, the same tattoo mark that is on Kiley's arm was placed on the arm of the man who is to represent him. Now, Kiley introduced the blonde woman to you as his wife. She may be such, and she may not be. But rest assured they make the world believe that she is.

"Now, men are not in the habit of finding pleasure in seeing their wives' eyes, or anything connected with their wives, tattooed on the arms of other men. Many a divorce case has had its beginning with a woman's likeness being found on the wrong man's dresser, or in his watch case. So it follows logically that this prisoner is to be presented to some one, together with the public at large, as Austin Kiley, and also as the husband of this woman Wyn. Is that all clear?" "Perfectly," she told him. "You think the society, then, is merely a blind?"

"Perhaps. Whether it is or not, though, is not significant just now. It will take weeks for this man's tattoo mark to heal; and whatever is to be his fate, then, nothing will be done until it has healed, so that it will resemble the older mark on Kiley's arm."

Mercer absently turned a paper weight over and over on his desk.

"If only you had been successful in prevailing upon Kiley to come for you again for the retouching of the work," he said. "Then I could have had a man hidden in your studio, who would trail Kiley or the woman back to this mysterious house when they came for you. But so long as you could not do so—"

"Why, I almost forgot!" she broke in excitedly. "I was so upset that I neglected to tell you the main thing of all. They will come for me again, Mr. Mercer, and quite soon, too."

"How's that?" he cried.

"They will come for me," she repeated. "You see, when I realized that Kiley would say they would not need me again I played a trick on them to make them come for me."

"Go on! Go on!" he urged.

"Well, you see, it is the business of a tattoo artist to undo work as well as to do it. In time most people regret having had themselves tattooed and look about to see if there is any way of removing the designs from their persons. There are several processes, one of which I use. Into a design I tattoo a certain chemical which, after repeated applications and much pain, causes the ink to fade, leaving the scars, however. In the case which I keep always ready to use when called to work away from my studio, I have everything necessary to my craft. For one thing, there is a bottle of this ink-removing chemical.

"Now, it begins to work very quickly on old designs; therefore I concluded that its action on fresh ink would be very rapid indeed. So when I got ready to tattoo the woman I mixed with my ink some of this chemical. And I think that long before their artist's broken arm has healed they will come to me with the complaint that the design on her arm is mysteriously fading away."

Jefferson Mercer slapped his thigh, sprang to his feet, stalked around his desk, and held out his big hand to the diminutive Nan.

"Put her there!" he cried, his eyes beaming.

CHAPTER X
ON KILEY'S TRAIL

In anticipation of the conspirators' return to Nan Sundy's studio as soon as the tattoo design had begun to fade, Jefferson Mercer sent a man to remain on duty there and be ready to trail them to the mysterious house.

A thorough search of the city directory failed to show the name, Austin Kiley. Moreover, Mercer learned that there was no such building as the Manners Building in San Francisco. No real estate men, no oil speculators, no one in investment circles ever had heard of Kiley.

Mercer had expected this to be the case, but in his painstaking way he began at the bottom in his gradual exhaustion of all possible clews.

Now he gave his attention to the many book stores of San Francisco, hoping to find a salesman who had sold *Thou Art the Man* the day before, or perhaps previous to that. He was taking the great chance of wasting time; but it had occurred to him that the book, because of its significant title, had been introduced into the plot for some distinct purpose. In which case it doubtless had been secured on the spur of the moment to fulfil that purpose.

His search was long and tedious, but along towards four o'clock that afternoon, in a little downtown store, he found a book dealer who recalled selling such a volume the previous day.

"I couldn't help remembering," said he, "because that was the only copy in stock, and a dealer wouldn't sell one of them a year."

Mercer made known his identity, and the book-store man became intensely interested.

"He was a large man," he said, "and I think his hair was dark. Well dressed? Yes, if I remember correctly. Wait a minute now; I remember something quite distinctly.

"It was evening, just before closing time—the slowest hour of the day, with us. I was straightening the piles of magazines in the window and happened to see this man coming across the street from the barber shop, over there.

"He came into the store and stood with his face to the front, apparently looking over the contents tables of the magazines. I didn't ask him if he wanted anything in particular because I'm used to having bookworms nose about by themselves.

"Presently he left the magazine stand and began looking over some bargain books on that little table there in the main aisle. This book, *Thou Art the Man*, was one of the lot. Pretty soon he called me and handed me the book. 'I'll take this,' he told me and reached for his purse.

"And that's about all. I wrapped it hurriedly, for my clerks were then closing the windows and getting ready to lock up. If he had bought the book at any other time I might not have remembered as much as I do of the simple transaction."

"You didn't see him pasting anything in the book before he called you, did you?" Mercer asked.

A negative reply was made, and Mercer thanked the bookseller and walked across the street.

The barber shop that the book dealer had indicated was a high-class concern, operating many chairs. He was soon in consultation with the head barber, but learned nothing whatever from him or his fellow workers.

"You might try in the Turkish bath that's run in connection with the shop," suggested Mercer's interlocutor. "The entrance is outside, to your left."

The manager of the Turkish bath conducted Mercer into the steaming mysteries beyond, and soon he faced a gigantic negro, nude but for the coarse towel about his middle.

"Kiley? Kiley? Kiley?" repeated the African, rolling his eyes retrospectively. "Ah don' know dat gemman, suh. What foh a lookin' gemman is dis heah Mistah Kiley, suh?"

Mercer drew on his meagre stock of descriptive data, and when he mentioned the tattooed eye on Kiley's arm the negro's pupils began to dilate.

"Yes, suh. Ah knows dat gemman, suh. Tips me a dollah every time he comes heah, suh. He was in heah yesterday, er day befoah, Ah forgets which. Soused to de eyeballs, suh. Looked lak he nevah knew me. Had another gemman with 'im, an' dey both went through, this heah Mistah Kiley tryin' to sober up, Ah reckon. Got 'im to bed, an' de other gemman pulled out. Den nothin' would do but dis Mistah Kiley had to go hunt 'im up right afterward."

"Describe this other man, please," said Mercer.

"Big gemman—about lak dis heah Mistah Kiley. Black hair, lak Kiley's, too, suh. Didn't have much to say."

"And you say Kiley comes often?"

"Yes, sah—once a week, maybe. Tryin' to reduce, Ah reckon, when he ain't tryin' to steam off a jag." The negro showed his white teeth in a grin. "Been comin' heah six months, Ah'd say."

Mercer took out his purse, and there passed from him to the bath attendant a bank note which would surpass the amount of Austin Kiley's tips for many weeks to come.

"You-all sen' youah man heah, suh," said the recipient, grinning, as Mercer started to leave. "When his heah bird wid de eye on his arm shows up Ah'll suah tip 'im off to youah man, suh."

To all appearances the walls were pressing in rather closely about Mr. Austin Kiley as Mercer left the bath house and drove to Nan Sundy's studio.

"I've seen nothing of them yet," was Nan's report. "Your man is hidden in the back room, ready to follow at a word from me. I don't expect them for a week, though; and then I fancy they'll come at night. I think I'll keep open quite late every night, to be ready for them."

Mercer approved this plan and returned to his office, well pleased with the progress that had been made.

For several days nothing occurred; then, at three o'clock one afternoon, Mercer answered the telephone to hear Nan Sundy's silvery tones over the wire.

"They've been here!" she cried excitedly. "The man and the woman, too. Already the design has begun to fade, and they are hopping mad. I told a beautiful little fib, saying I'd used a new and untried brand of ink that night. I got terribly agitated and offered to do anything to remedy my mistake. But her arm was too sore for me to work on it today, so I told them that when it had healed a little more I would go again to their house, and do the work over with my old ink. Kiley told me rather huffily that they would come to the studio instead, and they took their leave in the limousine."

"Yes, yes—and then?"

"Oh, your man was after them in his little runabout before they were out of the block. I do hope he contrives to trail them down!"

"So do I," said Mercer grimly.

For twenty minutes or more he paced the floor, waiting for a telephone call from his shadow. None came, however, and he buried himself in work and tried to forget.

But he could not, and once more he rose and paced about, more fretful than he ever had been on a case before. If only Nan Sundy had pricked the chemical under the man's skin instead of the woman's. That would have made it necessary for her to go again to the house to do her work over. Whereas the woman could go to her. But it might be just as well as it was. The man he had set on their trail, Steve Glidden, was an expert. There was every reason to hope—

Br-r-r-r-r-r!

Jefferson Mercer jumped at the telephone and whipped off the receiver.

"Mercer!" he cried into the mouthpiece.

"Hello! This is Steve, Mr. Mercer."

"Yes, yes! Did you run them down?"

"Yes, I ran them down," replied Glidden slowly, "down to the water-front. And before I knew what was up they were in a fast little motor boat heading out into the bay. I grabbed the limousine driver before he could get away. He'd never seen these people before, he claimed. He runs the car for hire—has a stand on Post Street. I took his name and number, but I think he told the truth. And by the time I'd got through with him and was looking about for some sort of a craft that I could hire, the motor boat had disappeared somewhere out there in the bay. I'll have a fast put-put here in a minute or two, and will be after em. But I've got only a slim chance of getting on their trail again. The bay's black with boats today."

"I see," said Mercer quietly, and hung the receiver on its hook.

CHAPTER XI
THE CABIN IN THE PINES

Lying once more on the bed in the closed-in room of the mystery house on Cedarview Avenue, Tyler succumbed to the intense strain and fell asleep. When he regained consciousness the second time that night he was tossing slowly back and forth on a narrow bunk. In his ears was a noise which, it seemed, he had been hearing for days and days; but now it was louder and more distinct. It was five minutes before he realized that the sounds represented the quick exhausts of a gasoline engine, and that the rocking was caused by the motion of a boat.

He believed that while he had slept chloroform at last had been successfully applied to his nostrils, and that while under its influence he had been carried from the house on Cedarview Avenue and taken aboard a boat.

Again he slept. He was too weak and dull to move about, or to speculate on his fate. When he awoke once more he was being lifted from the motor boat. Later he knew that he had been dumped into the tonneau of an automobile. He heard the crash of breakers on a rocky coast. He succumbed to drowsiness again as the automobile rushed away into the night.

Hours later—they seemed like years—he was awakened by being dragged from the car. Now he smelled on the cool night air the breath of pine trees. He smiled and dozed once more as he was jolted along, finally to be dropped in total darkness—where, he did not know or care.

When consciousness suddenly came to him after another long interval he found himself lying flat on the hard ground in semi-darkness. A blinking survey of his surroundings at last showed him that he was in a tunnel, a cave, or some underground chamber. On both sides of him gaunt rocks protruded from the earth that held them in place. Such light as penetrated to the remote place came through piled-up stones at what must be the entrance.

Wearily he tried to rise. He heard the clank of iron. A weight dragged on his ankle. Wonderingly he looked at it, to find that a heavy steel band encircled it, to which was fastened a chain, the chain in turn being held by a ring cemented into a bowlder larger than his body.

As he still stared at this the stones at the opening began moving. He saw hands taking them away one by one, and the light grew stronger with their displacement. Then the light was shut off entirely as a bulk crowded through the resulting opening, and a moment later Austin Kiley, in rough outdoor garb, stood over him, chuckling sardonically.

"Well, you're alive, I see," he remarked lightly.

Tyler made no reply.

"Wouldn't make much difference if you weren't alive," Kiley offered.

Still the prisoner remained silent.

"I've brought your breakfast," Kiley added. "Better eat and go to sleep again."

He returned to the entrance and lifted in a wooden box containing food, which he set at his captive's side.

"See you later," he said nonchalantly, and crawled out, replacing the loose stones after him.

It was nearly three weeks before Tyler Lake saw Austin Kiley again. The man with the broken arm had attended to the prisoner's wants during this period, sometimes aided by the woman. Always one or the other carried an automatic pistol when dealing with him. Neither had had much to say to him, and he was too proud to question them as to their motive for mistreating him.

Often during this period he thought of the girl who had promised to help him. Nothing had come of this promise. Now he realized that she probably was unable to render aid. It occurred to him that she might have been smuggled into the house to do that mysterious tattooing and taken away again without knowledge of where she had been. If only he had thought to paint on her white arm that night the address of the house on Cedarview Avenue. He wondered if she was trying to help. He believed she was. He liked to believe this, anyway; for the unknown girl who had been brought into such strange contact with him fascinated and mystified him.

He had kept track of the days, and on the nineteenth night since he had called at the house on Cedarview Avenue, the man called Cass Starr lifted down stones at the entrance of the tunnel and crawled inside.

As usual, his left hand held an automatic pistol. Tyler noticed that tonight, for the first time since their encounter in the hall, his right arm was not in a sling.

"Stand up," he ordered, stopping a few feet from Tyler.

Cheerfully Tyler obeyed. Inaction was torture.

"Turn around," came the next command.

The man approached closer when Tyler had followed this injunction. He stooped at Tyler's back and unlocked the padlock that held the chain to Tyler's leg.

"I'm going to take you to the cabin," he said, rising. "Go ahead. Remember my arm's getting well now. I can handle you. I'll pump you full of lead if you make a break."

Tyler said nothing, but started for the entrance. There his jailer made him stand back, while he crawled through ahead of him, backing out, the pistol trained on the other throughout the manoeuvre.

At his command, given from the outside, Tyler followed. He had smelled liquor on the man's breath. His hope that this might mean an opportunity for escape grew strong.

"Go towards that light," ordered Cass Starr. "I'll be right behind you, with the gun at the small of your back."

The moon was up. In its soft light Tyler saw a rugged, hilly country, studded with pines and oaks and irregular outcroppings of rock. A light gleamed through the pines a short distance away, and towards it he walked, glad of the chance to be outdoors once more, and of the longed-for opportunity to pit his wits against these mysterious conspirators.

Presently they entered a cabin, and Cass Starr, always ready with the automatic, told Tyler to seat himself. Tyler chose a seat near an oilcloth-covered table, on which stood a crock of dry beans. On the other end of the table stood a glass and a bottle of whisky. The walls of the cabin were of rough boards, the furniture of the plainest. The odour of whisky was in the room as well as on the breath of Starr.

The man seated himself at the other end of the table and looked across at Tyler.

"Folks went off and left me all alone," he confided. "And I got lonesome for somebody to talk to. I took a few drinks, and then I wanted to talk to some one all the more. I'd talk to a cow when I'm drinking. So I thought I'd bring you in and tell you a few things."

"Thanks," said Tyler dryly.

Starr's eyes lighted on the crock of beans. "By golly," he muttered, "Wyn told me to put those beans to soak. Put 'em there so I couldn't forget. But I forgot to pour water over them."

He arose and walked to a bucket of water in one corner of the room. Tyler eagerly watched his steps for evidences of unsteadiness, but was disappointed. The man's back was turned to him only an instant while he filled a dipper from the bucket. But in that short space of time Tyler's hand dived noiselessly into the crock of beans and came away filled, to rest again in his lap underneath the table.

Cass Starr poured water into the crock; then, handling it a bit awkwardly with his gun hand and its injured mate, he carried the crock and set it on a shelf.

When he returned to his end of the table he carried another whisky glass, which he set within Tyler's reach. Then he seated himself and pushed the whisky bottle across the oilcloth.

"They say a condemned man gets anything he wants on the night preceding his execution," he said with a laugh. "So I thought I'd extend you this privilege. Drink up. There's plenty more of it here. Get good and pickled if you care to. That's what I'd do if I were in your fix."

Tyler's cheeks paled in spite of him, but his eyes snapped.

"Condemned? Execution?" he said. "What do you mean?"

Cass poured himself a drink, and once more shoved the bottle toward Tyler.

"Just what I said," he replied, draining the liquor. "Better drink a lot of it. It'll be easier for you. That's why I'm drinking tonight. I'm not keen about this part of Kiley's scheme. I'm a crook all right, I guess, but a pretty poor murderer. But it's Kiley's business—not mine. So I'm going to be soused to the eyeballs by the time he pulls it off. But say, don't get hopeful. I can handle lots of this stuff. I won't drink so much while you're here that I'll get careless and let you make your get-away. Don't try it, Lake. I'm a dead shot with a pistol, drunk or sober."

"Perhaps you'll explain more," suggested Tyler.

"I might as well tell you everything," mused Cass. "You won't care to talk about anything else, anyway, and I've got to talk about something to somebody when I'm drinking. Kiley's idea was to tell you nothing—just bump you off without a word of warning. But I've got to tell you, it seems; and with this to back me up"—he tapped his whisky glass—"I've got the nerve to talk about it."

Tyler nodded gravely. The beans he held in his clinched hand under the table grew suddenly wet and clammy.

Starr poured for himself another drink and leaned forward over the table, his eyes on Tyler, his automatic firm and steady in his hand.

CHAPTER XII
NAN TURNS DETECTIVE

There was a look of worriment on Jefferson Mercer's face as he entered Nan Sundy's studio on the eighteenth morning after she had brought to his attention the mystery of the prisoner in the house without a number. Steve Glidden, his shadow, had failed to find the motor boat on San Francisco bay that morning, and since then nothing more had been heard of Austin Kiley or his wife.

"They haven't showed up?" he asked.

Nan, unoccupied at the time, shook her head.

"This is the eighteenth day," he said gravely. "How long does it usually take tattoo wounds to heal, Miss Sundy?"

"It seems to depend a great deal on the individual," she answered. "If he is in good health, and his blood is in active circulation, they will heal much sooner than in the case of a sickly person."

"Of course—naturally," he said musingly. "I should say that the man you described is robust and in good health. This being the case, do you think his wounds should be healed by now?"

"Just about," she replied.

His face was graver than usual as he started to take his leave.

"What is it?" she queried. "Why did you ask what you did?"

He hesitated. "I'm worried now," he confessed. "I'm afraid that whatever is to happen to this unfortunate man is destined to occur just as soon as the tattoo marks have healed."

"I don't understand," she faltered.

"To be blunt, then," he said, drawing in his breath, "when his tattoo mark has healed it will resemble the one on Kiley's arm. Then they can—can—"

"Yes—go on!"

"Can kill him," he said.

She clutched at his arm. "You don't mean that! You're trying to frighten me, Mr. Mercer!"

She knew he was doing nothing of the sort; her words were involuntary. In her heart she had feared just this all along.

"I'm afraid that's what it all means," he said soberly. "Murder—pure, deliberate murder. And we seem helpless to stop it. I think they must have missed the eye that you removed from that book, Miss Sundy, and accordingly have grown suspicious of you. In that case, they'll not be likely to come here again. If the woman's mark is healing as it should she ought to have reappeared before this. I think they are waiting for their own artist to finish the job, or have decided to let it go in the woman's case. Her arm being tattooed is not absolutely necessary to their plans, it strikes me."

"Do you know anything of their plans, Mr. Mercer?"

"I suspect—that's all. But I'd rather not talk about it. It would only worry you."

Mercer went into Nan's back room and talked a few minutes with the detective he had stationed there, then took his leave, graver of face than Nan ever before had seen him. He had not been gone twenty minutes when Austin Kiley, immaculately dressed, appeared in the door of the studio, smiling blandly.

Nan caught her breath and struggled for composure.

"How do you do, Madame Sundy?" was Kiley's greeting.

She bowed her head, her lips white.

"Has Mrs. Kiley been here?" he asked.

"Not—not recently," said Nan inanely.

He elevated his dark eyebrows. "I was to meet her here about this time," he said, consulting a thin gold watch. "I'm late, as it is. She was to come here to see if you could go over her design again."

"I've not seen her," Nan told him.

Mr. Kiley frowned. "Well, considering the time it would require for you to retouch the work, she should have been here half an hour ago—if she meant to be ready to go with me at the time she set. That means she has changed her plans. I'll not wait. If she does come, please tell her that I have gone on home without her."

He lifted his hat and closed the door.

Nan sprang to life. In a flutter of excitement she burst into the back room and confronted the stolid Steve, shrouded by a cloud of cigar smoke.

"Hurry!" she cried. "The man was just here. He has—"

The detective bounded from his chair and ran with her to the front door.

"There!" she breathed, pointing down the street. "That large, black-haired man with the derby hat."

"I got him," muttered Mercer's man and glided out into the street.

He disappeared instantly from Nan's view, in a crowd of pedestrians.

It was about fifteen minutes after this that the blonde woman whom Nan knew as Mrs. Kiley entered the studio.

Again Nan stood trembling.

"Has Mr. Kiley been here?" asked the caller, smiling her cold smile. Nan explained.

"Oh, why couldn't he wait a minute?" she said, pouting. "But now that I'm here I want you to look at my arm, Madame Sundy."

Nan seated her and examined the results of her work. There

remained few signs of the eye she had tattooed on the smooth skin that memorable night. The wounds were now nearly healed, but soreness still remained.

"I can do nothing with this at present," said the tattoo artist.

"I was afraid you couldn't," said the woman as she pulled down her sleeve, "but I thought I'd have you look at it. Do you mind if I wait here a little for Mr. Kiley? He may look in again before he starts home. I know him pretty well, you see." She smiled thinly as she seated herself in one of Nan's soft-leather chairs and picked up a magazine.

Nan returned to her pen-and-ink creation of a new design to tempt the frivolous, but she trembled so violently that she could not work. She pretended to be deeply engrossed, however, and hoped no one would come in until the woman had taken her leave.

The minutes dragged, and still the blonde sat and turned the leaves of the periodical. Then the sharp ringing of the telephone bell brought Nan to her feet with a nervous start.

"Bad news, Miss Sundy," came over the wire in Mercer's voice. "Steve has just phoned in that he lost this man Kiley in a crowd on Market Street. Something strange about that. Steve's the best shadow I ever employed. It strikes me that this man must have known he was being followed, or he couldn't have shaken Steve."

"Oh!" cried Nan. "I—I—" She came to a full stop. She dared say almost nothing about the matter, with the blonde woman seated there not twenty feet from the telephone.

"Steve's returning to you on the chance that the woman may come, after all. But he thinks it is a—"

There came an interruption. The blonde woman had risen, and was moving toward the door.

"Oh! Oh!" wailed Nan, clutching her breast.

"What's the matter?" asked Mercer.

"I—I—"

The door opened and closed.

"She was here!" Nan screamed into the transmitter. "I couldn't say anything. Now she's gone—and there's no one here to follow her! She'll get away if—I'm going after her myself!"

"Don't! Listen here—"

Mercer's words tinkled in the receiver unheard by Nan. She had dropped it and was struggling into her coat. With one hat pin held by her white teeth, and both hands thrusting another through her hat and hair, she ran out to the pavement.

A few doors distant she saw the blonde woman moving away, loitering from one show window to another. Nan locked her door and waited close to the building. The blonde left off her gazing into windows and started briskly down the street. Nan followed.

One hour later she had crossed on a ferryboat to Oakland and boarded an eastbound train. At the other end of the Pullman sat the woman Wyn. Much to the conductor's chuckling amazement, Nan paid her fare from station to station, as she had no idea of the quarry's destination. About thirty miles out of Oakland she sent the Pullman porter out with a telegram to Mercer, explaining her move, and telling the direction in which she was travelling. Then she settled down to see that the blonde did not leave the train without her knowledge, and to keep herself from being seen by her.

CHAPTER XIII
BEANS

Tyler Lake and Cass Starr still sat facing each other across the oilcloth-covered table in the cabin. Starr helped himself to another drink of whisky and once more pushed the bottle toward his prisoner. Tyler shook his head.

Cass Starr was growing more and more loquacious after every drink; but so far Tyler had not been able to detect any sign of what he had been hoping for. Starr handled his liquor well; not once did the automatic waver in his hand; there was no indication of heedlessness in his eyes. Tyler kept his hand clinched on the beans that it held, and waited for the whisky to do its work.

"Well," said Starr, "you're wondering about the tattooed eye on your arm, and the rest of it, aren't you? It's quite simple, after all.

"You see Kiley, as we call him, is an expert at insurance frauds. He has engineered two or three big ones, with certain other people as principals. This time he's acting as principal himself—with Wyn Godfrey posing as his wife. I don't mind mentioning names, you see, because they're fictitious—and anyway you won't be here when—But I'll not rub it in.

"Well, in the present instance Kiley has insured his life with a New York insurance company to the amount of a hundred thousand dollars. He did this a year ago. Wyn, as his wife, is named as beneficiary.

"Before he presented himself for examination Kiley had a reproduction of Wyn's eye tattooed on his arm. He used to belong to a criminal ring that followed this custom, and he got the idea from that. I did the work. I'm an expert tattoo artist; and that's what gave me my part in the plot. So it's in the insurance company's descriptive record of Kiley that his wife's eye is tattooed on his arm. Furthermore, there is on file a photograph of that tattoo mark.

"This attended to, Kiley waited a year, to throw off suspicion, and then began looking up a man who resembled him to an extent that would make it easy to fool the insurance company. You are that man.

"You and Kiley are about of an age, nearly the same height, and your complexions are the same. When Wyn Godfrey presents your body to the insurance company and claims it to be that of her husband we except little difficulty in making them believe it."

"*My body!*" cried Tyler.

"Yes, your body," coolly echoed Starr. "Tomorrow you are to be killed in a mine accident. Your body will be packed in ice and shipped to New York for identification. We travelled clear across the continent to get a man—we thought it safer."

Tyler Lake's eyes burned, and the cold sweat oozed out on his forehead.

"Take a drink," urged Starr. "Surely you need it now."

Still Tyler shook his head. "Go on with your story," he said.

"Well, that's nearly the whole of it," returned the other. "You broke my arm that night, so I couldn't tattoo Wyn's eye on your arm. That was necessary, you see. It will be about the only means of identifying your body as that of Kiley's, for you'll be pretty well messed up after the explosion in that tunnel where we're keeping you. But we'll see to it that the tattoo mark is not obliterated. You'll be chained down, you know, and your tattooed arm will be protected from the shot with stones piled over it. Funny how lightly I can talk about it. It's the booze that makes this possible. Personally I'm not a bloodthirsty man at all. Kiley's different."

"Go on," said Tyler in low tones.

"Well, we were fortunate in getting a good tattoo artist to take my place. I'll bet you were surprised when you came to and found you'd been tattooed. We've been waiting for it to heal, of course. It's well now, and Kiley means to pull off his climax tomorrow morning. The eye on your arm is so well done that it will correspond nicely with the photograph of Kiley's tattoo mark in the files of the insurance company.

"Oh, it will be easy; but, to make things doubly sure, we had Kiley's eye tattooed on Wyn's arm. Kiley thought it might help. But something went wrong, and Wyn's design began to fade immediately. We weren't suspicious till Wyn missed from a book that was connected with the deal—in fact, the book you delivered that night—a photograph of Kiley's eye, which he had pasted there.

"That was only yesterday; and we decided that this little tattoo girl had stolen it because the leaves, where it had been pasted, were crinkled and stuck together. We decided that she'd sponged it off when Kiley left her for a minute, to call the car. Then I knew she'd doped her ink when she tattooed Wyn, in order to make Wyn come back to her. So we decided to let Wyn's design fade out and not use it, as it is not absolutely necessary to the scheme.

"This tattoo girl doesn't know anything, of course, but it worried us. So today Kiley and Wyn went down to San Francisco to tend to her. Kiley was to go to her studio and pretend that he expected to meet Wyn there. Not finding her, he was to say he wouldn't wait, and take his leave at once. He thought maybe this Madame Sundy had shown the eye to a dick and told of her strange adventure. In which case, a man would likely be waiting in her studio to follow Kiley or Wyn if they showed up again.

"So Kiley figured to go there and draw this man off on his trail. He knew he could lose him easily. It's not hard to lose a shadow if you know one's after you. Meantime Wyn would present herself at the studio, asking for Kiley. With the dick already trailing Kiley, they figured there would be no one there to shadow Wyn when she took her leave. That is, no one but the tattoo artist herself. And they hoped she'd be game enough to make a try at it, seeing it was up to her if it was to be done at all. Wyn will lead her here, of course. Then we'll find out what she knows and what she has done in the matter; and Kiley will hold her here till our plans are completed, and Wyn and I are well on our way to New York with your body.

"Of course we don't know yet whether the scheme will work with the tattoo artist, but Wyn ought to be showing up pretty quick. I heard the train come in.

"This is a lonely place, as you may have guessed. We've made it our headquarters for some time, and everybody about here thinks we're mining. We bought an old abandoned mine for a song. So it will all seem quite regular when a 'premature' explosion bumps you off. See that battery box over there in the corner? All we have to do is throw the switch, and—bang! The charge is all laid in the tunnel where you're kept—wires all connected. You've been sleeping near it for over two weeks. Oh, you can't reach it so long as you're chained. Surely you'll take a drink now? No? Well, I need another one, at any rate."

Tyler scarcely had listened to the latter part of Cass Starr's recital. He was struggling with the cold horror within him, trying to force his brains to think. He looked up suddenly and managed a cackling laugh.

"Very fine—but for one thing," he said, with all the scorn he could muster.

Starr looked politely inquisitive.

"I wasn't under the influence of chloroform when I was tattooed," said Tyler.

Starr's eyes narrowed. "No?" he said. "Well, prove it."

Tyler did so by telling of the fictitious society, the masks, and of his being carried in on a stretcher covered with a sheet.

Starr looked puzzled and not a little worried.

"The tattoo artist made you people stand away from her, you will recall," Tyler went on. "Then she slipped a brush into my hand, and I painted what I wanted to tell her on her arm." So far this was all true, but now Tyler began lying desperately. "I gave her the number of the house," he said. "She made it known to me that she would get in touch with the police at once. I overheard a lot of your conversation, and knew all about your plans. I've not been worrying, because I knew you didn't dare kill me till the tattoo marks had healed. I let the girl know this, and she perhaps has told the police there was no immediate danger. So that's why you haven't been arrested. I'm positive you've all been under surveillance ever since the tattoo artist left the house that night. The police are merely waiting to get you red-handed in the very act of preparing to kill me. I haven't the slightest doubt in the world but that detectives are listening at that window behind you this very moment!"

Tyler shot out the last sentence with dramatic force, and the eyes of Cass Starr bulged almost comically. He made a slight motion as if to turn his head, and Tyler tightened his muscles for a quick leap across the table.

But Starr did not turn. His eyes began receding, and his colour came back. A slow smile crossed his lips as he said:

"Fairly clever, my boy! Fairly clever! But it didn't work, did it? I'm too old a head to fall for anything so raw as that. I'll admit, though, that for a moment I was nervous—you told it so well. But common sense ought to tell a fellow that, even though you might have communicated something to the girl that night, you hadn't time or opportunity to write all that you have claimed."

Tyler was pretending that the other's words were unheard. He fixed his glance on the window back of Starr and allowed his lips to part as if he were intently watching something behind his jailer.

"Fairly good, old man!" repeated Starr, laughing. "Don't overdo it, though. When you're convinced that I know you're staring at something of absorbing interest taking place behind my back, you ought to pretend that you're *pretending* indifference. You're a fair actor, Lake, but you slur the finer details. Come now—accept a drink!"

Tyler's glance did not waver. He even allowed it to travel slowly from the window to a point directly behind Starr's chair, as if he were following the stealthy progress of some one stealing upon his tormentor.

"Good! Good!" said Starr, chuckling. "You refused to give up, didn't you? But my pistol hand is as steady as ever, you see, and nothing seems to impel me to look back and give you a chance to spring at my gun. Go on, Lake. What next? About time for that dick to jump on my back, eh? Takes him quite a time to sneak over here from the window. Oh, stop it, boy! I admit you're clever, but—"

At this instant there came a slight rattling sound over near the window at Starr's back. With his hand under the table Tyler had flipped two of the beans past Starr's legs.

Once more the man's eyes bulged. His body jerked forward, and it seemed that only a supreme effort kept him from wheeling about.

"By golly, Lake," he said, laughing, "that sound behind me almost did the work. Even the mice are on your side. This old cabin is full of them, and I remembered just in time. Go on with the show, Lake—I like to watch you. Of course I wouldn't hesitate to bore you, you understand. It wouldn't affect our plans, now that your tattoo mark has healed. We could blow your dead body to fragments as thoroughly as if you were alive, you know."

Tyler paid absolutely no attention to his bantering chatter. He continued to look fixedly behind Starr's back, and once more flipped a bean from under the table. Again Starr stirred uneasily as the bean rattled against the wall behind him.

Now Tyler flipped three beans at once. They rattled on the floor. Still Starr jeered at him with his eyes, though Tyler noticed his growing uneasiness. Slowly he moved his right hand to the edge of the table. He balanced a single bean on his thumb nail and made ready for the supreme moment. Aiming directly at the window glass, he shot the bean and made ready to leap upon Starr.

The sharp *tink* which sounded when the bean struck the glass proved too much for Starr. Mice might rattle things about the floor at a moment when the actor across from him needed their aid, but mice did not make such sounds as that. He jerked back his chair and sprang to his feet. He pointed the automatic directly at Tyler's breast, then, with whitening cheeks, swiftly turned his head towards the window.

In that instant Tyler Lake leaped across the table at the gun. He grabbed the wrist of the hand that held it. There came a deafening roar. Acrid powder smoke filled Tyler's nostrils. Starr wrenched his wrist and fired again, then swung around the table towards Tyler.

They clinched. Tyler drew back a fist and shot it straight into the other's face. With a groan Starr collapsed. Tyler grabbed the pistol with his other hand and wrenched desperately at it. He felt the weakening of the other's grip. One twist and—

For an instant there appeared at the window a white, tense face; then it vanished as quickly as it had come. There came a singing in Tyler's ears, and bright sparks shot before his eyes. With a low moan he crumpled and staggered forward, losing his hold on the gun and on Cass Starr's wrist.

From behind a pair of arms encircled him as he fell; then for a time he knew no more.

CHAPTER XIV
ANOTHER CAPTIVE

Tyler Lake's head was aching when he regained consciousness. A crimson drip trickled down the back of his neck. He found himself sitting upright, bound to a straight-backed chair. Before him sat Cass Starr. Near the door stood the woman Wyn.

"Cass," she was saying, "Kile will half kill you for this. What d'ye mean by taking a chance on bringing this bird in here? You're soused, that's what. I told Kile you'd get at the booze if we left you here alone; but I didn't think you'd do anything so crazy as this. If I hadn't run in and soaked him with the door weight just when I did he'd have knocked you out and made his get-away. Good thing for you it wasn't Kile that saved your bacon!"

Cass Starr seemed half stunned. In a dazed manner he fingered the jaw upon which Tyler's terrific blow had landed.

"How'd you get here, Wyn?" he asked.

"I just got in from San Francisco," she snapped. "Everything worked fine and dandy. She followed me, and ought to be showing up any time now. I walked slowly through the woods in the moonlight, and if she lost me she's a fool. I was waiting out on the porch to see if I could lamp her before coming inside; and then I heard you shoot. I ran in, grabbed up the door weight, and cracked this guy just in time. Now get busy! Sneak out and be watching for that Jane. I'll keep my eye on this fellow here. Nail her and bring her in. Hurry, for—"

Here Tyler interrupted her by shouting at the top of his voice:

"Go away! Run! You've walked into a trap! Run for help!"

In a twinkling the woman's hand was snapped over his mouth. Savagely he bit at it. She whipped it away and grabbed a towel. But before she could slap it over his lips he had repeated his loud-voiced warning to the person outside, whose face he had seen for an instant at the window. He knew that face. It was that of the little tattoo artist. She had fooled Wyn, it seemed, and approached the cabin from another direction while the blonde was waiting on the porch.

With the towel over his mouth and twisted at the back of his neck he could make no further outcry. Cass Starr had sprung to life and now rushed out into the night. Both Tyler and the woman listened with bated breath, until presently, from a distance, there came a piercing scream. Three minutes later Cass Starr opened the door and led Nan Sundy in by the wrist.

Her face was pallid and she trembled, but her dark eyes shot defiance at her captor. Starr rudely pushed her onto a chair and locked the door.

"Take the towel away now, Wyn," he said, chuckling. "Lake and his lady friend may wish to say 'How d'ye do' to each other."

Wyn untwisted the towel. Tyler and Nan gazed into each other's eyes.

"You did your best, and I thank you," said Tyler. "Don't worry a bit now. These people don't dare harm you. I suppose the police are right behind you."

Nan took her cue and nodded.

Starr and Wyn laughed outright.

"Good work!" cried Starr. "And the little lady plays right up to you, too. I've seen some wonderful acting tonight, Wyn."

"You'd see more than that if you had about three more drinks," sneeringly said Wyn. "Well, we've got both of 'em. Now get at the girl and see if you can make her tell what she knows."

"Maybe we'd better leave that for Kile, since you think I've made such a mess of things," said Starr loftily. "Will he get in tonight?"

"Sure. He was to come in the machine after he'd ditched the

dick. He was shadowed from the studio, all right. I was watching from the window of the drug store on the corner. It will take him longer to get here than it did me—an hour more, I'd say. You take Lake back to the tunnel."

"No, not till Kile comes," said Starr. "I've told Lake what's to happen to him, and he'll take any chance now."

"You ought to've thought of that before you brought him in and spilled it to him," she said witheringly. "Tie the girl up, then, and we'll wait for Kile."

Starr acted on this advice. Nan seemed too terrified to struggle, and soon she was roped to her chair. She and Tyler sat looking miserably into each other's face. Wyn Godfrey went about certain slipshod household duties. Cass Starr buried himself in the city papers that Wyn had brought.

Tyler's eyes asked a question. Nan sorrowfully shook her head. Then he knew that she had in reality been drawn into Kiley and Wyn's trap, and that she had played a lone hand to save him. He wondered if she liked his looks, now that she had seen him unmasked. He knew that he wanted her to, whether or not they were destined to escape with their lives.

Almost two hours had passed before a heavy step sounded on the little proch of the cabin. Wyn and Starr sprang to their feet. Starr unlocked the door, and in came Austin Kiley, as immaculately dressed as ever.

"Oh-ho!" he cried jovially, devouring Nan Sundy with his eyes. "Good work, Wyn! She fell nicely, didn't she?"

He wheeled and scowled at Tyler. "What's this bird doing here?" he asked, eyebrows drawn down.

"Oh, Friend Cass began hitting up the booze and got lonesome," drawled Wyn. "So he brings this fellow in to have somebody to talk to. And he tells him everything—and I got here just in time to keep—"

"Shut up, can't you?" growled Starr. "No harm's been done. You talk too much!"

At any other time Austin Kiley might have been angry with his fellow criminal. Now, however, he only laughed lightly. It was apparent that his mind was engrossed with something else. Tyler Lake soon interpreted the meaning of this, when he caught Kiley casting surreptitious glances of admiration at the demure tattoo artist. Wyn Godfrey saw it, too, and angrily gnawed her lips.

"You shook the dick all right, did you, Kile?" she asked crisply.

"Easy," returned the other. "I saw him go in a drug store and telephone his chief that he'd lost me."

"And I waited in the studio till the chief telephoned the result to the girl here," said Wyn. "It was laughable, Kile. With me right there, she could only stutter. Then I went out, and she was obliged to follow at once or let me get away."

"Well, let's take Lake back to his hole," suggested Kiley. "Then we'll see if we can find a way to learn what this Jane knows. Keep the ropes about him. I guess the two of us can handle him."

One on each side of him, both armed, the men led Tyler Lake through the door. With his last look into the cabin his eyes were on Nan Sundy. He smiled as best he could to cheer her up. She tried to smile back at him, but her eyes filled with tears, and she burst into low sobbing.

In the tunnel Kiley and Starr chained their intended victim to the heavy stone once more, Kiley flashing a spotlight over the rocky walls.

"The dynamite's buried there," said he, pointing to a spot in the dirt floor several feet out of Tyler's reach. "I thought you might care to know."

Tyler Lake made no reply.

Kiley and Starr went out and piled rocks in front of the tunnel entrance. Faint moonlight streamed in between them. A little later Tyler heard the closing of the cabin door.

CHAPTER XV
THE SWITCH

In the cabin Nan Sundy, bound to her chair, bravely faced Wyn Godfrey, Austin Kiley, and Cass Starr.

Kiley leaned forward, rested his forearms on his knees, and locked his fingers.

"Now," he said, "I want you to tell us what you did after doping the ink with which you tattooed Mrs. Kiley, stealing the photograph of my eye from the book, *Thou Art the Man*, and went away from us that night."

"And I don't propose to tell you one single word," Nan told him through her white teeth.

Kiley leaned back and surveyed her speculatively.

"I rather like you," he remarked.

"Cut out that bunk, Kile," Wyn ordered harshly.

Kiley shrugged and winked at Cass Starr. "Don't butt in, Wyn, dear," he drawled.

"Don't 'Wyn dear' me!" snapped the blonde woman. "I'm on to you, you rattlesnake! Get busy with the girl. Let's finish our job and get the money; then I'll get out of your sight forever."

Kiley shrugged again and addressed himself to Nan.

"So you won't tell one single word," he mimicked. "But I imagine you're going to change your mind about that. Listen, now. Do you see that battery box over there in the corner? Well, I'm going to tell you what's scheduled to happen tomorrow morning when the switch is closed. After you hear that I think you'll be glad to do about anything I say."

"I wouldn't tell her, Kile," put in Cass Starr. "I believe she knows a lot too much already."

Rapidly he recounted what Tyler had told him of his asking for help by painting messages on Nan's arm.

Kiley stared at him. "But he couldn't have conveyed much by that method," he protested.

"I know more than you think," Nan gravely bluffed, "and there are certain things that you don't know. I may seem to have walked into your trap today, but—" She came to a dead stop and tried to look chagrined at her own frankness.

"Another good little bluffer!" exclaimed Cass, laughing.

"Pure bluff," added Wyn. "No one followed her; I took pains to see about that."

"And I'm sure I lost the dick that was trailing me," put in Kiley. "No, Nan, your little bluff won't work. So get busy and tell us what you've done. If you don't I'll have to make you—though I hate to, I assure you."

He waited expectantly, but Nan said nothing.

"Afer we blow this man up in the tunnel tomorrow and ship his body East," said Kiley, watching closely for the effect of his words, "we'll have to keep you here under my kind care until the bereaved widow and friend Cass can attend to our business in New York. I assure you I'll be a tender guardian. But you won't be set free for a month, at least, I think. Insurance companies are slow and cautious when they are asked to let go of their money. You won't mind staying here for a month with me, will you, Nan?"

Her dark eyes flashed fire at him.

"You'll have to stay, whether you like it or not," he went on. "But right now we must know what you did after you left us that night with the photograph of my eye. And right now you're going to tell us all about It."

Nan elevated and lowered her eyebrows in high disdain.

"Oh, well," said Kiley, yawning as he rose, "I'll heat the poker. Take off one of her shoes, Wyn."

A chill coursed through Nan Sundy from head to feet as Wyn, with a malignant laugh, stooped before her and removed one of her shoes. Kiley had stepped to the cookstove and thrust a poker through the grate into the glowing coals.

"I don't like using this stuff, especially on you," he said sincerely, turning to Nan. "But we've simply got to know whether any detectives are watching for us. We know that you went to one, because I was followed from your studio; but we don't know who is at the head of the business. If he is clever enough to suspect an insurance fraud he could take the photograph of my eye to all the companies and have it compared with their lists of descriptive records. Mine is on file in New York, of course; but the company has a branch in Frisco. We must know all about it, to avoid running into a trap later on."

He removed the poker from the fire. It glowed red and sputtered. In horrified fascination Nan gazed at it. He replaced it in the coals and turned to her once more.

"Come, tell us everything," he urged. "Next time I take the poker out, I'll— Well, you'll see!"

Nan clenched her teeth and closed her eyes. Her brain reeled, and a nauseating sickness crept over her.

The only sound to be heard now was the low song of the night wind in the pine trees about the cabin. Wyn Godfrey's face was white but determined. Cass Starr moved uneasily from time to time, and, with his eyes on Wyn, slyly poured a stiff drink of whisky and tossed it off. Only Austin Kiley seemed complete master of his emotions.

Once more he removed the poker from the coals. It was at white heat now. He walked with it towards Nan and stooped before her.

Nan's breath seemed almost to choke her. Dizzily her senses swam away into oblivion, only to return with sickening suddenness. She tried to cry out, but no sound came from her lips.

"Will you tell?" said Kiley's low voice through the tense stillness of the room.

There was a moment's wait. Nan could not have spoken a word, had she wished to. She could not even nod her head. She prayed for unconsciousness, but total unconsciousness would not come to her relief.

She felt Kiley's strong fingers twining themselves about her ankle. She was powerless to prevent him from lifting her foot. Nearer and nearer came the white-hot poker. Through her stocking the sole of her foot felt the hot breath of the iron, growing fiercer and fiercer as Kiley slowly moved the poker closer. A little moan escaped her. Once more her eyelids fell.

"Your stocking's beginning to scorch," warned Kiley with cruel gentleness. "The iron will soon touch your foot. Better tell."

Another wait which seemed like hours. Then she heard Kiley's strong teeth gritting with angry determination.

"All right," he said. "Here goes."

His fingers tightened on her ankle. At last a scream rang from her lips, and she struggled desperately. Then—

Crash! Crash! The windows on two sides of the cabin burst into a thousand fragments. The door went spinning from its hinges. Through a red haze Nan saw men clambering in both windows,

with automatic pistols levelled. Others rushed in from the door.
Wyn Godfrey screamed piercingly.

A heavily shot foot hurtled between Nan and the stooping Kiley,
and the implement of torture went spinning over the floor. With
a bellow of rage Kiley sprang to his feet, struck Jefferson Mercer
a stunning blow in the face, and, dashing detectives right and left,
leaped towards the battery box.

"You got me!" he yelled. "But I'll send one man to his doom, at
any rate!"

He pounced upon the box and grabbed the switch. Revolvers
barked snappily, and Kiley, mortally wounded, reeled backward on
his heels. But he caught himself, reached out once more, and shot
the switch into place.

A deafening roar. The cabin rocked. Dishes leaped from a cupboard and crashed on the floor. Outside, the limbs of the pines lashed
the cabin in tempestuous fury. Through the clouds of powder smoke
Nan saw Kiley grin fiendishly, then fall dead across the battery box.

Nan fell back in somebody's arms. Her eyes looked up into the
eyes of the owner of the arms, then she fainted quietly away.

Strange indeed was the scene that confronted her when, a little
later, she came back to consciousness. She had been unbound, and
her shoe had been replaced on her foot. Still those arms were about
her, and she did not struggle to free herself as she gazed at the
ruined room, the bleeding body of Kiley, Mercer, and his squad of
detectives, and the handcuffs on the wrists of Wyn Godfrey and Cass
Starr. Half heedingly she listened to Jefferson Mercer's words, as he
spoke to the man upon whose shoulder her head lay so peacefully.

"It was the photograph of the eye that Miss Sundy got that
cleared the mystery," he said. "I scented an insurance fraud, as
everything pointed that way. I had all the San Francisco insurance

companies look up their records; then, as they found nothing, I had them wire their home offices. At last one located the tattooed eye in New York City. I sent the photograph, and received a wire telling me that the eye corresponded with the photograph of the tattoo mark on record.

"I didn't tell Miss Sundy outright that a man's life hung in the balance. I thought it best not to do so. Plucky girl. I couldn't stop her. She walked right into their trap."

"I couldn't imagine who it was when your men came crawling into the cave and turned me loose," said the voice of Tyler Lake. "How did you know I was in the tunnel?"

"We were listening at the window," replied Mercer. "This is a mining country. I saw the battery box. Then I heard a tunnel mentioned and sent a couple of my men to hunt for it. I knew at once how you were to be disposed of. The time they took to find you forced us to let the attempted torture of Miss Sundy go as far as it did. I was afraid this Kiley would jump for the electric switch if we broke in. So I had to wait till you were safely out of the tunnel. That Kiley was a vindictive crook. I knew him the moment I saw him, though his name's not Kiley. I took no chances when he jumped at the switch of the battery box, even though I knew you were out of the tunnel. I didn't know but that the cabin might have had dynamite planted under it, too, with the idea of blowing it and everything in it to atoms if the conspirators realized they were to lose. So I had ordered the boys to let Kiley have it if he jumped for the switch. And there he lies."

"But how did you get here in the first place?" queried Tyler. "Were you following Miss Sundy?"

"No. They got away clean with her. And Kiley actually lost my shadow in San Francisco. But after he'd done so he foolishly went to have a Turkish bath. And for three weeks I've had a man waiting for him in the bath house. He phoned me when Kiley came in; and when Kiley left, pink and fresh, we trailed his car to the edge of these woods, and followed him afoot to the cabin."

Mercer paused, and his eyes twinkled. "Isn't Miss Sundy conscious now?" he asked. "Perhaps she doesn't need your arms about her any longer, Mr. Lake."

"I think," said Tyler slowly, "that before very long I am going to ask her if I may keep them about her for the remainder of our natural lives."

The little tattoo artist closed her eyes so that the man who held her would not know that she was conscious and had heard.

THE STARFISH TATTOO (1921)

Arthur Tuckerman

Arthur Tuckerman (1896–1955) was an American educated in Britain at Oxford and, as a boy, at the prestigious Cheltenham College, an experience he would later recount in his first book *The Old School Tie* (1954). Tuckerman produced a steady stream of short fiction for British and American magazines between 1918 and 1925 (with a handful more later), many of which set their action in Africa, where he travelled with his family as a young man.

As the title suggests, "The Starfish Tattoo" is another story with a nautical background though it is not the tattoo's maritime connections that provides its primary significance here. "The Starfish Tattoo" draws on a tradition of representation in which tattoos become important in legal questions of identification and inheritance. This theme is prominent, for instance, in Henry Rider Haggard's 1888 novel *Mr. Meeson's Will*, in which a shipwrecked and ailing publisher, finding no paper to hand, has his will tattooed on his wife's back. Haggard's novel in turn draws on the famous Tichborne Case from the 1860s and 70s when a claimant to the Tichborne baronetcy was refused when it turned out that, unbeknown to the claimant, the genuine, missing baron had extensive tattoos. In Tuckerman's tale it is the impoverished figure of Royden, who trying desperately to restore his ruined fortunes, is called upon to negotiate the singularity of the tattoo as a marker of identity.

THEY WERE SEATED AT A RICKETY LITTLE TABLE IN A Pernambuco drink shop, Royden and his friend Cawlish. It was an untidy, evil-smelling place, tucked away in a dark alley not far from the water-front—the kind of place that seems instinctively to cringe from the candid glare of a noonday sun.

Royden surveyed the swaying figure opposite him with a sense of growing disgust.

"Downhill, Cawlish," he said. "Every day a little lower. Pretty soon they'll call us just plain beach combers—the both of us."

Cawlish stared at him, a look of vague distress in his watery blue eyes. He made a palpable, rather pitiful effort to pull himself together, and he seemed suddenly apologetic.

"You don't have to go down with me, Royden. You got a chance left; you can leave the stuff alone, and I can't. Listen. Last night I got to thinkin' about you. Why don't you go back—to the States—and start again? You can do it, because you're young and you got the advantage of bein' well born. See what I mean, Royden?"

He paused a moment, to gulp down the vicious contents of the glass before him.

"What I mean is," he went on with a kind of drunken persistency, "you've got the right makins'. Why, dammit, look at the very way you *sip* your liquor, instead of swilling it down—like the rest of us swine. Beat it, Royden, before this place gets you!"

Royden laughed harshly.

"Shut up, Cawlish. You weren't born to be a preacher."

Cawlish was always absurd like this—when he was drunk. But the thing was true, just the same. There came into Royden's mind, then, a dim but vaguely beautiful picture—a big, comfortable, white house surrounded by green lawns, an old-fashioned garden of hollyhocks and Canterbury bells, a peaceful New England road, arched with leafy elms—he had been a decent fellow then, the pride of a proud old family. They had sent him to college. All that, of course had been years ago.

A sudden spasm of pain crossed his brow as his thoughts turned to that tragic night at college, when he had risen unsteadily from the card table and crept to his room—every cent he had, and a great deal more, pledged to his friends. A night of agony, and the next morning—a forged cheque; it had been so simple.

Later on, discovery—and flight.

Of the intervening years his impressions were varied, and lacking any coherent sequence, a series of vivid cinematic impressions; many ships, many ports, many lands; brutal dockyard work in a British seaport; a longing for something better, and then a year in a foreign regiment at a torrid Sahara post, where there was a relentless, pitiless, white sun. Desertion, sudden and swift, when he could stand it no longer. Then the Brazilian rubber plantation, which turned out a failure, like the rest. And now he was down to the very dregs.

Cawlish began droning again.

"There's a yacht down at the harbour, a big, white yacht—bound for New York. Fellow on board her told me a steward died last night, of fever. You could do that, Royden. An' then—in New York you could find somethin' to do worth-while. See what I mean?"

Royden shot him a vicious glance.

"You're an idealist, Cawlish—and a hell of a poor one at that."

Nevertheless, as he left the drink shop Royden paused to glance at himself appraisingly in a cracked mirror near the door. He saw himself, a tall, loose-limbed figure, with sharp and bitter features. He looked, almost, as if he hated the very world he lived in. His clothes were worn and faded, a heavy, reddish beard sprouted from his gaunt chin. He laughed again, so suddenly and bitterly that Cawlish staggered away from him, cringing with fear.

That very evening Royden brushed his clothes carefully and strolled down to the harbour. He had secured the steward's berth aboard the yacht *Thessaly* by six o'clock.

The *Thessaly* was a palatial craft. From the crew Royden learned that her owner, John Blackstone, was an American—the man whose brains and money had made the great Amazon railroad across Brazil a human possibility; he had made the building of it his life's greatest work. And now, after ten long years, Blackstone was returning home to enjoy the fruits of a gigantic success.

As the yacht swung her nose to sea, Royden, clad in a new, white uniform, served dinner to Blackstone in the pink and gold luxury of a Louis XIV saloon amidships. Dish after dish, cooked to perfection by a French chef, came from the galley, while Blackstone ate in silence—seemingly oblivious of Royden's presence. By the time the meal was over Royden felt an inexplicable sense of hatred toward this man who had everything.

The delicate luxuries of the yacht had, as a matter of fact, brought back to Royden certain vivid memories of the past, of the things that had once been his for the asking, and which he had placidly accepted as his natural right. The softly upholstered armchairs; the silver that gleamed brightly under the rose-tinted lamps; the fine, white damask; the cut-glass decanters containing rich, rare wines—all these things affected him queerly. He found himself wishing, bitterly, that he had stayed down there with Cawlish—in the dregs, where he now belonged.

Off the coast of Martinique a week later the *Thessaly* plunged into a thick, deadening fog. Royden, in his bunk, heard the mournful shriek of the fog horn, and cursed it because it had awakened him. This was about midnight. Presently he dropped off again into a fitful sleep.

Hours later he regained his senses—very slowly, as if he were emerging from some deep trance. He found himself lying on the cabin floor, his head throbbing painfully where it had struck the door, when he had been flung from his bunk. He sat up suddenly and opened his eyes—to find the cabin in pitch darkness. He shouted, then, at the top of his voice in a sudden, unreasoning fear. But no answer came.

In a frenzy of fear he flung on his clothes and staggered out of the cabin. The whole ship was in darkness. No sound broke the stillness, except the padding of his own stockinged feet. Eventually he managed to grope his way to the deck.

The night was thick with a swirling, enveloping dampness that hid all but a few feet of deck from view; it made him feel suddenly clammy from head to foot; the silence was complete but for the sullen lapping of the becalmed sea against the yacht's hull. He made his way forward along a deck that was slanted at an ugly angle, and discovered a gaping wound in the starboard bow, where the jagged edge of a reef—ambushed in the grey blanket of fog—had dealt the yacht a cowardly blow. Royden knew that she was sinking—but very slowly, almost imperceptibly.

And then he saw that all the lifeboats were gone, that every davit was empty. Apparently the captain, the crew, and Blackstone had fled in a wild panic—without a thought of him. The cowards! He cursed them one and all, loudly.

He turned aft, unsteadily, owing to the absurd angle of the deck, trying vainly all the while to pierce the thick darkness with his eyes. He searched with his hands for the touch of a lifeboat, a raft, anything upon which he might make his escape. As he breasted the chart house his feet tripped suddenly upon a heavy object lying across the deck, and he sprawled to his knees.

He fumbled in his pocket and found a match; lighting it, he held the yellow flare above the thing he had tripped upon. It was the body of John Blackstone; his high, white forehead fearfully marred, where some falling deck tackle had struck him a mortal blow. Something in the dead man's face made Royden look again. An uncanny feeling crept over him. It was as if he were looking at himself. In death the wrinkles had left Blackstone's features, making him look some ten years younger. Blackstone was tall, and loosely built, just as Royden was; Blackstone's hair was of a sandy reddish colour—so was Royden's; they were about the same weight.

In two points only did they differ; Blackstone was clean shaven, while Royden wore a heavy russet beard. The other thing Royden did not notice until later, when he had read the letter in Blackstone's pocketbook. They were, of course, dressed as differently as two men could be. Blackstone wore a heavy suit of rich grey tweed while Royden was clad in a white duck uniform.

Presently Royden went into the chart house and found a lamp; he brought it out on deck and placed it beside Blackstone's body. Then, coolly and deliberately, he proceeded to search the dead man's clothes.

He found a thin diamond-studded watch, a gold fountain pen, and a pocketbook. In the pocketbook were some eight hundred dollars in Brazilian currency, several visiting cards, and a letter bearing a New York postmark, addressed to Blackstone at Pernambuco.

Royden opened the letter and read it by the feeble orange glow of the lamp. The heading bore the name of a well-known New York club. The letter ran:

> DEAR JOHN: All your old friends, and I particularly, were very glad to get the news that you were coming home after all these years. I think you'll drop back quickly into the old ways. Cedar Point is in order, in fact I went over it thoroughly the other day, and I've managed to get a few good servants. We long for your safe arrival; some of us old stick-at-homes persist in thinking that a long sea voyage is always attended with nameless perils, in spite of wireless and such things—

Royden smiled grimly. He continued to peruse the letter hurriedly, until he reached the final paragraph. This he reread several times; a cunning gleam of light came into his eyes—at the birth of a sudden, fantastic idea:

> After ten years we'll hardly know you. You must have changed like the rest of us, but the old crowd is still here, John, ready to welcome you—Lefferts, Van Bruns, and the rest, grey-haired and fat in their middle age. And even if you've changed a whole lot, I told the fellows—jokingly—that we'd always be able to recognize you by that queer little starfish tattooed on your wrist! Remember that night, years ago—after one of your big parties—when we all went down to the harbour, and several of us insisted on making an old sailor tattoo us? A foolish prank, but it amused us at the time. Always your old friend,

> HARRIS FLETCHER.

Royden replaced the letter in the pocketbook and peered sharply at the dead man's hands. Upon the left wrist he discovered a five-pointed starfish, tattooed in bright blue ink.

He smiled slowly as he thought of Blackstone's house, illuminated and warm and hospitable, filled with well-trained servants, waiting in vain for a dead man. To live for a month—even for a week—amid those comforts which had been his birthright! To escape, just for a little while, from the everlasting hardship, the grime and filth, the brutality of the life that he had led for all these years! If only he could do that!

He took the lamp below and made a hurried inspection of the hold; the water was filtering in very slowly. There would be time. Eyes filled with deep purpose, he hurried aft to Blackstone's cabin; there he found what he wanted—a pair of scissors, a safety razor, a cake of soap.

At dawn on the following morning the Panama-Atlantic liner *Culebra*, bound for New York, sighted a piece of floating wreckage off the southern coast of Martinique. A lifeboat was launched immediately, while the liner hove to. When the rescue crew returned, fifteen minutes later, they brought with them a clean-shaven, affluent-looking man dressed in grey tweed. To avoid notoriety this gentleman fled to a cabin, requesting the purser that his identity be kept secret, if possible. It soon became rumoured, however, that the shipwrecked man was John Blackstone.

It was some time before Royden could accustom himself to the deference with which he was treated aboard the *Culebra*; he began to realize, slowly, the power of Blackstone's name. He remained as much as he could in the solitude of his cabin, and found stewards at his beck and call to obey his slightest command. It was all very new and pleasant, and as the ship approached New York his plans took definite shape within his mind.

He was too level-headed to presume for an instant that he could carry the thing on indefinitely without discovery. He came to the conclusion, that the sensible thing for him to do would be to live Blackstone's life for a period of a few weeks only, in which time he could draw from the dead man's bank some fifty thousand dollars. Fifty thousand dollars! It was hard to realize those figures! And then—before it became necessary for John Blackstone to look up any of his old friends, and plunge once more into the intimacies of social life—he would disappear—into oblivion. He would go to South Africa, or Australia perhaps, where there would be little likelihood of being traced. His working days would be over, too!

As the *Culebra* left quarantine and slowly passed by the Statue of Liberty, Royden noticed a bronzed sailor polishing the brass of the taffrail at his side; the man had a python and a dancing girl brazenly tattooed upon his muscular forearm.

"Who did that work of art for you?" Royden asked, nodding at the tattoo with casual good humour.

The sailor straightened up and grinned.

"Old fellow by the name of Skinner. Watchman at the Cuban fruit docks, near the Brooklyn Navy Yard. He often makes a little spare cash doing that kind of thing." He gazed for a moment, proudly, at the dancing girl and then resumed his polishing.

Royden landed at noon; he hailed a taxicab as soon as he had left the pier.

"Go to the Cuban fruit docks," he told the driver.

The tattooing proved less painful than he had anticipated.

★

When Royden reached Cedar Point, that night, he was overawed. The great marble house, the terraced rose gardens, the sloping lawns, the lofty rooms, stunned him with their sheer magnificence. The servants, all of them new to the place, gave him little cause for worry it was obvious that they suspected nothing. Evening clothes lay ready for him upon an armchair in the great white-and-gold bedroom overlooking the garden which he understood had always been his; and an obsequious valet prepared for him a steaming bath.

"Mr. Fletcher thought you would want your old room," said the valet, "so we prepared it for you. Is everything quite right, sir?"

Royden nodded quickly.

"Is—is Mr. Fletcher in the house now?"

"No, sir. He was sorry not to be able to welcome you, but he said it would be impossible for him to leave town for several days. He didn't expect the yacht in so soon, sir. You wrote him that you would stay over in Havana a few days, I believe."

"So I did," said Royden, and breathed an unconscious little sigh of relief. He must avoid seeing this man Fletcher.

For an hour Royden revelled in his newfound luxury. At the sound of a sonorous gong he went down to dinner. The delicacies which were served to him seemed strangely new, but none the less palatable; strangely enough, all those hard years had not succeeded in banishing the latent sense of the epicure within him.

After dinner he found his way to the library, a place of wainscoted walls and priceless carved oak. He sank into an armchair before a crackling fire, lighted a large Havana cigar, and gave himself up to the ecstasy of sheer contentment. His optimism grew; he began to entertain hopes of a prolonged stay at Cedar Point. Perhaps he might even draw a hundred thousand dollars before he decided to sink into oblivion. Why not? The thing was so much easier than he had expected!

He went to New York the next morning in the buff-upholstered limousine which he found waiting for him. In the busy, hurrying crowds of Wall Street he met no one who seemed to recognize him. As he entered the Hudson National Bank, where Blackstone kept his money, he felt a sudden qualm of terror. Supposing he should fail—at the critical moment? Presently he recovered his self-possession sufficiently to send one of Blackstone's cards into the vice president's office.

A stout, nervous little man came hurrying out to meet him. He grasped Royden's hand eagerly.

"Glad to see you home again, Mr. Blackstone. Many years since I've seen you, isn't it? I hope we managed the Amazon transactions to your satisfaction. And that last loan, to the Para people, how about that?"

Royden nodded hurriedly.

"I'll have to go into that with you later."

The little man babbled on.

"You've changed somewhat, Mr. Blackstone, but I never forget a man's face—once I've seen it. It must have done you good down there. You actually look younger that when you left—ten years ago, wasn't it?"

He broke off, suddenly aware that Royden was growing impatient.

"Is it a cheque today, Mr. Blackstone?"

"Yes," said Royden, "I'm afraid I'll have to trouble you for a pretty big one. Lost all my ready cash when my yacht sank—you've probably read about it in the papers. Well, you'd better give me—say—five thousand, in thousand-dollar bills."

The vice president smiled.

"We're used to big sums when dealing with you, Mr. Blackstone."

In the privacy of his cabin aboard the *Culebra* Royden had given Blackstone's signature infinite study. And so, for the second time in his life, he put his pen to a check and signed, with a careless assurance, a name that was not his. He left the bank ten minutes later.

To Royden that first day in New York was like a strange, vivid dream. Everywhere he went the mere mention of Blackstone's name evoked deference and respect. The Fifth Avenue tailor, from whom he ordered several suits of the finest imported cloth, took infinite pains with his measurements. He dined at the best hotels, upon the fat of the land, and spent the evening witnessing a Broadway musical show from the isolated splendour of a twenty-five-dollar box.

It was some time after midnight when his limousine drew up before the marble steps of Cedar Point. Royden found his bedroom uncomfortably close that night, and just before getting into bed he crossed over to the window to draw apart the heavy silken curtains. A faint, rose-scented breath of air drifted in from the terraces below. He drew the curtains swiftly apart; a man stepped out from behind them. Royden saw the gleam of a revolver levelled at his head and threw up his hands instinctively.

The stranger, a wizened, shabbily dressed little creature, backed him step by step towards the bed.

"John Blackstone," he said, "I've been waiting fifteen years for this moment. Sit down on that bed, don't move—and listen to me."

He was an old man, puny and wrinkled, but the unflinching purpose in his steely grey eyes made Royden suddenly afraid. He sat down hurriedly upon the edge of the bed.

"Blackstone," said the other sharply. "Do you remember the Golden Arrow copper mine?"

Royden had, of course, never heard of the Golden Arrow, but he nodded instinctively. It was becoming second nature with him to play the part of John Blackstone. But he wished fervently that the old man would put down that revolver.

The stranger nodded toward an ormulu clock ticking on the marble mantelpiece.

"It is now ten minutes before one, Blackstone. At one o'clock I am going to shoot you. And if you shout, or try to offer any kind of resistence before that time, I'll not hesitate to put a bullet through you at once. Still, I think it's only fair to let you know why you're going to die—so I'm going to tell you my story."

Royden felt the sweat beading upon his brow. Who was this creature who had hidden himself to await his coming? A madman, probably. Perhaps he could humour him—until relief came. Just then the hands of the ormulu clock jumped a fraction of a minute, with a nerve-wracking little whirr and—

"Listen," he began desperately, "I'm not the man—"

But the other motioned him to be silent.

"I know all about it," he said with a grim smile. "You took all my money, and the money of hundreds of others, with your sweet promises. And you knew all the time the thing wasn't worth a damn cent, curse you!

"On account of you my wife is dead, of a broken heart—she died penniless—and my children are slaving their youth away in a factory. Oh, I know you all right, John Blackstone. Don't think I'm mad—I learned of your trickery after you'd fled to Brazil, and I vowed that if you ever returned to this country you wouldn't live forty-eight hours—and I'm here to keep that vow!"

Royden's voice broke the stillness then, and it was shrill with terror.

"How do you know that I'm John Blackstone? You can't prove it!" The little man sneered.

"Of course I know you. It was you, yourself, who persuaded me into that devilish scheme. I was a clerk in the National Wheel Company, when you were president of it. I suppose you'll say you don't remember that morning when you called us into your office—"

"No!" Royden shouted. "I don't remember. Because I'm *not* Blackstone!"

The stranger stared at him for an instant, and then burst into laughter.

"My God! You've got a sense of humour, haven't you—to think I'd swallow that? You've grown a little thinner, perhaps—maybe you had to work down there, instead of growing fat on poor men's money—"

Royden glanced fearfully at the clock. It lacked but four minutes of one.

"For God's sake," he whimpered, "listen to me! I'm not Blackstone. He's dead—at the bottom of the sea. I'll tell you how it happened—only, put that thing away—give me a chance!"

The stranger was fingering his revolver.

"I suppose I'll have to listen," he said wearily, "but you'll die just the same—so what's the use?"

Then Royden poured out his story in a torrent of words, almost incoherent at times, while the other listened with a contemptuous curl of his lips. In frantic haste he outlined everything that had happened to him since the yacht struck the reef, but he kept his head enough to omit any mention of the tattoo. He felt, somehow, that that part of the affair would seem incredible—and the other man had apparently failed to notice the blemish upon his wrist. He slipped his hands furtively into the pockets of his dressing gown. At two minutes before one he finished his story.

"So you see," he concluded breathlessly, pleadingly, "I'm no more John Blackstone than you are, and—"

"It's ingenious," snarled the other, "mighty ingenious. But I don't swallow it. In a moment that clock is going to strike one—"

His bright little eyes shone with sudden triumph.

"But listen. I'll give you a sporting chance. There's one way— only one—in which you can convince me that you're not John Blackstone. He had a starfish tattooed on his wrist—we clerks used to joke about it, I remember. Seems he had it done when he was a kid, after a wild party."

Royden's cheeks were white as death itself.

"You've no right—" he whimpered, but the old man had risen from his chair, flourishing his weapon.

"Quick! Show me those hands!"

Royden's hands shot above his head. Upon the tanned skin of his right wrist a five-pointed starfish was tattooed.

"Ah!" shouted the other triumphantly. "I thought so. There's the proof."

He raised his revolver swiftly. Royden's muscles tensed; he was all alert, ready to spring; he wasn't going to die like that—without putting up a fight. Just then the ormulu clock whirred—and struck one.

The old man's brows were knitted in a puzzled frown; he kept his revolver levelled, but he seemed suddenly and curiously baffled.

"Don't try to move," he commanded, "but answer me. Where did you get that tattoo—if you're not John Blackstone?"

Royden felt certain now that the man was crazy.

"It was done when I landed," he said, "to imitate Blackstone. For God's sake—why do you ask that?"

The old man smiled—a queer, twisted little smile.

"Because," he said very slowly, "you've saved yourself—by a fool's mistake. John Blackstone's tattoo was on his *left* wrist!"

Suddenly he darted across the room, and flung open a closet door. Two men, in evening clothes, stepped out, blinking in the sudden glare.

"Gentlemen," said the old man, "you have heard the confession. The moment I saw this fellow in a Fifth Avenue tailor's this morning—and heard him give Blackstone's name—I knew that he was not my lifelong friend. His slip in the tattoo matter only served to confirm my suspicions. Instead of denouncing him there I decided to make him confess. You bet me that I couldn't; I think I've won my bet—in ten minutes."

To Royden, haggard and miserable, he turned with a smile.

"You see," he explained softly, "I happen to be Harris Fletcher, whose letter you stole from John's body. My poor fellow—besides that trivial mistake of the tattoo, you made another and much bigger error; you overlooked one thing—that when a big, lovable man dies, his friends live—to protect his memory."

THE SECRET TATTOO (1927)

Frederick Ames Coates

Frederick Ames Coates (1890–?) was a prolific author of pulp detective fiction and an occasional dabbler in Westerns who was active from the 1920s until the early 1940s. Apart from listings of the stories he published and some brief details on his family, very little information on Coates is available, perhaps a necessary hazard of a writer who devoted his creative energies to the most ephemeral form of fiction.

"The Secret Tattoo" is another tale that engages with tattooing's association with criminality, a connection that has both a social and a narrative dimension. On the one hand, the long history of the tattoo as a mark of the outsider makes it a frequent sign of the outlaw or the degenerate, forging an illicit living on the fringes of respectability. On the other hand, tattoos often play a very useful role in the plotting of detective mysteries as a clandestine way of communicating misbegotten information, such as, most commonly, the whereabouts of the hidden loot. Coates' story makes use of both of these motifs. A criminal gang display their allegiance in a collective tattoo design, while the proceeds of a bank job can only be recovered if the secret tattoo of the story's title can be located. If this seems to make for a rather conventional detective-fiction take on the tattoo, Coates has a surprise in store with an ingenious twist in the tale.

S O RAPIDLY DID AL BRECK SLIDE DOWN FROM HIS PERCH IN THE tree that the rough bark cut his hands and nearly tore the bandage off his wrist. He cursed softly but savagely at the twinge which came from his injured member. Quite characteristically, it did not occur to him to blame his own heedless haste: a haste which was entirely unnecessary. He had just seen, across the railroad cut which separated him from the fringe of the village, a car drive out of the garage and on to the road beyond; had heard the creaking gate at the end of the driveway closed; had seen the car, with headlights turned on to dispel the early gathering dusk, start along the highway toward downtown. "Mouthpiece" Wilkes, living there entirely alone except for the dog, took his meals at a hotel in the village. He would not be likely to return from supper for an hour at least. One hour was time enough for what Breck planned, without crowding the minutes.

He thrust his way through the thicket, pushing aside the wet-leaved branches that seemed possessed to slap into his face. He paused on the brink of the grassless slope which led down to the tracks, and again indulged in purposeless anger. The freight train, which had been standing there only a moment ago, was now in motion. Far in the distance, towards the village station, he saw the lights of the caboose. It was one of those interminably long trains; a train of empties, of which an engine can pull thrice as many as it can loaded cars. It would be a good ten minutes, at the rate it was going, before it passed and left the track clear for him to cross.

Ordinarily, Al Breck would have thought nothing of making his way across a slowly moving freight train. One does not get any practice in hopping freights in a prison, however. Also, the rain which was helping him by bringing early darkness added to the hazards of the attempt.

The direction in which the train was going made a left-handed leap necessary. It was Al's left wrist, which was throbbing beneath its bandage, which would momentarily have to bear the bigger part of his weight. The man no longer hesitated, however, when he reached the cinder bed of the railroad. He took a few running steps alongside the train, made a leap and a grab, and, in an instant, had got a foothold on the slippery strap-iron step. He quickly swung himself around the corner onto the ladder at the end of the car. Then came a moment of greater danger as he made his way, with legs wide-straddled, between the two car ends to the iron ladder on the other side.

With a sigh of relief, he flung himself clear of the train and dropped to the ground. The rain-softened gravel of the embankment gave way under the impact of his feet, and started him sliding down towards the rails and the deadly wheels. Clawing with hands and knees, he stopped his sliding in time and crept up to safety. Savagely, he chalked it all up to the account of the man he was going to interview, the man who was going to pay for it all, just as he was going to pay for those prison years.

First, though, there was the matter of the dog. The ex-convict would get a pleasant foretaste of revenge by settling that score. The manner of settlement was already in mind; the means already at hand. In the long grass which throve in the protection of the wire fence of the Burney place, lay a broken-tined pitchfork which Breck had found yesterday. The man picked it up and thrust its cruel points through one of the rectangular openings in the wire fence, where it was accessible for use, but equally invisible from either side, owing to the rank grass. The fence itself was one of the modern kind so popular with progressive farmers: horse-high, hog-tight, and bull-strong. It would prove an effective barrier for a savage dog, though not for a man who had a pair of wire cutters in his pocket.

Al Breck stood for a moment surveying the Burney place from the rear. It was not a farm; though the house was an old one, reno-vated, which had originally been a farm homestead. Neither was it pretentious enough to be classed as an estate. Dan Burney, going into hiding, had certainly chosen an effective concealment. None of the old gang would have looked for him in so quiet a village, so far from the bright lights and the marts of spending. That was probably why, unlike so many crooks, Burney had finished his days in peace; had cheated his former pals by dying a natural death.

The garage, which had formerly been a woodshed, was attached to the house. Beside it, equally discernible from here or from the highway at the other side of the plot, was the diminutive hut where the unchained dog made its headquarters. Probably the animal was inside now; the rain would have driven it to shelter.

Al Breck picked up a stone. After a cautious glance about him, he heaved it with true aim, and it bounced hollowly from the roof of the kennel. He was rewarded with the sound of a quick growl. In a moment the animal was outside, sniffing suspiciously: a huge collie. Two more quickly flung stones thudded into the sod near the dog's feet. With savage satisfaction, Breck saw the animal turn and come bounding toward him through the dusk. It was an ideal watchdog in at least this particular: one did not have to spend much time or effort in getting its attention.

Without underestimating the ocular powers of the dog, or its power of scent, Breck made assurance doubly sure. He took a small flash light from his pocket, and, with his left hand, switched it on for an instant. Straight towards the point whence the flash had come, straight towards the man crouching in the gloom against the fence, the animal dashed. Its savage onrush was matched by the savage anticipation of the ex-convict who awaited it. His right hand grasped the long pitchfork handle; slid it backward on the smooth wire.

At just the proper instant, Breck lunged with all his strength. The two unbroken tines of the rusted fork found their mark in the throat and shaggy chest of the watchdog. Its angry barking degenerated to a gurgle. With cruel delight, Al Breck twisted the weapon about in both hands, throwing the writhing body of the dying animal from one side to another. Its struggles grew feebler. Soon it was only the dead weight of the dog that he was handling.

When he was quite certain that his four-footed enemy was no longer dangerous, the man tilted the pitchfork, grasped it at the top near the animal's body, and slid it through and over the wire fence. It was as well, however, not to leave the body lying here, too large to be effectively hidden in the grass; even though darkness had fallen, and though trespassers along the railroad right of way were likely to be few, if any.

The long train of empties was still passing, a short distance below him; slowly gathering speed on the long up grade Breck made out the yawning blackness of an open box-ear door coming towards him. He grinned at the easy solution of his problem.

He was poised and ready when the car came abreast. With a quick heave on the pitchfork, he threw it and its impaled burden into the blackness of the empty car. He heard the body slide across the floor and strike the closed door on the other side. No brakeman would find it there until the car reached its destination. Dan Burrney's watchdog was as dead as its master. Its final resting place, however, would be hundreds, perhaps thousands, of miles away from the resting place of the man who had trained it to repel intruders.

Al Breck, though of superstitious nature, was no better educated in superstitions than in other kinds of lore. The curative powers of "the hair of the dog that bit one" were unknown to him. The death of the animal, which had inflicted the wound on his wrist, however, did seem to ease the pain of the wrist. He forgot the ache as he applied himself to the completion of his task.

Cutting several strands of wire, he made a hole in the fence large enough to let his body wriggle through. Once inside the grounds, he wasted no time on unnecessary caution, but made his way directly to the house. The only danger had already been eliminated.

The house itself offered no effective barriers to the entrance of a man skilled in the ways of crime. Its neighbours, too, were sufficiently distant to render the danger of being seen or heard a negligible one.

Al Breck entered by the kitchen, but passed on quickly. The living room, too, he left for further inspection. A small study in a rear corner of the house held a desk that invited inspection. Making certain that the shades were drawn, he switched on his flash light and set to work.

He was rather disappointed at finding the desk not even locked. The contents of it proved as valueless for his purposes as the fact had led him to assume. Only one thing he found which challenged his attention: a loaded revolver. His eyes glistened; he slipped the weapon into his pocket. It clanked against the one which he already carried there.

Then he gave a chuckle, and removed the gun which he had found. He carefully extracted all its cartridges, and replaced it in the desk drawer where he had found it.

His search of the house was swift but thorough. In the flat drawer of the living-room table he found another gun, which he unloaded and left in its place. Aside from that, he found nothing to interest him. He was hardly disappointed, for he had really expected no better luck.

He was in a room in the upper storey when he heard the rusted hinges of the driveway gate creaking. He peered out and saw the lights of the car that headed in. He saw Lawyer Eugene Wilkes reascend to the seat and drive the car into the garage. By the time the attorney's footsteps crunched along the path toward the house, Breck was in the front hall behind the entrance door, so that, as it swung open, it would conceal him.

He waited, grinning, with his finger on the trigger of the gun in his pocket, while the bolt turned in the lock and the door opened. Even as it closed again, he did not move; for, in the dark hall, Lawyer Wilkes turned from him and made his way to the living room. The lights were snapped on; even in this village most of the houses were wired for electricity. The creak of a chair told him that the other man had seated himself, probably beside the table. Not the slightest suspicion of an alien presence had been aroused.

Breck steppd softly to the open door. Not until he spoke, did the other have an inkling that he was there.

"Hello, Mouthpiece!" he greeted.

Lawyer Wilkes nearly jumped from the chair with a ludicrous start. His jaw sagged open. He snapped it partly to as he recognized the apparition. "Oh, it's you! Breck, ain't it? Al Breck."

"You got me right, brother," said Breck with glinting eyes. The face of the man of law was crafty and cunning; but it could not conceal the dismay that shone from the little eyes.

"When were you 'sprung'? I wasn't expecting to see you," said the lawyer.

"I didn't think you was! But just sit right there comfortable. We're going to have a little talk." Breck removed his right hand from his pocket, but he patted the pocket significantly. "I understand you're executor, or whatever they call it, of Dan Burney's estate."

Lawyer Wilkes nodded. "That's why I'm here."

"Who get's the estate? How's it left?"

The lawyer fidgeted. "Well, you see, Dan didn't leave much of anything. By the time affairs are settled up—"

"You're a brimstone-eating liar," declared Al Breck calmly. "He left a plenty. And it wasn't his to leave, either. Them last two pay-roll jobs alone netted over a hundred thousand. There'd been no split made of it—unless you got yours, maybe. Dan Burney, as head of the gang, knew where it was cached; and he was the only one that wasn't jugged when they rounded us up. I aim to live fat from now on; fatter than old Burney lived in this out-of-the-way dump."

The lawyer opened his eyes wide, in pretended astonishment that did not deceive his captor. "Why, Dan did tell me, on one of the visits that I paid him here before he died, that he had a little something buried in a certain place in the middle of a flower bed in the yard. I had no idea it was any considerable amount. Let's go out there now; I'll get a spade."

Al Breck laughed harshly. "No good, Mouthpiece! I ain't fooled a bit. I know why you want to get me out in the yard; but it's no good even if I went. That dog of Burney's—"

He saw hope die in the lawyer's eyes, and laughed again. "That mutt's fangs ain't going to bother me any more! Oh, he got me once yesterday." Anger mounted to Beck's eyes at the memory. He advanced and showed his wrist, with an improvised bandage of iodine-stained gauze and surgeon's plaster. "Couldn't even go to a local doctor to have it dressed right, for fear he'd recognize the tattoo mark on my wrist. The same kind of a mark that all the other members of the gang had; that helped to identify us when we were pinched." He reached forward suddenly and grasped the lawyer's left hand, yanking it forward to expose the under side of the wrist, "You ain't got it on your wrist: the mark of the skull with red eyes. He didn't put it on you."

"I never was a member of your gang or any other," said Eugene Wilkes stiffly. "I'm a member of the bar!"

"Yes!" sneered Breck. "Dan Burney kidded us into letting him put that mark on all of us. He was a tattoo artist, as well as a double-cross artist! If it hadn't been for those marks, some of the crowd, including me, would never have been picked up and sent to the stir. I wouldn't put it past Burney to have spread the word—maybe through you—to the bulls to pick up any man with that red-eyed skull on his wrist. Him sitting back safe, with you telling him how to stay safe and let the rest of us take the rap!

"Dan didn't have it on his own wrist; claimed it took two hands to work the tattoo instruments, so he couldn't do it to himself. We were young fellows. We felt big and romantic at having the secret insignia of the gang on our skins. Felt proud to tie up with a big-time crook like Dan Burney! Only him and you didn't have the mark. Dan enjoyed the swag the rest of his life—and I curse the day that he died in bed! You was going to enjoy it after him. But you got another think coming about that, Wilkes, you double-crossing crook!"

The lawyer's chair suddenly tipped to the floor. The table drawer rasped open, and Wilkes backed away holding a levelled revolver. "Stand right there, Breck, or I'll shoot!" he barked.

Breck's lips curled back from his teeth in savage defiance. He clenched and unclenched his hands slowly, and then raised them in front of him. He took a step forward.

Wilkes at the same instant, stepped back. With the revolver steadily levelled at his enemy's middle, he pulled on the trigger. It snapped almost soundlessly, and the lawyer's face went suddenly pale. He pulled again and again.

Beck grinned as he grabbed the useless weapon from the other's hands and flung it to the floor. "Not a shot in it!" he taunted. "What do you think I've been doing, while I was waiting here for you? I won't forget, though, what you would have done if you could!"

He struck the lawyer a resounding slap on the jaw with his open hand, making him reel and totter. Then he suddenly yanked the smaller man around by the shoulder. "Just to make sure," he muttered.

Resistance would have been useless; and the lawyer offered none as the ex-convict grabbed his two wrists behind him in one strong hand. Breck fumbled in his pocket and brought out a roll of surgeon's plaster: the residue of that which he had used on his injured wrist. Quickly wrapped it, in several layers, around the lawyer's wrists, pinioning them effectively in helpless position. Then, with a shove, he sent Wilkes staggering back into a chair.

He could not resist the temptation to gloat. "Bet you're wishing I hadn't found you—and wondering how I did it," he said. "I wasn't really interested in you. It was Dan Burney I was after—not knowing that he'd cheated me by dying. It was only after I couldn't find any trace of him that I thought of you, knowing how thick the two of you had been. Oh, you ain't got any double crossers in your office; don't worry. But I followed one of your clerks home, and cornered him in a dark alley. I put a little fear into him—not mentioning a few bruises and a sore throat, just as a foretaste. He told me where I could find you, because he had to. I must have frightened him good: so good that he didn't even dare to send you word I was coming."

The lawyer ventured an uneasy, placating laugh. "I've got to hand it to you, Breck," he complimented. "But, of course, you've a right—a moral right to share, along with the other members of the gang, in what Burney left. Only I'm telling you he didn't leave a great deal. Not so much as you seem to think."

"I ain't worrying about the other members," said Al Breck frankly. "No more than Burney or you worried about me. I'm going to get mine while the getting's good. I'll be treasurer for everybody's share, including yours." He laughed at his own little joke; and Wilkes shrivelled under the laugh, which seemed more terrible than direct threats, "As for there not being much, I want it all. And you got to convince me that what I get *is* all! And first thing, I want to see the sight of it, and get the feel of it. Real money! Crisp, cash money! Where is it?" He thrust his face close to that of the cowering man in the chair.

"I don't know! Honest, Al, I don't know how much there is, or where it is!"

"You—don't—know!" growled Breck with slow, scornful emphasis. He took his own revolver from his pocket, and drew threatening aim. "Mouthpiece, you're slick and crafty; but it ain't going to do you any good. You hold out that secret on me, and the secret's going to die with you, see?" His finger nursed the trigger caressingly. He stepped back a pace, as if for better aim; and there was gloating in his eyes.

The lawyer writhed helplessly, and a growing horror twisted his face into a grimace. Suddenly, the tension was broken as Wilkes laughed.

"You'd never do it!" he shrilled in hysterical glee. "You want the money more than you want my life. If you killed me, your last chance would be gone! You'd never get it then!"

His insight was sure. The baffled look that came over the ex-convict's face showed him how sure it was.

Breck swore and wavered. The hand that held the gun dropped slowly. He restored the weapon to his pocket. For the moment, he realized, the crafty lawyer held the whip hand. It wasn't enough, it seemed, to be strong, and pitiless, and to have the right of the matter on your side; to have earned the reward by long years' served behind grey walls, while others stayed "outside" and lived on fat. Brains won every time. You had to meet brains with brains, or you didn't have a chance.

Gradually, the scowl disappeared from Breck's face. The corners of his lips lifted. He walked to the nearest window, pulled the shade aside for a moment, and saw the raindrops beating against the pane. He turned again to his prisoner and voiced an order.

"Stand up! Walk out to the kitchen."

Some advantage to an old-fashioned house like this! An advantage which, having discovered it in his previous careful search of the premises, he could use! He walked behind the lawyer as the latter wonderingly walked to the designated room.

Wilkes stood in a corner to which he had been motioned while Al Breck stooped to the painted floor and grasped an iron ring set in flush with the boarding. An inkling of what was in store came to him as Breck raised the flat trapdoor whose visible edges were perfectly familiar to the man who had been occupying the house.

"I suppose this rain-water cistern has been here since before the house was piped for village water," commented Breck. "I plumbed it with a stick while I was looking for likely hiding places for the swag. It's just about deep enough. And in you go!"

He laid the door back, and led Wilkes to the square opening in the floor. The lawyer, with his hands pinioned behind him, could not effectively resist. Neither could he lower himself into the cistern unaided. Breck willingly gave help, lifted the shrinking lawyer clear of the floor, dangled him downward.

Wilkes' wondering horror gave way to relief as his feet struck solid bottom. The chilling water came up to his neck; and, without the free use of his hands, he knew that he could not clamber up again. Unseen inlets were pouring water into the cistern from conductor pipes that led from the roof gutters of the house. But there was an outlet also, to prevent flooding; an outlet which would not permit the water to reach a higher level than it now held.

Breck glared contentedly at his immersed captive for a moment, and then swung on his heel and left the room. The lawyer had not yet fathomed what the plan was. His eyes were some six inches below the level of the kitchen floor, as he stood erect. It was hopeless to attempt to escape unaided, for the floor timbers overhung the sides of the cistern by a considerable distance, and the cemented sides themselves were slimy and slippery. Breck had shown no overconfidence in leaving him alone. He was as securely imprisoned as if in a cell! and less comfortably; for he must continue to stand erect, and the water was chilling his thin blood already. In time, of course—one or two hours, perhaps—the surgeon's plaster which bound his wrists would soften, and he might regain the use of his arms and hands. It would be easy then.

A pounding noise came to his ears: a noise that seemed transmitted in waves through the water. The lawyer listened in apprehension. He had not grasped the full significance of it yet, when Breck's step sounded again above, and Breck's face leered down at him.

"I just plugged up the overflow outlet—on the outside of the house, where you can't reach it," he announced. "Whittled a wooden plug, and drove it into the pipe. All the water that comes into this cistern now, will stay here. And it's still raining; harder than ever."

The leering face disappeared. Breck's footsteps walked across the creaking floor toward the door. There was a pause there, and his voice called back. "I'm going into the living room, to sit down and take it easy. Might even take a nap. You had the right dope, Wilkes, when you thought I wouldn't shoot, and end all my chances of getting the money. But this is different. I won't even see you here; won't know when the water reaches a point high enough to drown you like a rat! I'll just let nature take its course: let the rain keep filling up the cistern. Nature ain't soft-hearted, as I'm likely to be. Nature don't think. It just does its work, and nothing can stop it. Only, just listen to this, Wilkes. When you get so's you want to talk, be sure you reach that decision before your mouth's under water. Because if you don't, you might not be able to make me hear you. And then it wouldn't do either of us any good!"

He went, and there was silence. Wilkes heard the water still entering the tank through the unseen inlets. He had a premonition that he was beaten. It might take some time for the level to rise to a dangerous point. Unless the rain stopped very soon, it would eventually rise there. The inevitability of it was the thing that terrified. Breck had turned a good trick at psychology. It was one thing to face death at the hands of a man whose determination might waver, or whose finger might tremble or slip. It was quite another to stand in water which crept up by fractions of an inch; to stand there and keep a secret whose telling would release him; to keep it perhaps until that fatal moment when he would no longer be able to tell it!

Lawyer Eugene Wilkes was on tiptoe, and his lower lip was wet, when he finally opened his mouth in a frenzied call. "Al! Al Breck! I'll tell! I'll—" His voice died in a gurgle as he took in a mouthful of water. His head began to swim, and he almost lost balance. No sound! What if Breck had indeed gone to sleep! "Breck! For Heaven's sake!"

Slow steps creaked across the floor. The ex-convict stood calmly above him; saw his tight-closed lips and the eddies of water playing underneath his nostrils, through which he was breathing heavily. "Who's the anxious one now?" asked Breck with caustic sullenness. Slowly, he knelt on the kitchen floor at the edge of the cistern. He reached out one strong hand, placed it under the submerged man's chin, and tilted the chin upward, wrenchingly, clear of the water. "Want to talk, do you?"

"Yes!" gasped Wilkes, his neck straining from the weight of his body on it. "The money's in a safe-deposit box in a New York bank. I've got the key to the box in a pocket of my clothes, right here."

"Don't they have a password that you have to give, before they'll let you use the key?" asked Breck deliberately.

"Yes. I've got that, too. Copied on a slip of paper, the identification word that Burney gave me. Haul me out of here, for Heaven's sake! It's all yours, the money. You've got me. I'm licked!"

"What's the name of the bank?" demanded Breck.

Even desperation did not blind the shrewd lawyer to his danger. "Tell you that, and have you leave me here to drown?" he gasped. "You've got half the information; and the key's in my clothes. Get me out of here safe first, before I give you the rest. I won't hold out on you; but I do want to live!"

For a moment, as Breck released his captive's chin, Wilkes' head went under water. The next instant, hands grasped him beneath the shoulders. He was hauled up, scrapingly, past the board edges of his submarine prison, and landed in a sitting posture on the floor with a dexterity which a life guard could not have excelled. "Now get that cursed bandage off my wrists!" he shivered.

Al Breck slashed the bandage in two with a knife, heedless of the cut that he inflicted on his victim's skin. Wilkes was heedless of it, too. He raised himself to his feet, and tottered to the living room, where he sank into a chair, with the water dripping in pools onto the floor about him.

"What bank?" demanded Breck again, standing over him. "There's hundreds of banks in New York."

Lawyer Wilkes fumbled in a wet pocket and brought out a key and a bit of soggy paper, which he handed over. "I don't know the name of the bank," he said.

"What?"

Wilkes cringed. "I'm not trying to cross you!" he whined. "That's true. But I can get the information, and I'll tell you how to get it. Just what Burney told me! I didn't want to raise any suspicion among the neighbours, so I was waiting until I settled affairs up here, and sold this place, and was ready to start back to the city."

"Suspicion? Neighbours? What do you mean?"

"If I killed it," said Wilkes cryptically, "they'd notice; they'd miss it. These country neighbours notice everything. If I shaved it, they'd notice even more. There was no sense in broadcasting the secret to everybody, was there? Especially when the secret was so safe."

"Killed what? Shaved? Have you gone clean out of your senses, Wilkes?" The voice was both threatening and apprehensive.

"The dog!" explained Wilkes. "Dan Burney's collie watchdog! The dog you killed! I'd like to have killed it myself, the brute! It bit me twice before it got used to me, even though it had seen me here on visits before Burney died."

"What about the dog?" demanded Al Breck.

"We'll have to shave the shaggy hair off, just back of its left shoulder. That's where the secret is: the name of the bank. Nobody but a tattoo artist, like Dan Burney, would have thought of it. He shaved the dog, tattooed the name of the bank on its skin, and then let the hair grow out again. In that case, nobody could steal the secret or get the swag, not even if they had the key and the password!"

Al Breck tottered with the suddenness of his dismay. He leaned on the table for support. "That mutt! That dead mutt that I tossed into an empty box car, going west. Heaven only knows where it is now; and there's hundreds of banks in New York!"

Wilkes leaned forward with glistening eyes. "You did what? In a box car?"

Breck nodded and laughed with a harsh, mirthless cackle. "Clean beaten—both of us! Beaten by a dead man, and by a natural mistake. Eighty or a hundred grand rotting in some vault where it'll do nobody any good. Trimmed by a dead man!" He paused for a savage grimace, and his hands clutched empty air.

"And to think that he died in bed!"

THE TATTOOED CARD (1937)

William E. Barrett

William Edward Barrett (1900–1986) was a writer who played a notable role in American popular culture mainly through the development of three of his novels into films, most prominently *The Lilies of the Field*, a movie that saw Sidney Poitier become the first black artist to win an Oscar for Best Actor in a Leading Role. The focus in *Lilies of the Field* on an itinerant African-American's chance encounter with a community of German nuns reveals an interest in spirituality and social justice characteristic of Barrett's writing.

"The Tattooed Card" is the thirteenth of sixteen detective stories featuring Needle Mike, a tattoo artist and amateur sleuth who represents a unique creation in the literary history of tattooing. Mike is actually the alter ego of a wealthy socialite Ken McInally who periodically swaps his privileged existence for a grimy tattoo parlour at the wrong end of St. Louis. As McInally dons his disguise (primarily scars, a limp, and the reek of rough booze), he enters an underworld where he stumbles into a series of crimes, usually involving his clients. While the Needle Mike stories affirm tattooing's darker side, Mike is also an accomplished artist who learned to tattoo in Japan. "The Tattooed Card" sees Mike become involved in an elaborate murder mystery that his career as a tattoo artist enables him to solve.

CHAPTER ONE
TO BE HANGED BY THE NECK

NEEDLE MIKE'S TATTOOING SHOP WAS A GRIMY HOLE IN THE wall on South Broadway in St. Louis. Over the doorway, a gaudy sign swung—

> Needle Mike's
> Tat-2-ing done Neatly
> Day or Night

The window had a large and dirty pane and the shop had a wide assortment of mismatched furniture. The man who ran the shop, and owned the furniture, was the son of a millionaire.

Kenneth McNally didn't look like a scion of wealth. He sat in a wired-together chair, with his feet on a scar-laced table. He looked like an old sailor with a taste for whisky. The powder burns on his cheek were measle scars retouched, and his tangled mop of hair was chemically streaked with grey. Chemicals, too, had given him a slightly yellow complexion. Tiny wads of parrafin had changed the shape of his nose and mouth. His glittering gold tooth was a clever dental bridge. To South Broadway, these things were neither artificial nor unreal. Part of his neighbourhood, he was a man whose periodical absences were charged off to drunkenness. He was Needle Mike.

McNally looked out of the window. It was a quiet evening, and such evenings made him restless. He had embarked on this fantastic existence along the fringe of the St. Louis underworld to escape the upperworld's boredom and to flirt with danger of a kind to which he had not been born.

Across the street, there was a flood of humanity pouring from the doors of the Apollo Theatre. Flaring posters before the Apollo proclaimed the fact that one could see *Real Burlesk. Pretty Girls. Star Comedians. A Feature Picture and a News Reel*, all for the sum of twenty-five cents. The crowd that was leaving now had seen the pretty girls and comedians. They were not tarrying for the feature or the news reels. The weather-beaten clock on McNally's wall bonged the half hour for ten-thirty. There was a shuffling step along the pavement, and McNally's knob turned.

McNally looked up.

The man who slouched in the doorway could have stepped out of a comic strip or magazine cover. He was the tramp artists imagine. His clothes were worn and torn and visibly held together in spots by the free use of pins. Long and lean, all that could be seen of his face beneath the pulled-down soft hat, was dirty and beard-blue. His shoes were broken across the toes. He lacked, however, the usual geniality of his kind. Half crouched there in the doorway, he exuded a sullen air of menace.

McNally looked him over with the uncompromising hostility of Needle Mike. "What am I supposed to do, take your photograph?" he growled. "Or do you talk sometimes?"

The man came into the room behind a baritone grunt. He fumbled in the pocket of a greasy coat, that had once been grey, and brought out a single playing-card. He tossed it face up upon the table between McNally's feet.

"How much would you charge to needle that on me, as is?" he asked.

McNally got a glimpse of the card, and his feet came down from the table with a bang. It was the trey of clubs. He looked up sharply. The tramp was standing so that his back was to the low-powered lamp inside the door, and his shoulder half turned to drop light above McNally's workbench. His face was deep in shadow, but McNally felt the burning intensity of the man's eyes.

McNally frowned at the card. "As is, with the little pips in the comers, I'll do it for five bucks."

The ragged man didn't move a muscle of his body. "On my chest and on my forearm—both."

McNally looked up again. He was startled, and, for a second, he showed it. The bulking shadow of another blotted out for a moment the glare of the theatre sign across the way. He was coming towards McNally's window from the curb. The tramp took a scarcely perceptible step, threw a look towards the window. McNally looked up, too. He suppressed a growl of annoyance. Rex Milligan was coming over for one of the visits that lately were almost a nightly occurrence.

The tramp tugged at the brim of his battered hat and sidled toward the door. "Check it, professor," he said. "I'll be back."

He squeezed past Milligan in the doorway, without looking at him.

Milligan looked after him, removed his hat, and passed a handkerchief around the sweatband. "Hope I'm not driving away customers, Needler," he said.

McNally turned the trey of clubs face down on the table. "Nope," he said. "Lots of 'em shop when they haven't got dough. Once a guy gets the bug for needlework, it's like collecting stamps. He either gets needled or he goes around getting prices."

"Is that a fact? I'm glad I never let you get started on me."

*

Milligan sat down without invitation. He was a blocky man, a few years past forty. His hair was thinning but he was in good shape physically. He grunted and groaned and planted himself around like a fat man, but had no bay window. He wore a Vandyke beard, blond, inclined to be straggly, and a source of annoyance to McNally. There was a tradition behind Vandyke beards, but Milligan had the beard without the tradition. He wore ill-fitting clothes badly, had stubby fingers with dirty fingernails, and collected dirt in the large pores of his face. He was a partner in the Apollo Theatre.

"I'm tired, Needler," he grunted. "I came over to take a drink. I can't start doing it in my place or the customers will start doing it, too. It's bad enough now. Have one?"

He set a pint whisky bottle on the table. It was bonded whisky. Milligan always had good whisky. It was his one high-grade trait, and he explained it by the fact that he had been poisoned badly once by whisky that wasn't good. He never drank in any of the South Broadway saloons.

"Don't care if I do," McNally accepted the invitation.

He picked up the bottle. Needle Mike had to live always in character, and Needle Mike wasn't the type to refuse a drink of bonded liquor. He drank, and wiped his lips.

Milligan drank right after him, and set the bottle down with a sigh. "I get wore out these days, Needler," he said. "I got to keep checking up on Walker. Getting absent-minded, he is. Got something on his mind, and acts like he's worried as hell. Queer kind of a guy. Keeps bottled up. I don't know nothin' about him, and I'm his partner."

McNally looked out of the window. He could see Walker out in front of the theatre removing the framed photographs of the "pretty girls", preparatory to closing up. McNally didn't know much about

Walker, either. The man was surly and unsociable, about the same age and build as Milligan but seemingly without Milligan's interest in people. In their Apollo partnership, the men split duties according to their talents. Milligan was the front office and handled the crowd; Walker was stage manager and handled the properties.

"Another?" Milligan held out the bottle.

"Sure." McNally appeared to drink deeply, but he was cautious.

Milligan took the bottle back and corked it. "I'd like another myself," he said, "but I've got a dirty headache. I'm going down to the drug-store for an aspirin. Sorry about the customer, Mike."

"Think nothin' of it. He'll be back. Probably thought you were a dick." McNally laughed in the deep bellowing fashion of a tattoo artist with a couple of drinks.

He watched Milligan walk stiffly down the block toward the drugstore on the corner. The laugh died out of his voice and manner as soon as the necessity for it was past. His eyes were thoughtful. He had come very close to telling Rex Milligan that the tramp had been asking him about the price of a design similar to the one that he had tattooed nearly a year ago on the arm and chest of Phil Walker.

McNally turned, and hobbled over to the table. His limp was the last careful touch to his adopted identity. There was an ovular device of cork and rubber, on his right kneecap, that held his leg stiff. He could never forget, even in a moment of stress, to walk like Needle Mike. While he wore the clamp, he could walk no other way. He reached the table-top, and stopped short.

The trey of clubs stared up at him. He had turned it face down, when Milligan entered. Sometime during the visit, it had been turned around. He picked it up thoughtfully, and put it in his pocket. He went back to the window and looked out.

★

It was one of those dull quiet evenings that come along so often when spring is early and people aren't ready for it. There were a few more stragglers drifting out of the Apollo, and all of the sign lights were out. The feature would be over in a few minutes, and Walker would close up the theatre. McNally wondered about Walker, and also about the bum, but this puzzling didn't hold his interest. There was no drama in it.

"As far as excitement goes, I might as well be home," he growled. "Somebody might drop a teacup, or something, and give a man a hell of a flutter."

He stretched wearily and started back to the chair in which he had been sitting when the tramp came in. He got halfway across the room when the lights went out. There was just the short warning flicker, and, after that, darkness. He swore softly. Both lights had gone simultaneously so that he knew it wasn't a bulb burnout.

"Fuse probably."

He hobbled toward the back room where the fuse-box was. It was misty-grey in the shop, and it got darker the farther he went from the window. At best, he got little illumination from outside on Broadway once the theatre lights went out. He was reaching in his pocket for a match, as he opened the door to the back room. He never lighted it.

Powerful hands reached for him out of the darkness, and he felt strong fingers at his throat.

McNally tried to turn and break the grip, but the fingers pressed harder against his windpipe, and his eyes seemed to pop. The room spun, and, out of the spinning mist, he tried to ram his fists into his assailant. The man was behind him, and McNally's fists beat against the air. The other's weight seemed to bear him down, legs twisting in a scissor-grip. Then the bottom dropped out of everything, and McNally's brain was a whirling pinwheel of light in a pit of darkness.

There was a blank, then, out of which McNally roused briefly to the completely physical sensation of a rough rope against his neck and his body lifting free of the floor. He choked and tried to fight, and the blackness crowded back over him. Some part of his brain, impervious to the punishment of his body, mocked him as he slipped off into unconsciousness.

"Hanged by the neck until you are dead," it said. "Until you are dead—dead—"

There was movement behind Needle Mike—sinister, powerful movement—but he knew nothing of it at all. He was out, like a man drowned in a bottomless sea.

CHAPTER TWO
BLOODY BURLESQUE

The tramp was bending over him when he opened his eyes, and there was a candle flame dancing upon the table-top.

"Swallow it, bo—you need it." His voice came from afar off.

McNally swallowed because it was too much effort not to swallow. It was vile whisky, and blazed its way down his gullet but there was life in it. McNally felt warmth flow back into his veins. He choked, strangled, and raised his two hands to his throat. His fingers gripped the rough strands of a rope, and the shock of the contact snapped his brain back out of the darkness. He sat up.

"Yep, I left the rope on yuh," said the tramp. "I cut it in the middle."

He was down on one knee. He took a short pull at the bottle from which McNally had been drinking.

McNally blinked and looked up. The light from the candle was a dancing light, but he could see the end of rope lashed fast around the transom frame. He touched the loosened noose around his own neck, and looked down upon the cut length of rope that matched the rope-end above. He felt as sure of himself as a dizzy man balancing on a window-ledge about thirty floors up, but the mist was clearing from his brain. There was a chair lying on its side in about the position that it would be if a man stood on it to hang himself and then kicked it away.

McNally opened his hand. There was something in it. It took seconds for him to recognize it as a clipping from a newspaper and seconds more before he could focus his eyes well enough to read it. It was a verse with a simple title—'The Bum'. McNally read—

> A man gets weary of life sometimes,
> Of the endless swim upstream,
> And he yearns to float where the current goes,
> To rest and to drift and to dream.
> The world shouts, "Weakling" and, "Swim, fool, swim!"
> But the current pounds at his breath
> And he wants to go with the stream in life
> As he'll go with the stream in death.

McNally grunted. It was bad, maudlin verse, but the kind that a shabby down-and-outer might read when his cup of despondency was about filled to the brim. He passed it to the tramp.

"With that in my fist, I'd be a clean case of suicide," he said. The words rasped from his lips, as he forced the air through his tortured windpipe.

The shabby stranger scarcely glanced at the clipping. "Sure," he said. "I figured that. Somebody fixed your clock, and the cops wouldn't fuss with no murder clues. There you'd be, and you'd be dead. Suicide goes nice on a blotter, and it don't make a cop much work." There was bitterness in the man's tone. He rose slowly from his knee.

McNally loosed the noose and dropped it on the floor, a cold feeling moving along his spine. "How did you suspect?"

The tramp was standing, and the candlelight flickered over his ragged outfit without touching the face beneath the pulled-down hatbrim. "I saw a guy doing a fast fadeout from the back of your joint, so I came in for a look," he said.

"What kind of a guy?"

"Just a guy. It's dark outside."

The shabby man was evasive, but he was studying McNally from under the hatbrim. He shot his question suddenly. "Professor, I done you a turn. O.K. Do me one. Who's the guy that you needled the two treys on?"

"What two treys?" McNally frowned.

The man spat. "Don't be like that. You were remembering to beat hell, when I showed you that trey and told you where I wanted 'em put. Who'd you put them on?" He was crouched, grim. His eyes gleamed out of the shadow beneath the hatbrim.

McNally shrugged. After all, it didn't make a lot of difference. The man who had the marks had never tried very hard to conceal them.

"I needled them onto a fellow named Walker, over at the Apollo across the street," he said. "About a year ago, I guess."

The tramp straightened up. "I figured that," he said.

"Figured what?"

"Skip it!" The man snapped his fingers. "Hope you come along O.K., professor."

He turned on his heel and headed for the back door. He didn't shuffle now, but stepped out with a long stride. McNally tried to rise quickly, and dizziness swept over him like a wave. He had to spread his hands out on the floor to steady himself, and, when the whirling motion stopped, he was alone. He swore softly.

"Maybe it adds up," he said huskily. "But I'm too dumb to get the answer. Why try to rub me out?"

When he succeeded in gaining his feet, he crossed the room unsteadily and found the fuse-box. One fuse had been screwed out part way. He tightened it, and the lights went on in the other room. He rubbed his throat gingerly. There was a wash-basin in the front room. It took effort to reach it, but the cold water felt good on his face. There was less feeling of bulge behind his eyes.

The door of the shop opened, and he turned with the wet towel still in his hands. Detective Sergeant Mort Dickinson, of the homicide squad, was standing just inside of the door.

"What's the matter with you?" Dickinson growled.

McNally drew a handkerchief around his throat and knotted it. He didn't favour police investigations, whether in his favour or against him. He wanted none of them.

"Bad cold," he answered huskily. "Sore throat."

Dickinson sniffed. "And too much bad liquor to cure it. Put a hat on, Mike."

"What for?" McNally was startled.

"Identification. No pinch."

"Right away." McNally hobbled into the back room. He didn't know what was in the wind, but he was thanking his luck that Dickinson was on the job while Corbin enjoyed a vacation. Corbin, his old Nemesis, would have had him foul tonight. Dickinson was a routine kind of a dick who took things pretty much as he found them without sniffing out wild angles.

In the process of being hanged, McNally had lost the pieces of paraffin that reshaped his mouth. Dickinson stayed in the front room and gave him an opportunity of replacing them. He was just a minor witness in the case, to Dickinson; everybody from the mayor on down would have been a suspect to the absent Corbin. McNally took time to pass a grimy towel over his face to make up for any ravages caused by washing. He jammed a hat on his head, limped into the front room again.

They went across the street to the Apollo.

Phil Walker was lying on the floor in the cluttered office backstage. He had a hole in his face, just under the cheekbone, and a small automatic clutched in his hand. A fleshy woman, with dyed red hair, sat slumped in an old-fashioned swivel-chair that faced the visitor's side of the office desk. The front of her green dress was soaked with blood, and her eyes protruded glassily.

The office was filled with people, but they made room for Dickinson and McNally. There was a police inspector who had dropped in unofficially, a cop in harness, several newspaper reporters, and a couple of people from the Apollo theatre.

Dickinson waved his hand. "Know 'em, Mike?"

McNally looked down at the man. Walker's sleeves were rolled up, and the tattooed trey of clubs stood out on his right forearm, six inches or so above the gun that he clutched with dead fingers.

He had been a light-haired man with a blond moustache, husky but not fat.

McNally nodded. "I know him. He's Phil Walker—one of the fellows that own this dump."

"How about the playing-card? Did you needle it on him?"

"Yep—about a year ago."

"Why?"

"He wanted it."

"What's it mean?" Dickinson was shooting the questions.

McNally shrugged. "I wouldn't know. It was his idea."

Dickinson grunted. "How about the woman? Ever see her before?"

McNally looked at the lined face beneath the dyed hair. The rouge stood out with dark ghastliness against the pallid skin of death. Here was a woman of forty-five, or fifty, who had fought hard against the years. He shook his head.

"I don't spot her."

Dickinson crossed the room and lifted the woman's limp arm. "How about that playing-card? Did you do that, too?"

McNally stared. On the woman's right forearm was the six of spades. "I didn't do that," he said.

Dickinson sighed. A cop's life was being constantly marred by such disappointments. He'd gone after McNally, personally, because it would have been a nice break for him if he could walk in with an identifying witness while the inspector and newspapermen were in the room. Identifying Walker hadn't been a problem.

There was a stir at the door. A plain-clothesman came in with Rex Milligan. Milligan was mopping his hatband with a handkerchief and seemed highly agitated. "This is terrible, gentlemen, terrible. How did it happen? This man wouldn't tell me anything, and—"

"Do you know the woman?" Dickinson snapped the monologue in two with the question.

Milligan stared at the dead woman, shuddered, and shook his head. "Stranger to me," he said. "Didn't she have a bag or—or anything?"

"She didn't have a damned thing." One of the reporters supplied the answer, when Dickinson turned his back.

Dickinson turned around again fast. "Where were you when it happened?"

Milligan blinked. "I don't know. Walker was all right, when I left. I had a headache. I stopped and got some aspirin, and I went home."

Dickinson looked at the plainclothesman.

The man nodded. "He was in bed," he said. "He lives about six blocks away."

Milligan was patting his forehead with the handkerchief. He turned appealingly to the reporter who had answered his previous question. "What happened?"

The reporter jerked his thumb toward a collarless man in a grey suit who was holding a towel in his hands. The man was pale-faced, thin, smooth-shaven, and now stepped forward.

"I'm Padgett, comedian in your show, Mr. Milligan," he said. "You wouldn't know me. We saw Walker, usually. I went out and sat through the news reel, after the show, without taking off my make-up, so I was late cleaning up. Belle, over there, was late, too." He jerked his thumb toward a plump girl in a pink dress who was scrubbed clean of make-up in the presence of the press, and very unhappy about it.

Padgett cleared his throat. "I heard the shots—three of them. I ran up to Walker's office here, and the front door was locked. Belle was with me. I left her there at the door, yelling, and I ran down that

short flight of steps to the stage and around through the prop-room
to your office. This is how they were, and they looked dead to me.
I phoned for the cops."

"But the woman. Where did she come from? How did she get
in? There must be some clue." Milligan was looking around wildly
as if he had a chance of seeing a clue and catching it on the wing.

The reporter cut in: "She sat through the show, and asked for
Walker while the picture was on. We got that from an usher that
they picked up in the saloon down the block."

McNally drew back against the wall. He was conscious of the fact
that his disguise, simple thought it was and proof against ordinary
mishap, had taken punishment tonight and might gain him unfavour-
able attention under close police scrutiny. He was conscious, too, of
the fact that he was a more important witness in this murder case
than anyone suspected.

The fact that there was a shabby tramp asking about that trey-
of-clubs design tonight before the murder was committed had
heavy implications. That he, himself, was attacked murderously
was somehow significant, too. But he couldn't add the facts up,
himself, and he was willing to bet that the cops couldn't add them
up. If he opened his mouth, they'd hold him as a material witness.
Material witnesses were often sweated at H.Q., and he didn't kid
himself that he could stand the process without revealing himself as a man in disguise. Once let the fact of his disguise come
out, and he was lost. The cops would hang every unexplainable
fact around his neck. He shook his head. His play was to keep
buttoned up.

Dickinson looked across the room at him, nodded his head, and
waved.

McNally sighed, and turned to the door. Let them yammer about the case all they wanted to. Dickinson said that he could go, and there wasn't anything that he wanted more than that.

Dickinson was a routine cop and the case would blow over. Dickinson would sift the facts that he had and go before the coroner's jury probably with a clean case of murder and suicide. The woman had come out of Walker's past. She'd found him, and they'd quarrelled. Walker had killed her, and then taken his own life. It was as simple as that, and the tattooed playing-cards were just bits of business that the Fates had tossed in to make it tough for cops.

McNally hobbled across the street to his shop. "Me and Walker both," he muttered. "I committed suicide, too—but it didn't take."

CHAPTER THREE
DEATH DEALT FROM THE DECK

McNally sat a long while with his thoughts behind the grimy window that faced South Broadway. The bugles were blowing in his blood, but he couldn't answer them. Adventure had flitted past him, yet he had barely touched the fringe of its shining garment as it passed. There had been a bum, a trey of clubs, and a hangman's rope. Out of less than that, he had sometimes had experiences to curl a man's hair.

But there was no place to go from where he was now.

It would be foolhardy to mess with a murder case still fresh in the minds of the police, and he had no clue that would lead him to the ragged stranger who was, somehow, the key to the mystery of what had happened in the Apollo. McNally felt his throat. It still ached from the pressure of a strangler's fingers. He frowned at his own hands. Who had done that?

He thought of Milligan and the turned trey of clubs. Milligan was strong enough to be the strangler, if he had wanted to strangle him. McNally stiffened suddenly, and snapped his fingers.

"The bum!" he muttered.

Faulty reasoning starts from such obscure facts. Simply because the ragged stranger cut him down didn't mean that the man was innocent of stringing him up. The tramp had traded a favour for a favour. He had found out about the clubs that McNally had needled on Walker. He had found this out while McNally was still groggy, and probably under no other circumstances would he have found out so easily. The result might have justified the effort. Right after the man got his information, Phil Walker died.

The clipped poem, that McNally had had in his hand, was the type that a down-and-outer might have in his possession. McNally walked up and down.

"It adds up roughly," he said. "But there are holes. Why in hell should Walker be killed for a trey of clubs that I needled onto him? If it ever meant anything to him, except another skin-picture, he never showed that it did."

He went back and sat by the window. The street was quieting down. The morgue-wagon had come and gone. The morbid crowd had drifted away. One by one, the principals came out. Padgett, the comedian, who had found the body, left the darkened theatre with the girl called Belle, and parted with her out front. Rex Milligan made his exit in conversation, with one of the detectives, but walked down South Broadway, alone. Dickinson and the others left in police cars, and the theatre brooded in black darkness.

McNally watched it for a while and smoked. Then he rose and went into the back room. He had left the severed rope in there, and

he wondered what the police would make of it if they should decide
to take a look through Needle Mike's.

He turned on the light, and stopped short. In the centre of the
room, there was a batch of newspaper clippings in a broken envelope
held together by string. He picked them up gingerly and took them
to the table. Before untying the string, he locked the rear door, and
closed the door that opened on the big room in front. He could feel
the stir of excitement in his blood.

He took the clippings out of the envelope and spread the top strip
across the table. It, like the others in the envelope, was yellowed with
age. The type face was typically small-town and from some paper
that McNally did not recognize. The headline across the page read—

FOURTEEN DIE IN EXPLOSION AT HILLTOP MINE

His eye raced through the account. The Hilltop Mine was a coal mine
in a western state. Prior to the writing of this news story, there had
evidently been some labour unrest. At three-fifteen in the morning,
an explosion had destroyed two buildings in which a group of visiting company executives were temporarily housed. Four company
executives, a newspaper man, three engineers, and six employees
of the Hilltop Mine were killed in the explosion. The first account
carried very little more information than that. The other clippings
told most of the story in headlines—

FOURTEEN MEN MURDERED AT HILLTOP

COUNTY ATTORNEY CLAIMS EXPLOSION
WAS RESULT OF TERRORIST BOMB.

The clippings fell in order, according to dates—

DUPE OF TERRORISTS CONFESSES MURDER PLOT

BOMBING PLANNED BY AGITATORS, SAYS MINER.
STRANGE SECRET SOCIETY PLANNED MORE ATROCITIES.

TWENTY TATTOOED TERRORISTS ARRESTED

MEN NAMED BY TOM FENNER TAKEN IN CUSTODY. EACH MAN
TATTOOED WITH THE DESIGN OF A PLAYING-CARD.

MORE ARRESTS IN HILLTOP BOMBING

TOM FENNER TELLS HOW HE WAS FORCED TO JOIN
TATTOOED SOCIETY KNOWN AS THE "DECK".

The clippings ran on for nearly a year, with many dates missing but with the story fairly complete. McNally read through them, his face growing more grim with each unfolding detail. It was a tragedy of ten years ago, but there was a vivid reality to it in this dingy little room with a noosed rope coiled beside the yellowed pieces of pulp paper.

FENNER TELLS HOW HE BECAME THE TREY OF CLUBS
AND LEARNED PLAN OF THE TATTOOED TERRORISTS,
AS THIRTY FACE TRIAL FOR BOMBING.

The feature story covered the ground pretty well. There had been a labour lockout three months earlier at Hilltop Mine, and a group of miners had been fired upon by armed company guards. When the survivors gathered together, after three of their number had been killed, they found that there were exactly fifty-two of them. Out of that meeting had grown the idea of the "Deck"—suggested by the deck of cards. Each man had been dealt a card and was known by that card, thereafter, to avoid the dangerous use of names in the organization. Tom Fenner, the young miner who turned state's evidence, claimed that he was forced to join the organization under fear of death, and that, when one of the miners who understood the art, tattooed the members, he had to submit.

There were clippings, too, of denials—

ACCUSED MEN SAY THAT FENNER LIES

NO PLOT, MINERS CLAIM THE DECK ORGANIZED AS NUCLEUS OF LABOUR UNION.

FENNER SET BOMB, SAYS ORTH

LEADER OF DECK SAYS VIOLENCE WAS NOT IN ORGANIZATION PLAN.

Back and forth, through many papers, the controversy raged in type. Fenner stuck to his story and had company support. The miners were incensed at Fenner, and he was given armed protection. No place was there a picture of him, but again and again his identifying mark was mentioned. He was the trey of clubs.

The climax was a series of sentences. A miner named Orth and two associates were named as the actual bombers, and sentenced to hang. Twenty-seven other men went to jail for sentences averaging ten years. The last clipping was a picture of a woman with one hand in her hair, her other hand upraised. The caption read—

DEATH TO THE TREY OF CLUBS

MRS. FRANK ORTH, KNOWN AS "BIG SADIE" TO THE MINERS, SNAPPED AS SHE SWORE VENGEANCE ON TOM FENNER, STATE'S WITNESS AT THE TRIAL OF HER

HUSBAND WHO WAS HANGED TODAY FOR HIS PART
IN THE HILLTOP MINE BOMBING.

McNally stared a long time at that photograph, and the tragedy of
ten years back moved into the room where he sat. The face that
stared out of the time-dimmed picture was the same face that had
stared across Phil Walker's desk tonight in the stare of death.

The Trey of Clubs had been the betrayer of his mates, and the
woman who died in Phil Walker's office was the widow of a miner
who hanged.

The story of tonight's murder, then, had been written ten years
ago in a little western town about which few people in St. Louis
had ever heard. McNally shook his shoulders against the chill that
moved along his spine. It was deathly still in the back room of Needle
Mike's, but the ghosts seemed to move there through the yellowed
clippings and about the noosed rope.

"Somebody made a mistake," McNally thought. "Phil Walker
wasn't Tom Fenner."

McNally stacked the clippings neatly and put them away in the worn
envelope. There were no identifying marks on that envelope, unless
there were fingerprints on it, and the odds were that any fingerprints
would be badly smudged. He rose from the table.

"Who dropped them?" he muttered.

There had been two men in his back room, unless the tramp had
played two rôles. It had been the height of carelessness for anyone to
lose a clipping-collection like this—but here they were. He wrinkled
his brow with concentration.

Something was eluding him—something that should be obvious.
He wished that his head didn't ache quite so hard and that he

could remember a little more about the half hour before Dickinson
came over after him. He had been very close to death, and a man who
dangles over the brink of eternity does not come out of the experience with his brain clear and observant. The memory-pictures that
McNally was capable of calling back were blurred around the edges.

And he couldn't remember if that envelope had been on the floor
when he recovered consciousness. He had been on the floor, himself,
at about the point where the envelope had lain. He measured it off.

He went into the front of the shop, with a prescience of danger.
It was well after midnight, and South Broadway was quiet except
for the occasional engine throb of a passing car. A man desperate
enough to try for his life once, when the neighbourhood was alive
and nervous, could be expected to return.

Somebody, too—either the man who had attempted murder the
first time, or another—would have an inducement to come back.
There were the damning papers. They were dynamite, of course,
to McNally. But how could the other man know that?

The police were entitled to those papers. The man who lost
them would expect Needle Mike to turn them over and curry favour
at H.Q. He wouldn't know that Needle Mike couldn't stand police
scrutiny and police examination. As result, he would be back.

The warning bell rang again in McNally's consciousness, to
remind him of a slipped cog somewhere in his reasoning. But he
couldn't pin the error down. He shook his shoulders irritably, locked
his front door and put out the light.

He sat, then, in his rickety chair and stared across the street at
the darkened front of the Apollo Theatre.

Needle Mike's clock had just bonged once for the half hour of
two-thirty, when he saw Rex Milligan.

The theatre man came up South Broadway warily, and his heels didn't click on the pavement. He had his head held stiffly forward, like the head of a man who is listening, and his right hand was rammed in his pocket. He stopped just a few yards short of the theatre entrance, took a quick look up and down the block. Then he plunged into the black areaway that led to the stage entrance.

McNally sat where he was for a long five minutes, and no living thing stirred along the block. He took a deep breath, and rose to his feet. The weariness and the indecision dropped away from him. He had something to do and a beat in his blood that promised him excitement in the doing.

He left his place dark, and went across the street.

CHAPTER FOUR
A CORPSE FOR A CORPSE

The stage-entrance door was locked. McNally had expected that but he felt strangely baffled. His brain wasn't functioning well. He had neglected the little kit that he had assembled for dealing with recalcitrant locks. He didn't want to go back after it, and he moved cautiously around behind the theatre. There was a jutting platform there, on which props were unloaded, and a sliding door that led to the backstage area. McNally tried the door, more in hope than in faith. It slid back soundlessly.

He stepped into the thick darkness and stood with his back to the door. His heart was hammering. By no stretch of the imagination could he conceive of Rex Milligan entering the theatre by so clumsy a route as this. Milligan would have a key to the stage door, off the areaway, and would go in by that door. The police weren't in the habit of leaving the scene of violent death with doors unlocked.

"So the facts add up to two people ahead of me," he decided.

McNally moved slowly forward. In the entire catalogue of buildings there is none as completely spooky as an empty theatre. The stage curtain, that had been dropped for the showing of films, was still down, and he was spared the sight of ghostly seats stretching off into blurred distance. The stage, itself, was a hazardous passage. Sections of scenery, that had been the walls of a stage room, were standing at cockeyed angles to one another. There were odds and ends of paraphernalia scattered around, as well as coils of rope that were part of the scene-shifting system. He tripped over an end of rope, and then heard the scraping sound above him, to his left.

It was a slight noise, but the empty theatre magnified sound. McNally stopped and he could hear—or thought that he could—the pounding of his own heart. He moved in the direction of the sound and, although something within him was urging speed, he was forced to move at a snail's-pace. There was no light. He could not see obstructions until he was squarely upon them.

An iron-stepped stairway loomed ahead of him. He stretched out his hand to a railing that was cold to the touch. This would be the back stair to the little above-stage balcony upon which the two offices of the theatre were built. He was remembering the account of Padgett, the comedian, who had found the bodies. Padgett had gone up the front steps, that duplicated these, and, when he found the door to Walker's office locked, he had had to circle the stage— with the scenery, no doubt, still in place—then charge up these stairs to Milligan's office.

The murderer—if there were a murderer, and it had not been murder and suicide—would have had plenty of chance to run down these stairs and out into the alley behind the theatre.

These thoughts flashed through McNally's brain as he moved softly up the steps. The slight scraping of his feet, and the metallic response of the stairs to his weight, stirred echoes backstage and took on the characteristics of clatter.

There was no response to the sound, save the scraping noise again—closer now and punctuated with an occasional wooden thump. McNally crossed the short landing, and opened the door to Milligan's office. The office, like the rest of the theatre, was dark but the scraping sound became intensified at his entrance. He reached out, fumbled along the wall till he found the switch, and flooded the office with light.

Rex Milligan was securely trussed up in a straight-backed chair that had been shoved against the wall. His heavy, flat-topped desk had been moved so that its edge rested hard against his chest and robbed him of any chance that he might have had to squirm loose. A towel had been forced between his teeth, its ends tied with twine and looped around his head to a knot at the nape of his neck. His eyes blinked rapidly in the sudden light, then bulged with effort as he tried to flash a message of appeal to McNally.

McNally's eyes took quick inventory of the room. There were signs of struggle in the broken desk-lamp, the pile of photographs scattered around the room, the two torn books of Apollo Theatre press clippings on the floor. The door to the ill-fated Walker's office was closed, but near that door was a small pool of blood.

The top of Milligan's desk had been cleared of everything save a small clock and a black, rectangular box a trifle larger than a cigar box. McNally moved the desk towards the centre of the room, cut the gag-cord with his pocketknife and removed the towel from the theatre manager's mouth.

Milligan's face contorted like the face of a man with a sudden spasm. He gagged and sputtered, and drool flooded down upon the untied blond Vandyke. McNally's eyes were narrowed speculatively. He had been doing some clear thinking, since he entered the theatre, and he had literally stumbled into one vital clue that he should never have overlooked in the first place.

"What in hell's it all about, Milligan?" he growled. He was Needle Mike to the hilt now. The natural caution of an old neighbourhood character, who is on the fringe of the law, was his best card to play. He was in a position to trade for information.

"Let me loose and I'll tell you." Milligan's voice was thin and strained. There was agony in his eyes, and he kept looking at the clock.

McNally shook his head. "It's been a funny night," he said. "I ain't stepping into nothing till I know what's what."

"I'm your friend, Mike. Let me loose. I've got to—"

"Who tied you up?"

"Intruders. Two prowlers—"

"Yeah. They left your watch and that fancy chain and a ring on your finger."

"They got scared. I put up a good fight."

McNally was relentless. "What were you doing down here?"

Milligan squirmed impatiently. There was fire in his eyes and an angry twist to his lips. "Don't play copper, Mike. Cut me loose."

McNally had taken off the knee-clamp to facilitate fast action when he crossed to the theatre, but he remembered to hold the leg stiff when he moved up and down. He was in motion now, walking back and forth within a tight circle.

"Milligan, somebody tried to hang me tonight and make it look like suicide," he growled.

Milligan stopped squirming, body suddenly rigid. "Who?"

McNally stopped and levelled his forefinger. "The rope that was used on me is the same kind you've got outside for shifting scenery."

"That don't mean—Crysake, Mike—let me loose!"

Milligan was looking at the little clock again, and fighting the hard-tied twine.

McNally's jaw set grimly. "This slaughter up here was made to look like suicide, too." He jabbed his forefinger at Milligan's chest. "I figure it was the same guy's mind working both times. I figure that guy was planning the slaughter a long time. I figure that he tabbed me as dangerous because I was one guy who knew that Phil Walker wasn't Tom Fenner. I needled the trey of spades on Phil Walker, a year ago, and Tom Fenner had his ten years or more."

Rex Milligan's eyes were wild. He ran his tongue around his lips. "Mike, you've gone nuts. I don't know what you're talking about—"

"Sure, you do. If Tom Fenner was a smart guy, he'd know that the lads out West, who drew ten years, would be coming out pretty quick. He'd want to be dead in a big way—dead in headlines, so they wouldn't look for him. Maybe he'd be smart enough to fix it up a year in advance and pick up some dumb sucker who was about the same build and colouring like himself. He'd talk that guy into getting a trey of clubs tattoo with some gag or another and make him a partner in a business where he could watch him and keep him handy."

"Cut me loose, Mike. You're crazy—"

"If I'm crazy, you're not Tom Fenner." McNally's eyes were narrow slits. He took a step forward, snapped the button off the man's shirt cuff with one thrust of his finger and rammed the shirt sleeve back to the elbow.

Stark-blue against the man's hairy flesh was the tattooed trey of clubs.

"Very cute, professor, but I'm running this show." The voice broke softly from the door to Walker's office.

McNally spun around. The ragged man was leaning against the door jamb, his shabby hat pulled low. In his hand, he clutched a short and ugly automatic, its muzzle unwaveringly upon McNally.

McNally backed up. "So what?" he said.

"So you're a good guy if you don't get in my way." He flicked a bitter look at Milligan. "You, Fenner, will I take this guy away and let you listen to the tick alone, or will you write it out?"

The sweat was pouring down Milligan's face. He looked frantically at the clock. "I'll write it—anything," he whispered hoarsely.

"Write the truth and remember that I know what the truth is." The tramp still leaned against the door. He nodded to McNally. "Take that box off the desk and set it on the floor," he said. "Treat it gently."

McNally shrugged. He picked up the black box, and Milligan gave a gasp of terror. "That's a bomb."

McNally almost dropped the box out of sheer surprise. He bent over it and could hear a steady ticking like that of a clock. He looked toward the man in the doorway. He was between the man and Milligan. He couldn't see the man's eyes, but he read the mocking twist of the lips, or thought that he could. There could be no more racking third degree than a ticking mystery in a box. He set the box down.

"Now, loosen his right arm, professor. He's tied so that you can do that. There's pen and ink and paper in that left-hand drawer."

McNally obeyed instructions. Milligan had been cleverly trussed up by a man who knew knots. There was an egg-shaped lump over the man's temple, too, which indicated that he might have been knocked out pretty cold before he was tied.

Milligan whimpered like a whipped puppy and cursed futilely. Then he took the pen and wrote. McNally stepped back and watched him. The room was suddenly silent, save for the faint scratching noise of the pen against the paper. Milligan finished, and sat back.

The man with the gun gestured wearily. "Read it to me, Mike—as is."

McNally took the sheet and read the contents aloud, pausing to wonder—

"I am Tom Fenner. In 1926, I worked in the Hilltop Mine. Fifty-two of us, who were fired on by company guards in July, 1926, formed a society called the 'Deck'. We each drew a card. I was the trey of clubs. The idea of the Deck was like the idea of a labour union, collective bargaining. If any of us left Hilltop, we swore we would start another Deck wherever we went. Frank Orth, our leader, had a notion that the Deck idea would take and that we'd grow big."

McNally stopped reading and looked towards the man in the doorway.

The man nodded grimly. "O.K., so far. Read on."

McNally read slowly. The words that followed were a bad taste in his mouth—

"The state had a big reward for the arrest of anyone using explosives to damage private property and the company had rewards, too. I went in on a scheme to set off two bombs and blame the Deck for it. A private detective, named Messner, figured out the scheme. He's dead now. We didn't mean to kill anybody, but the bombs were too strong. Messner and I set

off the bombs. Thirty members of the Deck were convicted
for it. I testified against them.

(Signed) Thomas Fenner."

McNally threw a look of contempt at the man he had known as
Milligan—a fiend who had schemed and betrayed for his own ends
and who had never reformed, who had formed a partnership with
another man for the purpose of killing him and who had worked
with that man for a year before he acted. He had deliberately built
up a friendship with Needle Mike so that he'd know his habits and be
able to eliminate him, too, when the time came to die as an identity
through the deaths of others.

Milligan had quieted down. His eyes were watchful now, craftily
confident, somehow. There was no shame apparent in him over the
reading of this confession that had been so despicable to the man
who read it. He was like a poker player who had made a bet, and
watched the other players.

The man in the doorway didn't move. "Address an envelope to
the governor of the state that we both came from, Milligan," he said.
"I'll mail it. The governor's name is Andrew J. Baker."

Milligan addressed the envelope without hesitation. McNally
sealed the confession in it and passed it over to the ragged man.

Milligan's voice broke the sudden silence. "A bargain's a bargain,"
he said. "Let me go."

"I didn't promise you anything, rat. Think back. Tie him up again,
professor. I'm not through with him."

McNally hesitated, but he was remembering the man who held
the whip hand had not commanded any confession or admissions
about tonight's killings. There was merit in admitting the wisdom

of the man who held a gun. He tied Milligan up against protest and invective.

"He was figuring that an unwitnessed confession isn't any good and that neither of us want to talk to cops, professor. You tipped your hand, when you didn't report that hanging. Come outside a minute."

Milligan was almost hysterical, but McNally went out with the ragged stranger. The man had showed headwork so far. They moved slowly out of the theatre and down the alley. Where the light from a street lamp filtered in through the alley's mouth, the tramp stopped and sat down on the paving. He took a clipping from his pocket and handed it over. It was a personal clipped from a paper.

TREY OF CLUBS ST. LOUIS APOLLO THEATRE NAME OF WALKER.

"That ad's been running for months in the mining towns out in our country," the man said. "Fenner put it in, himself, of course, but nobody was expected to figure that. They were supposed to figure it was one of the Deck passing a tip." His voice softened. "Poor old Sadie figured that way. She was the one who spotted it and came on here. Her husband hanged." He stopped for a moment. "I spotted it myself, but I was careful. I didn't want anybody to die but Fenner. I was too late to save Sadie." He sighed deeply. "You knew I was dying, didn't you?"

McNally was startled. "No."

"Sure. That dirty son shot me when I jumped him. I knew that he'd come back to the theatre. He was worried because the cops didn't find those clippings he'd planted. He wanted those bodies identified. He came back because he was worried—"

McNally was barely listening. He was opening the man's shirt, examining the wound in the chest that was tattooed with the eight of diamonds.

The man shook his head. "I've been bleeding to death, inside, for an hour. I'm just waiting a while. Nothing you can do, professor. Mail the letter."

He passed it over, and brushed the hat off his face. McNally gasped. Seen thus, the face was that of a man wearing theatrical make-up. Under the skilful make-up was the lean face of Padgett, the comedian, who had discovered the bodies.

He smiled wearily. "I was a tramp comedian. This was a cinch. Varied my make-up. Swiped those clips and dumped them in your place, after the cops let me go. Figured you'd hang onto them. Smart figuring. You're all right, professor—"

The man closed his eyes. "I did ten years," he whispered. "Innocent as a babe. Good men, with kids, did time. Men hanged. Nothing could do any of us any good now—not even that confession—"

"What about Milligan? What'll I do?"

Padgett roused himself, stiffened. He held his watch up and strained to see it. "The mine blew up at three-fifteen a.m.," he said grimly.

McNally had a horrible tight feeling in his scalp. He looked at the watch. The minute hand was quivering on the quarter hour of three-fifteen now.

There was a blast that rocked the block, and a blinding sheet of flame. The whole back end of the theatre seemed to go out.

For a stunned second, McNally crouched there.

The man smiled faintly. "You don't think I'd bluff with that killer, did you?" he whispered. "O.K., professor—"

He was dead before the minute hand hit three-sixteen.

The neighbourhood was banged out of slumber, and McNally had only split seconds. He faded into the side street, and, at the corner he mailed the envelope to a governor of a western state. He didn't think that it would do any good, but Walker would probably be buried as Fenner, and there wouldn't be any of the real Fenner found.

"That body in the alley will be a headache for the cops," he muttered shakily.

He was heading for the haven of Needle Mike. He wasn't a cop, and he was glad of it. This case would never be solved, and only he could tell the truth of it. If he did, who would believe an old tattoo artist with a reputation as a drunkard—or believe a man in disguise? His hand closed on a playing-card in his pocket, and he tore it up before he threw it away. He didn't look at it because he knew what it was. It was the trey of clubs.

SKIN (1952)

Roald Dahl

The prolific writings of Roald Dahl (1916–1990) and especially his stories and poems for young readers have made him one of the best-loved writers of his generation. As well as writing children's classics like *Charlie and the Chocolate Factory* and *James and the Giant Peach*, Dahl was something of a Renaissance man: fighter pilot, spy, and, perhaps most surprisingly, a notable contributor to a number of significant medical innovations, in each case inspired by the illness of a close family member.

Both Dahl's children's work and his writing for adults have an inclination towards the macabre. His 1952 story, "Skin", was first published in the *New Yorker* and then collected in *Skin and Other Stories*. Like Saki's "The Background", at the centre of "Skin" is a backpiece tattoo that becomes the focus of intense interest in the art world. The down-on-his-luck war veteran Drioli discovers that the tattoo of his wife by the master artist Soutine has ironically acquired great financial value as he has been languishing in poverty. While in a sense there is nothing more personal or intimate than a tattoo, Dahl's dark tale shows how tattoos also transcend their wearers to exist in the world in a way that the tattooee cannot necessarily anticipate or control.

T HAT YEAR—1946—WINTER WAS A LONG TIME GOING. Although it was April, a freezing wind blew through the streets of the city, and overhead the snow clouds moved across the sky.

The old man who was called Drioli shuffled painfully along the sidewalk of the Rue de Rivoli. He was cold and miserable, huddled up, like a hedgehog, in a filthy black coat, only his eyes and the top of his head visible above the turned-up collar.

The door of a café opened and the faint whiff of roasting chicken brought a pain of yearning to the top of his stomach. He moved on, glancing, without any interest, at the things in the shop windows—perfume, silk ties, and shirts, diamonds, porcelain, antique furniture, finely bound books. Then a picture gallery. He had always liked picture galleries. This one had a single canvas on display in the window. He stopped to look at it. He turned to go on. He checked, looked back; and now, suddenly, there came to him a slight uneasiness, a movement of the memory, a distant recollection of something, somewhere, he had seen before. He looked again. It was a landscape, a clump of trees leaning madly over to one side as if blown by a tremendous wind, the sky swirling and twisting all around. Attached to the frame there was a little plaque, and on this it said: "Paul Tichine (1894–1943)."

Drioli stared at the picture, wondering vaguely what there was about it that seemed familiar. Crazy painting, he thought. Very strange and crazy—but I like it... Paul Tichine... Tichine... "By God!" he cried suddenly. "My little Kalmuck, that's who it is! My little Kalmuck, with a picture in the finest shop in Paris! Just imagine that!"

The old man pressed his face closer to the window. He could remember the boy—yes, quite clearly he could remember him. But when? When? The rest of it was not so easy to recollect. It was so long ago. How long? Twenty—no, more like thirty years, wasn't it? Wait a minute. Yes—it was the year before the war, the first war, 1913. That was it. And this Tichine, this ugly little Kalmuck, a sullen, brooding boy whom he had liked—almost loved—for no reason at all that he could think of, except that he could paint.

And how he could paint. It was coming back more clearly now— the street, the line of refuse cans along the length of it, the rotten smell, the brown cats walking delicately over the refuse, and then the women, moist fat women sitting on the doorsteps with their feet upon the cobblestones of the street. Which street? Where was it the boy had lived?

The Cité Falguière, that was it! The old man nodded his head several times, pleased to have remembered the name. Then there was the studio, with the single chair in it, and the filthy red couch that the boy had used for sleeping; the drunken parties, the cheap white wine, the furious quarrels, and always, always the bitter, sullen face of the boy brooding over his work.

It was odd, Drioli thought, how easily it all came back to him now, how each single small, remembered fact seemed instantly to remind him of another.

There was that nonsense with the tattoo, for instance. Now, *that* was a mad thing if ever there was one. How had it started? Ah, yes—he had got rich one day, that was it, and he had bought lots of wine. He could see himself now as he entered the studio with the parcel of bottles under his arm—the boy sitting before the easel, and his (Drioli's) own wife standing in the centre of the room, posing for her picture.

"Tonight we shall celebrate," he said. "We shall have a little celebration, us three."

"What is it that we celebrate?" the boy asked, without looking up. "Is it that you have decided to divorce your wife so she can marry me?"

"No," Drioli said. "We celebrate because today I have made a great sum of money with my work."

"And I have made nothing. We can celebrate that also."

"If you like." Drioli was standing by the table unwrapping the parcel. He felt tired and he wanted to get at the wine. Nine clients in one day was all very nice, but it could play hell with a man's eyes. He had never done as many as nine before. Nine boozy soldiers— and the remarkable thing was that no fewer than seven of them had been able to pay in cash. This had made him extremely rich. But the work was terrible on the eyes. Drioli's eyes were half closed from fatigue, the whites streaked with little connecting lines of red; and about an inch behind each eyeball there was a small concentration of pain. But it was evening now and he was wealthy as a pig, and in the parcel there were three bottles—one for his wife, one for his friend, and one for him. He had found the corkscrew and was drawing the corks from the bottles, each making a small plop as it came out.

The boy put down his brush. "Oh Christ," he said. "How can one work with all this going on?"

The girl came across the room to look at the painting. Drioli came over also, holding a bottle in one hand, a glass in the other.

"No!" the boy shouted, blazing up suddenly. "Please—no!" He snatched the canvas from the easel and stood it against the wall. But Drioli had seen it.

"I like it."

"It is terrible."

"It's marvellous. Like all the others that you do, it's marvellous. I love them all."

"The trouble is," the boy said, scowling, "that in themselves they are not nourishing. I cannot eat them."

"But still they are marvellous." Drioli handed him a tumbler full of the pale-yellow wine. "Drink it," he said. "It will make you happy."

Never, he thought, had he known a more unhappy person, or one with a gloomier face. He had spotted him in a café some seven months before, drinking alone, and because he had looked like a Russian, or some sort of an Asiatic, Drioli had sat down at his table and talked.

"You are a Russian?"

"Yes."

"Where from?"

"Minsk."

Drioli had jumped up and embraced him, crying that he, too, had been born in that city.

"It wasn't actually Minsk," the boy had said. "But quite near."

"Where?"

"Gorodok, about fifteen miles away."

"Gorodok!" Drioli had shouted, embracing him again. "I walked there several times when I was a boy." Then he had sat down again, staring affectionately at the other's face. "You know," he had said, "you don't look like a western Russian. You're more like a Tartar, or a Kalmuck. You look exactly like a Kalmuck."

Now, standing in the studio, Drioli looked again at the boy as he took the glass of wine and tipped it down his throat in one swallow. Yes, he did have a face like a Kalmuck—very broad and high-cheeked,

with a wide, coarse nose. This broadness of the cheeks was accentu-
ated by the ears, which stood out sharply from the head. And then
he had the narrow eyes, the black hair, the thick, sullen mouth of a
Kalmuck; but the hands—the hands were always a surprise, so small
and white, like a lady's, with tiny, thin fingers.

"Give me some more," the boy said. "If we are to celebrate, then
let us do it properly."

Drioli distributed the wine and sat himself on a chair. The boy
sat on the old couch with Drioli's wife. The three bottles were placed
on the floor between them.

"Tonight we shall drink as much as we possibly can," Drioli said.
"I am exceptionally rich. I think perhaps I should go out now and
buy some more bottles. How many shall I get?"

"Six more," the boy said. "Two for each."

"Good. I shall go now and fetch them."

"And I will help you."

In the nearest café, Drioli bought six bottles of white wine,
and they carried them back to the studio. They placed them on
the floor in two rows, and Drioli fetched the corkscrew and pulled
the corks, all six of them; then they sat down again and continued
to drink.

"It is only the very wealthy," Drioli said, "who can afford to
celebrate in this manner."

"That is true," the boy said. "Isn't that true, Josie?"

"Of course."

"How do you feel, Josie?"

"Fine."

"Will you leave Drioli and marry me?"

"No."

"Beautiful wine," Drioli said. "It is a privilege to drink it."

Slowly, methodically, they set about getting themselves drunk. The process was routine, but all the same there was a certain ceremony to be observed, and a gravity to be maintained, and a great number of things to be said, then said again—and the wine must be praised, and the slowness was important, too, so that there would be time to savour the three delicious stages of transition, especially (for Drioli) the one when he began to float and his feet did not really belong to him. That was the best period of them all—when he could look down at his feet and they were so far away that he would wonder what crazy person they might belong to, and why they were lying around on the floor like that, in the distance.

After a while, he got up to switch on the light. He was surprised to see that the feet came with him when he did this, especially because he couldn't feel them touching the ground. It gave him a pleasant sensation of walking on air. Then he began wandering around the room, peeking slyly at the canvases stacked against the walls.

"Listen," he said, at length. "I have an idea." He came across and stood before the couch, swaying gently. "Listen, my little Kalmuck."

"What?"

"I have a tremendous idea. Are you listening?"

"I'm listening to Josie."

"Listen to me, *please*. You are my friend—my ugly little Kalmuck from Minsk—and to me you are such an artist that I would like to have a picture, a lovely picture—"

"Have them all. Take all you can find, but do not interrupt me when I am talking with your wife."

"No, no. Now listen. I mean a picture that I can have with me always... forever... wherever I go... whatever happens... but always with me... a picture by you." He reached forward and shook the boy's knee. "Now listen to me, please."

"Listen to him," the girl said.

"It is this. I want you to paint a picture on my skin, on my back. Then I want you to tattoo over what you have painted, so that it will be there always."

"You have crazy ideas."

"Not crazy at all. Not even new—completely. I heard a man once telling about some such thing."

"It is still crazy."

"I will teach you how to use the tattoo. It is easy. A child could do it."

"I am not a child."

"*Please.*"

"You are quite mad. What is it you want?" The painter looked up into the slow, dark, wine-bright eyes of the other man. "What in Heaven's name is it you want?"

"You could do it easily! You could! You could!"

"You mean with the tattoo?"

"Yes, with the tattoo! I will teach you in two minutes!"

"Impossible!"

"Are you saying I do not know what I am talking about?"

No, the boy could not possibly be saying that, because if anyone knew about the tattoo it was he—Drioli. Had he not, only last month, covered a man's whole belly with the most wonderful and delicate design composed entirely of flowers? What about the client who had had so much hair upon his chest that he had done him a picture of a grizzly bear so designed that the hair on the chest became the furry coat of the bear? Could he not draw the likeness of a lady and position it with such subtlety upon a man's arm that when the muscle of the arm was flexed, the lady came to life and performed some astonishing contortions?

"All I am saying," the boy told him, "is that you are drunk and this is a drunken idea."

"We could have Josie for a model. A study of Josie upon my back. Am I not entitled to a picture of my wife upon my back?"

"Of Josie?"

"Yes." Drioli knew he only had to mention his wife and the boy's thick brown lips would loosen and begin to quiver.

"No," the girl said.

"Darling Josie, *please*. Take this bottle and finish it, then you will feel more generous. It is an enormous idea. Never in my life have I had such an idea before."

"What idea?"

"That he should make a picture of you upon my back. Am I not entitled to that?"

"A picture of me?"

"A nude study," the boy said. "It is an agreeable idea."

"Not nude," the girl said.

"It is an enormous idea," Drioli said.

"It's a damn crazy idea," the girl said.

"It is in any event an idea," the boy said. "It is an idea that calls for a celebration."

They emptied another bottle among them. Then the boy said, "It is no good. I could not possibly manage the tattoo. Instead, I will paint this picture on your back and you will have it with you so long as you do not take a bath and wash it off. If you never take a bath again in your life, then you will have it always, as long as you live."

"No," Drioli said.

"Yes—and on the day that you decide to take a bath, I will know that you do not any longer value my picture. It will be a test of your admiration for my art."

"I do not like that idea," the girl said. "His admiration for your art is so great that he would be unclean for many years. Let us have the tattoo. But not nude."

"Then just the head," Drioli said.

"I could not manage it."

"It is immensely simple. I will undertake to teach you in two minutes. You will see. I shall go now and fetch the instruments. The needles and the inks. I have inks of many different colours—as many different colours as you have paints, and far more beautiful…"

"It is impossible."

"I have many inks. Have I not many different colours of inks, Josie?"

"Yes."

"You will see," Drioli said. "I will go now and fetch them." He got up from his chair and walked unsteadily, but with determination, out of the room.

In half an hour Drioli was back. "I have brought everything," he cried, waving a brown suitcase. "All the necessities of the tattooist are here in this bag."

He placed the bag on the table, opened it, and laid out the electric needles and the small bottles of coloured inks. He plugged in the electric needle, then he took the instrument in his hand and pressed a switch. The instrument made a buzzing sound, and the quarter inch of needle that projected from the end of it began to vibrate swiftly up and down. He threw off his jacket and rolled up his left sleeve. "Now look. Watch me and I will show you how easy it is. I will make a design on my arm, here."

His forearm was already covered with blue markings, but he selected a small clear patch of skin upon which to demonstrate.

"First, I choose my ink—let us use ordinary blue—and I dip the point of my needle in the ink... so... and I hold the needle up straight and I run it lightly over the surface of the skin... like this... and with the little motor and the electricity, the needle jumps up and down and punctures the skin and the ink goes in and there you are... see how easy it is... see how I draw a picture of a greyhound here upon my arm..."

The boy was intrigued. "Now let *me* practise a little—on your arm."

With the buzzing needle, he began to draw blue lines upon Drioli's arm. "It is simple," he said. "It is like drawing with pen and ink. There is no difference except that it is slower."

"There is nothing to it. Are you ready? Shall we begin?"

"At once."

"The model!" cried Drioli. "Come on, Josie!" He was in a bustle of enthusiasm now, tottering around the room arranging everything, like a child preparing for some exciting game. "Where will you have her? Where shall she stand?"

"Let her be standing there, by my dressing table. Let her be brushing her hair. I will paint her with her hair down over her shoulders and her brushing it."

"Tremendous. You are a genius."

Reluctantly, the girl walked over and stood by the dressing table, carrying her glass of wine with her.

Drioli pulled off his shirt and stepped out of his trousers. He retained only his underpants and his socks and shoes, and he stood there swaying gently from side to side, his small body firm, white-skinned, almost hairless. "Now," he said, "I am the canvas. Where will you place your canvas?"

"As always, upon the easel."

"Don't be crazy. I am the canvas."

"Then place yourself upon the easel. That is where you belong."

"How can I?"

"Are you the canvas or are you not the canvas?"

"I am the canvas. Already I begin to feel like a canvas."

"Then place yourself upon the easel. There should be no difficulty."

"Truly, it is not possible."

"Then sit on the chair. Sit back to front, then you can lean your drunken head against the back of it. Hurry now, for I am about to commence."

"I am ready. I am waiting."

"First," the boy said, "I shall make an ordinary painting. Then, if it pleases me, I shall tattoo over it." With a wide brush, he began to paint upon the naked skin of the man's back.

"Ayee! Ayee!" Drioli screamed. "A monstrous centipede is marching down my spine!"

"Be still now! Be still!" The boy worked rapidly, applying the paint only in a thin blue wash, so that it would not afterward interfere with the process of tattooing. His concentration, as soon as he began to paint, was so great that it appeared somehow to supersede his drunkenness. He applied the brush strokes with quick, short jabs of the arm, holding the wrist stiff, and in less than half an hour it was finished.

"All right. That's all," he said to the girl, who immediately returned to the couch, lay down, and fell asleep.

Drioli remained awake. He watched the boy take up the needle and dip it in the ink; then he felt the sharp tickling sting as it touched the skin of his back. The pain, which was unpleasant but never extreme, kept him from going to sleep. By following the track of the needle and by watching the different colours of ink that the boy was using, Drioli amused himself trying to visualize what was going on behind him. The boy worked with an astonishing intensity. He appeared to have become completely absorbed in the little machine and in the unusual effects it was able to produce.

Far into the small hours of the morning the machine buzzed and the boy worked. Drioli could remember that when the artist finally stepped back and said "It is finished," there was daylight outside and the sound of people walking in the street.

"I want to see it," Drioli said. The boy held up a mirror, at an angle, and Drioli craned his neck to look.

"Good God!" he cried. It was a startling sight. The whole of his back, from the top of the shoulders to the base of the spine, was a blaze of colour—gold and green and blue and black and scarlet. The tattoo was applied so heavily it looked almost like an impasto. The boy had followed, as closely as possible, the original brush strokes, filling them in solid, and it was marvellous the way he had made use of the spine and the protrusion of the shoulder blades so that they became part of the composition. What is more, he had some-how managed to achieve—even with this slow process—a certain spontaneity. The portrait was quite alive; it contained much of that twisted, tortured quality so characteristic of Tichine's other work. It was not a good likeness. It was a mood rather than a likeness, the model's face vague and tipsy, the background swirling around her head in a mass of dark-green, curling strokes.

"It's tremendous!"

"I rather like it myself." The boy stood back, examining it critic-ally. "You know," he added, "I think it's good enough for me to sign." And, taking up the buzzer again, he inscribed his name, in red ink, on the right-hand side, over the place where Drioli's kidney was.

★

The old man who was called Drioli was standing in a sort of trance, staring at the painting in the window of the picture-dealer's shop. It had been so long ago, all that—almost as though it had happened in another life.

And the boy? What had become of him? He could remember now that after returning from the war—the first war—he had missed him and had questioned Josie.

"Where is my little Kalmuck?"

"He is gone," she had answered. "I do not know where, but I heard it said that a dealer had taken him up and sent him away to Céret to make more paintings."

"Perhaps he will return."

"Perhaps he will. Who knows?"

That was the last time they had mentioned him. Shortly afterward, they had moved to Le Havre, where there were more sailors and business was better. The old man smiled as he remembered Le Havre. Those were the pleasant years, the years between the wars, with the small shop near the docks, and the comfortable rooms, and always enough work, with every day three, four, five sailors coming and wanting pictures on their arms. Those were truly the pleasant years.

Then had come the second war, and Josie being killed, and the Germans arriving, and that was the finish of his business. No one had wanted pictures on their arms any more after that. And by that time he was too old for any other kind of work. In desperation, he had made his way back to Paris, hoping vaguely that things would be easier in the big city. But they were not.

And now, after the war was over, he possessed neither the means nor the energy to start up his small business again. It wasn't very easy for an old man to know what to do, especially when one did not like to beg. Yet how else could he keep alive?

Well, he thought, still staring at the picture. So that is my little Kalmuck. And how quickly the sight of one small object such as this can stir the memory. Up to a few moments ago, he had even forgotten that he had a tattoo on his back. It had been ages since he had thought about it. He put his face closer to the window and looked into the gallery. On the walls, he could see many other pictures, and all seemed to be the work of the same artist. There were a great number of people strolling around. Obviously it was a special exhibition.

On a sudden impulse, Drioli turned, pushed open the door of the gallery, and went in.

It was a long room with a thick, wine-coloured carpet, and by God how beautiful and warm it was! There were all these people strolling about looking at the pictures, well-washed, dignified people, each of whom held a catalogue in the hand. Drioli stood just inside the door, nervously glancing around, wondering whether he dared go forward and mingle with this crowd. But before he had had time to gather his courage, he heard a voice beside him saying, "What is it you want?"

The speaker wore a black morning coat. He was plump and short, and had a very white face. It was a flabby face, with so much flesh upon it that the cheeks hung down on either side of the mouth in two fleshy collops, spaniel-wise. He came up close to Drioli and said again, "What is it you want?"

Drioli stood still.

"If you please," the man was saying, "take yourself out of my gallery."

"Am I not permitted to look at the pictures?"

"I have asked you to leave."

Drioli stood his ground. He felt suddenly, overwhelmingly outraged.

"Let us not have trouble," the man was saying. "Come on now, this way." He put a fat white paw on Drioli's arm and began to push him firmly to the door.

That did it. "Take your goddam hands off me!" Drioli shouted. His voice rang clear down the long gallery, and all the heads jerked around as one—all the startled faces stared down the length of the room at the person who had made this noise. A flunky came running over to help, and the two men tried to hustle Drioli through the door. The people stood still, watching the struggle. Their faces expressed only a mild interest, and seemed to be saying, "It's all right. There's no danger to us. It's being taken care of."

"I, too!" Drioli was shouting. "I, too, have a picture by this painter! He was my friend and I have a picture which he gave me!"

"He's mad."

"A lunatic. A raving lunatic."

"Someone should call the police."

With a rapid twist of the body, Drioli suddenly jumped clear of the two men, and before anyone could stop him, he was running down the gallery shouting, "I'll show you! I'll show you! I'll show you!" He flung off his overcoat, then his jacket and shirt, and he turned so that his naked back was toward the people.

"There!" he cried, breathing quickly. "You see? There it is!"

There was a sudden absolute silence in the room, each person arrested in what he was doing, standing motionless in a kind of shocked, uneasy bewilderment. They were staring at the tattooed picture. It was still there, the colours as bright as ever, but the old man's back was thinner now, the shoulder blades protruded more sharply, and the effect, though not great, was to give the picture a curiously wrinkled, squashed appearance.

Somebody said, "My God, but it is!"

Then came the excitement and the noise of voices as the people surged forward to crowd around the old man.

"It is unmistakable!"

"His early manner, yes?"

"It is fantastic, fantastic!"

"And look, it is signed!"

"Bend your shoulders forward, my friend, so that the picture stretches out flat."

"Old one, when was this done?"

"In 1913," Drioli said, without turning around. "In the autumn of 1913."

"Who taught Tichine to tattoo?"

"I taught him."

"And the woman?"

"She was my own wife."

The gallery owner was pushing through the crowd toward Drioli. He was calm now, deadly serious, making a smile with his mouth. "Monsieur," he said, "I will buy it." Drioli could see the loose fat upon the face vibrating as he moved his jaw. "I said I will buy it, Monsieur."

"How can you buy it?" Drioli asked softly.

"I will give two hundred thousand francs for it." The dealer's eyes were small and dark, the wings of his broad nose-base were beginning to quiver.

"Don't do it!" someone murmured in the crowd. "It is worth three times as much."

Drioli opened his mouth to speak. No words came, so he shut it; then he opened it again and said slowly, "But how can I sell it?" He lifted his hands, let them drop loosely to his sides. "Monsieur, how can I possibly sell it?" All the sadness in the world was in his voice.

"Yes!" they were saying in the crowd. "How can he sell it? It is a part of himself!"

"Listen," the dealer said, coming up close. "I will help you. I will make you rich. Together we shall make some private arrangement over this picture, no?"

Drioli watched him with slow, apprehensive eyes. "But how can you buy it, Monsieur? What will you do with it when you have bought it? Where will you keep it? Where will you keep it tonight? And where tomorrow?"

"Ah, where will I keep it? Yes, where will I keep it? Now, where will I keep it? Well, now..." The dealer stroked the bridge of his nose with a fat white finger. "It would seem," he said, "that if I take the picture, I take you also. That is a disadvantage." He paused and stroked his nose again. "The picture itself is of no value until you are dead. How old are you, my friend?"

"Sixty-one."

"But you are perhaps not very robust, no?" The dealer lowered the hand from his nose and looked Drioli up and down, slowly, like a farmer appraising an old horse.

"I do not like this," Drioli said, edging away. "Quite honestly, Monsieur, I do not like it." He edged straight into the arms of a tall man, who put out his hands and caught him gently by the shoulders. Drioli glanced around and apologized. The man smiled down at him, patting one of the old fellow's naked shoulders reassuringly with a hand encased in a canary-coloured glove.

"Listen, my friend," the stranger said, still smiling. "Do you like to swim and to bask yourself in the sun?"

Drioli looked up at him, rather startled.

"Do you like fine food and red wine from the great châteaux of Bordeaux?" The man was still smiling, showing strong white teeth with a flash of gold among them. He spoke in a soft, coaxing manner, one gloved hand still resting on Drioli's shoulder. "Do you like such things?"

"Well—yes," Drioli answered, still greatly perplexed. "Of course."

"And the company of beautiful women?"

"Why not?"

"And a cupboard full of suits and shirts made to your own personal measurements? It would seem that you are a little lacking for clothes."

Drioli watched this suave man, waiting for the rest of the proposition.

"Have you ever had a shoe constructed especially for your own foot?"

"No."

"You would like that?"

"Well…"

"And a man who will shave you in the mornings and trim your hair?"

Drioli simply stood and gaped.

"And a plump, attractive girl to manicure the nails of your fingers?"

Someone in the crowd giggled.

"And a bell beside your bed to summon a maid to bring your breakfast in the morning? Would you like these things, my friend? Do they appeal to you?"

Drioli stood still and looked at him.

"You see, I am the owner of the Hotel Bristol in Cannes. I now invite you to come down there and live as my guest for the rest of your life, in luxury and comfort." The man paused, allowing his listener time to savour this cheerful prospect.

"Your only duty—shall I call it your pleasure—will be to spend your time on my beach in bathing trunks, walking among the guests, sunning yourself, swimming, drinking cocktails. You would like that?"

There was no answer.

"Don't you see—all the guests will thus be able to observe this fascinating picture by Tichine. You will become famous, and men will say, 'Look, there is the fellow with a million francs upon his back.' You like this idea, Monsieur? It pleases you?"

Drioli looked up at the tall man in the canary gloves, still wondering whether this was some sort of a joke. "It is a comical idea," he said slowly. "But do you really mean it?"

"Of course I mean it."

"Wait," the dealer interrupted. "See here, old one. Here is the answer to our problem. I will buy the picture, and I will arrange with a surgeon to remove the skin from your back, and then you will be able to go off on your own and enjoy the great sum of money I shall give you for it."

"With no skin on my back?"

"No, no, please! You misunderstand. This surgeon will put a new piece of skin in the place of the old one. It is simple."

"Could he do that?"

"There is nothing to it."

"Impossible!" said the man with the canary gloves. "He's too old for such a major skin-grafting operation. It would kill him. It would kill you, my friend."

"It would kill me?"

"Naturally. You would never survive. Only the picture would come through."

"In the name of God!" Drioli cried. He looked around, aghast, at the faces of the people watching him, and in the silence that followed, another man's voice, speaking quietly from the back of the group, could be heard saying, "Perhaps, if one were to offer this old man enough money, he might consent to kill himself on the spot. Who knows?" A few people sniggered. The dealer moved his feet uneasily on the carpet.

Then the hand in the canary glove was tapping Drioli again upon the shoulder. "Come on," the man was saying, smiling his broad white smile. "You and I will go and have a good dinner and we can talk about it some more while we eat. How's that? Are you hungry?"

Drioli watched him, frowning. He didn't like the man's long, flexible neck, or the way in which it craned forward at you when he spoke, like a snake.

"Roast duck and Chambertin," the man was saying. He put a rich, succulent accent on the words, splashing them out with his tongue. "And perhaps a soufflé aux marrons, light and frothy."

Drioli's eyes turned up toward the ceiling, his lips became loose and wet. One could see the poor old fellow beginning literally to drool at the mouth.

"How do you like your duck?" the man went on. "Do you like it very brown and crisp outside, or shall it be…"

"I am coming," Drioli said quickly. Already he had picked up his shirt and was pulling it frantically over his head. "Wait for me, Monsieur. I am coming." And within a minute he had disappeared out of the gallery with his new patron.

It wasn't more than a few weeks later that a picture by Tichine, of a woman's head, painted in an unusual manner, nicely framed and heavily varnished, turned up for sale in Buenos Aires. That—and the fact that there is no hotel in Cannes called Bristol—causes one to wonder a little, and to pray for the old man's health, and to hope fervently that, wherever he may be at this moment, there is a plump, attractive girl to manicure the nails of his fingers, and a maid to bring him his breakfast in bed in the mornings.

ALSO AVAILABLE

From atop the choppy waves to the choking darkness of the abyss, the seas are full of mystery and rife with tales of inexplicable events and encounters with the unknown.

In this anthology we see a thrilling spread of narratives; sailors are pitched against a nightmare from the depths, invisible to the naked eye; a German U-boat commander is tormented by an impossible transmission via Morse Code; a ship ensnares itself in the kelp of the Sargasso Sea and dooms a crew of mutineers, seemingly out of revenge for her lost captain...

The supernatural is set alongside the grim affairs of sailors scorned in these salt-soaked tales, recovered from obscurity for the twenty-first century.

A strange figure foretells tragedy on the railway tracks. A plague threatens to encroach upon an isolated castle. The daughter of an eccentric scientist falls victim to a poisonous curse.

For all its certainty and finality, death remains an infinitely mysterious subject to us all. The stories in this anthology depict that haunting moment when characters come face to face with their own mortality.

Spanning two centuries, *Mortal Echoes* features some of the finest writers in the English language – including Daphne du Maurier, Edgar Allan Poe, Graham Greene and H. G. Wells. Intriguing, unsettling and often darkly humorous, this collection explores humanity's transient existence, and what it means to be alive.

British Library Tales of the Weird collects a thrilling array of uncanny storytelling, from the realms of gothic, supernatural and horror fiction. With stories ranging from the nineteenth century to the present day, this series revives long-lost material from the Library's vaults to thrill again alongside beloved classics of the weird fiction genre.

We welcome any suggestions, corrections or feedback you may have, and will aim to respond to all items addressed to the following:

The Editor (Tales of the Weird),
British Library Publishing
The British Library
96 Euston Road
London, NW1 2DB

We also welcome enquiries through our Twitter account, @BL_Publishing.